# The Unthinkable Thoughts
# of Jacob Green

# The Unthinkable Thoughts of Jacob Green

*a novel by*

## JOSHUA BRAFF

ALGONQUIN BOOKS
OF CHAPEL HILL
2004

Published by
ALGONQUIN BOOKS OF CHAPEL HILL
Post Office Box 2225
Chapel Hill, North Carolina 27515-2225

a division of
Workman Publishing
708 Broadway
New York, New York 10003

Printed in the United States of America.
Published simultaneously in Canada by Thomas Allen & Son Limited.
Design by Anne Winslow.

Library of Congress Cataloging-in-Publication Data
Braff, Joshua, 1967–
    The unthinkable thoughts of Jacob Green : a novel / by Joshua
Braff.— 1st ed.
        p. cm.
    ISBN 1-56512-420-0
    1. Fathers and sons—Fiction.   2. Jewish families—Fiction.
    3. Suburban life—Fiction.   4. Teenage boys—Fiction.   5. New
Jersey—Fiction.   6. Brothers—Fiction.   7. Boys—Fiction.   I. Title.
PS3602.R344U57 2004
813'.6—dc22                                         2004046260

10 9 8 7 6 5 4 3

for Jill

# Acknowledgments

I had this girlfriend in New Jersey who liked the way
I wrote so I proposed to her in a story and she said yes
before it ended. That was a good day. I truly love this girl.

I am incredibly grateful and indebted to Debra Goldstein for
her unconditional guidance, encouragement, and expertise.

To my agent, Sonia Pabley, I can imagine no other
partner. Thank you for believing in the first one and for
knowing we were headed the right way.

My endless gratitude to my editor, Amy Gash. Thank you
for the tone and calm. I am also grateful to Robert Ray,
Ronald Spatz, Laurie Horowitz, Rabbi Barry Friedman,
Dean Rubinson, Carol and Steve Schulte, and my four
parents whom I love.

Do not reject the discipline of the Lord, my son;
Do not abhor his rebuke.
For whom the Lord loves, He rebukes,
As a father the son whom he favors.

Proverbs 3:11–13

# The Unthinkable Thoughts
# of Jacob Green

*Come Meet Your New Neighbors*

*THE GREENS*

*Food, Fun, and, Let's Hope, Sun—*

*Sunday the 23rd at 11:00 A.M.*

*1011 Westlock Dr. at the Corner of Saber St.*

*(Bring nothing but yourselves*
*and don't bother to knock.*
*We'll be home.)*

## Housewarming

I sit halfway up the staircase and listen to no one in particular. There are fifty-three people standing in the wide front hall of this new house. I counted. There are even more in the living room and some outside on an eating tour of the raspberry bushes. They keep arriving. Some carry wine bottles but most have flowerpots or tinfoil plates; the Litmans brought a Bible wrapped in newspaper comics. It's weird that a house full of people can sound like one thick and rumbled voice; a bass-y group chant that coughs here and there. Some of them have much smaller heads than others. Like the difference between cantaloupes and apples. I close my right eye and pick some of the fruit with my thumb and index finger. *Pluck. Squish.*

A "housewarming" party is what my father calls this one. The six of us are up before the sun: vacuuming, hiding unpacked boxes, calling to confirm the Saran-Wrapped platters and ice-sculpted G. Every friend he's ever made is invited, along with a dozen or more colleagues from the firm, temple congregants, new neighbors, and a waitress named Patty who served us the night before at the Ground Round.

My father wheels his tiny amp into the front hall. It makes a zapping noise as he kneels to plug it in. When he stands, he slaps the knees of his slacks and calls us over for a look before the introductions. Asher nearly passes but for his ratty brown hair that he likes to let hang in his eyes. He doesn't brush it on purpose, like he thinks he's one of the Sex Pistols. I happen to know he's got his "Eat Shit!" T-shirt under his striped button-down. He flashed me a peek as I struggled with my tie. My father removes a comb from his pocket and walks toward my brother.

"*I'll* do it," Asher says annoyed, taking it from my father's hand. Asher gets a stare for being aggressive but it ends quickly: there's a show to do. Dara does okay. She's got a loosened bow on the back of her yellow party dress and gets accused of cereal breath, but it's not a bad showing. My father spins her to retie the floppy bow, his brow ridge crinkled as if defusing a bomb. I do poorly. My tie is so askew that it needs to be removed like a snapped whip before being redone. From his knees, my father's nose nearly touches mine and I can see his bearded jaw beginning to churn with impatience. I keep my eyes lowered and my breath held; I too had Cheerios within the half hour. When he finishes he gets to his feet and begins to untangle the microphone wire.

"Daddy?" Dara says.

"What is it?"

"I have to go to the bathroom." She is five.

He jiggles and tightens the knot of his tie and releases a long breath with his eyes closed. He then points his chin outward to get some slack in the skin of his neck. "Asher . . . where's Asher?"

"I'm right behind you."

"Make sure the mike stays plugged in. If you want to tape it, fine, just do what you have to do to make it stay, all right? I want to avoid any of that buzzing or . . . or what's that . . . ?"

"Feedback."

"Right. That." He holds his dark frames in the air looking for smudges. "Remember the last time? Couldn't even hear the opener."

"Give it a try," Asher says from his knees.

My father puts his glasses back on and lifts the mike to his lips. "Hello, hello."

Dozens of heads turn our way. I get butterfly stings in my gut as some of the eyes meet mine. I wipe my palms on my new checkered pants and stand with my shoulders square. I'll just wave, I tell myself, then step behind Asher. At the "moving to Piedmont" party I chose to salute the audience just before my wave. It was a last-second decision that I wish I hadn't made. My father said it was "flip" and "discourteous to veterans" and made me apologize to Eli Gessow because his son served in Vietnam. Eli said he was in the crapper during the introductions and couldn't hear a word. He then kissed my forehead really hard and told me to get him some more lox.

"Okay, let's try it. Jacob, Dara, come stand by me. Enough, Asher, it sounds fine, up off the floor now. Let's see some smiles, yes? They're here for you. The Greens are in town today, right? Here we go now. Here we go." My father lifts the mike to his chin. "Hello and welcome to our new home."

Scattered applause.

"If I could have—what? Can't hear? Can I—can I have everyone's attention for a moment? Hello. Hi. Thank you, hello. Just settle down for a second or two. I want—thank you, Judith. Judith Meyer, ladies and gentlemen, helping me quiet the troops." He blows Judith a kiss. "Can you all hear me? Can I be heard?" he says, and taps the head of the microphone.

"Can't hear you," says a voice from somewhere in the living room.

"Okay, how about now?" he says louder.

"Better."

"All right. Hello and welcome. I—please, I need it quiet. I'm not sure if everyone can hear me. I see a thumbs up. Does that mean you can hear me, Liv? Okay. Thank you. If—no, no, still no? Perfect? Okay, here we go. Jacob?"

I step forward and wave.

"*No!*" he says, covering the mike. "I haven't introduced you yet. Where's your mother?"

"I don't know, Dad." I step back.

"Where the hell is she? I'm trying to start a party here."

"I saw her in the kitchen," Asher says. "She was hittin' a bag of ice with a hammer."

"That's just great."

"Should I go find her?" I ask.

"No. Don't move. We'll go without her."

"Daddy," Dara says.

"Hello and welcome to our new home."

The amp whines. My father cringes at it. Asher hits the top with his palm. The noise fades then stops.

"I . . . I hope you're all enjoying yourselves and getting enough to eat. Before I begin, has anyone seen my wife?

Claire, are you—she's—kitchen? Okay, would you tell her to come out here, please? I'd like to introduce you to my family but I'm missing my Gabriel and my wife. They're usually together."

Some audience laughter.

"Here she is, here's my lady."

Applause as my mother walks out from the kitchen with Gabriel in her arms.

"Hi, honey. Come on out and meet everyone. Many of you know my family but . . . I want you to see how wonderful they are and how beautiful my amazing and gorgeous wife is. Ladies and gentlemen, this is the mother of my beautiful children, Claire Green."

Applause. Some whistles. My father picks something off the shoulder of her sweater and puts his arm around her waist. He looks out at his guests with a tilted head, the microphone held loosely in his palm.

"'Along the garden ways just now / I heard the flowers speak; / The white rose told me of your brow, / The red rose of your cheek . . .'" He reaches to touch her face. "'The lily of your bended head, / The bindweed of your hair: / Each looked its loveliest and said / You'—Claire Green—'were more fair.'" He leans in to kiss her.

An *awww* rises from the room.

"A little balladry I found while unpacking. A poem I just *know* was written with my wife in mind. I . . . can't begin to tell you what it's like, to wake up every morning to this beautiful face."

*Awwwwwww.*

He leans in to give her another kiss, his hand on the back of her neck.

"Look at her," he says, then places a hand over the mike. "Want to do a small spin or . . . ?"

My mother shakes her head still smiling.

"Not one little one?"

"No, Abe."

"And this—can I have it a little bit quiet back there—please. This won't take long. I'd like to introduce you to my firstborn. This is my bar mitzvah boy. Two weeks ago, for those of you who weren't there, he became a man, a Jewish man in the eyes of God. My oldest son, Asher. He skateboards!"

Applause.

Asher steps forward and waves.

"Can ride the thing on his nose!"

Asher rolls his eyes and lifts his thumb in the air with a sarcastic smirk. The amp whines as his foot hits the cord and climbs to a screech before fading out.

My father shoves him away from it, back toward me.

"The blond boy," he says, still glaring at Asher. "Where's my blond boy? Hiding behind his mother, of course. This is my Jacob. Jacob is ten years old. He reads Hebrew so beautifully it'll make you cry. That's what five years of yeshiva gets ya."

Some audience laughter.

"Doesn't have a clue what he's saying but . . ."

More laughter.

"He also plays baseball. Show everyone your swing, J."

It's not the first time he's done this. At last year's Passover seder he ran into the garage to get me a Wiffle ball bat.

"Dad?"

"Just one swing."

"I look stupid."

He covers the mike. "It's gonna kill you to do one swing? Do it, please."

I swing an invisible bat to a smattering of applause.

"There it is . . . there it is. He plays Little League for the

Knights of Columbus. He pitches too. Show everyone a pitch,"
he says into the mike. "Come on, one pitch, here it comes . . .
wind up and . . . del-i-ve-ry, yes, beautiful. *Sandy Koufax,* ladies
and gentlemen. And no, he will *not* pitch on Yom Kippur."

Some laughter for the joke. Some applause for the pitch. I
step back.

"And this," he says, lifting her into his arms. "This is my girlie."
Applause.

"She swims like a fish. The butterfly. *Always* top three. You
can all come and see her race. The Jewish Y on Kingston Avenue. This is my Dara, folks. My one and only girl, my little
flower. Dara everyone!"

Applause.

"Now—although he needs no introduction whatsoever—
and I . . . I'd never say I saved the best for last because it's . . .
a silly thing to say, but, here he is, my baby, Gabriel. Gabriel
Green," he says over the applause. "He'll be three in April. I
made him with my own two fists! Isn't he beautiful?"

My father waves Gabriel's hand to the crowd. He turns and
tucks his face into my mother's neck. "Can sing 'Matchmaker'
perfectly, all the parts. Can we have a little of that, beautiful
boy? 'Matchmaker, matchmaker, make me a match.' Come on,
Gabey."

Gabe shakes his head hard, his face still hidden.

"All right, a little stage fright. So . . . we're so very happy
every one of you is here. We love all of you, we truly do. If you
need *anything,* just let us know." He covers the mike.

"Should I do a *hamotzi?*" he asks my mother.

"They're already eating," she says.

"People, people, one more thing. My son, *Jacob,* is going to
bless our food in Hebrew."

The burn in my stomach is startling. My father hands me

the mike and kisses the top of my head. "Relax," he says. "It's just the *hamotzi*. Every word's a jewel, right? Every word."

The head of the microphone smells like ass. "Baruch—"

"Louder," he says.

"Ata—"

"From the beginning."

"Baruch . . . ata, Adonai, Eloheynu, melech haolem, ha-motzi, lechem min haaretz." And the crowd says, "Amen."

My father lifts me from my armpits and floods my face with machine-gun kisses. His dark beard is like Brillo and rakes at the fair skin of my cheeks and neck. I smile through the bristles and the devouring of my face.

"One more thing," he says, after my feet touch the ground. "If you haven't had a tour of the house, meet me here in two minutes. I'll be your docent so don't be late. *Enjoy!*"

Some final applause.

He kneels to switch off the amplifier, then stands to face us. "Not too bad, not too bad."

The room grows crowded again with the rumble of voices. Asher yanks his tie off and runs up the stairs. My father watches him. "Where *you* goin'?"

My mother puts Gabriel on the floor and begins to remove his jacket.

"*Asher?*" he yells.

I walk over to the banister and look up.

"Where's your brother going?"

"I don't—"

"Just takes off," he says, facing me, and begins to coil the microphone wire. "Not too bad, Claire, right? Poem read well."

"It was fine."

"Could you hear me in the kitchen?"

"No, not really. It was muffled."

"Are there people still back there?"

She nods and folds the jacket over her arm.

"Could *they* hear me?"

"I don't know, Abe."

My father licks his thumb and wipes something off Gabe's cheek. "Why do you think—I have to beg for a spin, a little spin?"

"Mommy, I have to go to the bathroom," Dara says.

My mother grips my sister's hand and faces my dad. "I've told you I don't like that, Abram. When you do that. Haven't I?"

"A little spin."

"Mo-*mmy*," Dara says, her knees touching.

"Go right now, baby, you know where it is." Dara runs into the dining room and disappears among the bodies.

"Claire?"

She turns to him.

"I see nothing demeaning in it."

My mother ignores him and reaches for my tie. "You can take this off now," she says, and picks at the knot. "You hungry?"

"Claire?"

She faces my father with both hands on my tie.

"The poem," he says. "You've said *nothing* . . . about the poem."

# I

---

## 1977

## Ten Years Old

Tzitzit—You shall have it as a fringe so that when you look upon it you will remember to do all the commands of the Lord and you will not follow the desires of your heart and your eyes, which lead you astray.

Numbers 15:39

## Tzitzit

There's a soothing hum to the ride to Perth Amboy, especially when it's raining. The rhythmic *ping-pong* of windshield wipers, rubber on glass, the dense stretches of puddles on this parkway road. It's the week before my family leaves for Piedmont, New Jersey, and I watch my brother sleep on the van to yeshiva. We're not even past Sayerville on this chilly-wet morning, and Asher is long gone. One of his nostrils is wheezing on the exhale and his mouth is open a slit. It makes me tired just looking at him. I scoot closer to him and barely touch the side of my head to his shoulder, the thickness of his gray coat. I know he gets embarrassed when people see me do this but I won't wake him, no way. I'll just rest here a second and no one will know.

I always dream in these quick and faraway pictures that blur in the white noise of this long ride. Like today, I wear no tzitzit in my mind and so have committed the greatest of all yeshiva boy sins—an actual desecration of God. I reach for the four tzitzit tassels in my dream and when I wake I'm doing just that, frisking my own chest for what I cannot find. And I don't feel them. I don't have them. I slowly open my eyes and reach under my shirt.

"Asher?"

He says nothing. I lift my shirttails out of my pants and stare down at my stomach. "Asher."

A tzitzit is made up of four woolen fringes which are tied to the corners of a thin, white undergarment called an *arba kanfoth*. The garment resembles a tank top in that it has no sleeves but it's really more of a poncho in that it's open on the sides and drapes over the head. All males must wear one under sky blue dress shirts and each fringe that dangles from our pants must be kissed during *shaharith*, our daily morning prayer service. Every day at Eliahu Academy begins with a yarmulke and tzitzit inspection, which means a long-bearded rabbi in mid-head-bobbing prayer fondles each of the four strands. Failing this procedure is a *chilul* Hashem, or an act of great disrespect to God. This means detention and no way home without a ride from a parent. My father calls these breaches of faith "F jobs" and just loathes the embarrassment of fumbled rituals. I can picture where the stupid thing is sitting, washed and neatly folded in my sock drawer at home.

"Asher?" I say. "Ash?"

He sniffs and places a maroon prayer book between his head and the window. It's the book he's been studying from for months now, the *Humash* he'll read from at his bar mitzvah on Saturday.

"I forgot my tzitzit."

He doesn't move. It's as if he's unconscious.

Our father has invited 350 guests to hear Asher perform his allotted Torah portion; Parashah Noach; Genesis 6:9–11:32; and his haftarah, Isaiah 54:1–55:5. Cantor Goldfarb says it's a lengthy reading, longer than most, and for the last three weeks I've heard it rehearsed again and again through the door of my father's bedroom. Being that our dad is a veteran actor of the Rockridge Community Theater, but not a strong reader of the Hebrew language, his instructions focus on the projection of voice, body posture, and something he calls "pizzazz."

"*Bang* it off the back wall," I hear him say over my brother's singing voice as I lay in bed down the hall.

"Vayihee hageshem al haaretz—"

"You're emitting from here, do you see me? Look at me, from here, from up here. I want it down *here*. See me. It needs to rise and—"

"Arbaim yom hazeh—"

"Better, better. Keep that strength. Good. Each a jewel and—right! Better. From here!"

"Ba'etzem yom hazeh—"

"Stop, stop, stop. Just stop. *Listen*. It *must* come from lower and rise, got it? From the diaphragm, from way down, from here, touch it. You're all the way up here already and trust me, no one wants to hear it in your nose, okay? How many times do I have to say it? Fifty? Now find it down here and bring it all up, up here and appreciate each vowel, taste each bump, each swing. Now let's go again—please. From 'Vayihee.'"

It was past midnight when Asher left my father's room the night before. I listened for his footsteps to pass my room and for his bedroom door to finally click closed. I have never seen my brother so drained, so distant, so emptied by the months of invasive attention. There is not an ounce of this ritual he is doing for himself, not a day he doesn't wish it would all disappear. But when it does end, this Saturday morning, when the bar mitzvah has finally come and gone, our family will leave Rockridge, and Asher and I will enter public school for the first time in our lives. We have never been anything, he and I, but students under God: yeshiva boys.

I lean close to his ear and whisper once again. "Asher?"

He lifts his head off the book and looks down at me. "It's simple," he mumbles. "Wake me again . . . and I *rip* out your tongue."

Sometimes it's good to give Asher his space. Even me, and I'm very, very important to him. My mother says he came out with the umbilical cord wrapped around his neck a few times and he's been "trying to get free" ever since. He rests his head back on the window and tries to relax his eyes.

On his lap is a paperback copy of *The Man with the Golden Gun*. Roger Moore is firing a Walter PPK and stands bent-kneed between two women in string bikinis. Asher says the villain in this one has three nipples and goes by the name of Scaramanga. Waiting on the lawn this morning I remind him that Rabbi Belahsan doesn't like books with naked girls on the cover. *Diamonds Are Forever* bought him a two-hour detention last year and a call to our father at his office. The two girls on the book jacket weren't even in bikinis—they just had the silhouettes of their lips wrapped around the tip of a revolver. I glance down at the cover and slide my pinkie onto one of the ladies. She's got a moon-helmet afro and skin the color of cocoa. I touch her breasts, her knees, the flat between her legs.

"What the fuck are you doing?"

I flinch and pull my hand off the book. "Do you have your tzitzit?"

"You woke me up."

"I don't have my tzitzit."

"Where the hell is it?"

"I don't know."

"That's a bad answer."

"But I don't."

"Dickhead."

"Do you have an extra?"

"I don't sell them."

"What am I gonna do?"

"Where the hell is it?"

"At home I guess."

He nods a couple of times and looks out the window. "You're fucked."

"Don't say that."

"Dickhead."

"Don't say that either."

"Check right now," he says.

I reach under my dress shirt, trying to feel it, praying to feel it.

"No?" he asks.

I shake my head.

Asher looks around at the four other kids on the van. "Take Ezra's," he says, and leans his head back on the window.

"Take *Ezra's*? He's five years old."

"What do you want me to do?"

"Do you have yours?" I ask.

He lifts one of the fringes from his waist and lets it drop to his lap. I stare at it for a second before facing the boy behind me.

"Hi, Ezra."

"No!" he says, his *Fat Albert* lunchbox blocking his tzitzit.

I turn back around.

The van pulls to a stop in front of a green aluminum house, a few miles from the school. Seth Gimmelstein runs across his front lawn, his tzitzit hopping like the mane of a trophy horse. There's a black bobby pin anchoring his yarmulke to his scalp and a sharp crease in his charcoal slacks. I would trade lives with Seth Gimmelstein right now, grow old as him. When he sits in the seat in front of me, I tap his shoulder and ask if he's got an extra. He laughs with his mouth wide and asks if a dog ate my tzitzit. I'm in a great deal of trouble.

"Hey," Asher says, staring down at me. "What're you doing?"

I bring my lunch box on my lap and turn my back to him.

"You're *not* crying."

"Leave me alone."

"Are you really crying?"

"No."

"Jesus Christ."

"I'm *not*. Leave me alone."

He sits up and slams his *Humash* onto Roger Moore. "Listen to me, all right? Are you listening?"

I nod.

"You'll just . . . tell whatever Nazi they sic on you that . . . you're moving away in a week and your tzitzit's in a fuckin' box on a moving truck, all right?"

Seth finds this hilarious. "Classic," he says, his chubby shoulders jumping.

"It's your birthday on Wednesday," Asher says. "Tell 'em *that*."

I face him and his eyes widen. "I'm not telling them it's my birthday."

"It is, isn't it?"

"But they don't—"

"They don't *what*?" he snaps. "Believe in birthdays?"

The van stops a few houses down from Seth's. A seventh-grader named Mirium Levinson walks across her lawn with a Blow Pop in her mouth. Her red-headed brother, Noah, is six and runs to catch up to her. Asher sits taller in his seat and combs his hair into his eyes with his fingers. He fakes disinterest but I know he likes Mirium; all the boys like Mirium. In September she wore Tweetie Bird panties to school and couldn't help but prove it by lifting the back of her pleated gray skirt. I could see the crack in her *tuchis* through Tweetie's yellow head and I think about it every time she gets on the van now. Asher says she's the "foxiest" girl at Eliahu because she grew "titties" over the summer and her butt bubbles out. He also likes that she flips off the rabbis when they pass her in the hall and can curse like a felon.

"Good morning, kikes," she says, and plops down in front of us with Noah next to her.

Asher laughs out loud and actually claps. Mirium glances back at him, elated by the kudos, her face aglow. I think it's hilarious that her dark bangs are always crooked and snipped too high on her forehead. She brags of cutting them herself with scissors made special for lefties.

"Is this the bus to Dachau?" she adds through a smile. Asher loves this too and grins like Barbarino. She gets on her knees to face him, her hands squeezing the back of her seat. "I have a surprise for one of the Green boys." I look at her chewed-down fingernails, all dotted with chipped red polish.

"Happy birthday, little Greeny," she says, and hands me a wrapped gift.

"What is it?" I ask.

"Take it."

I tear a piece of the wrapping paper and can already see what's inside. I look up at my brother.

### Rule Number 1 of the Green House Rules

*Under no circumstance can any child in this family own or play with a toy gun. This applies to water guns, plastic guns, cork shooters, penny pistols, edible wax guns, and the miniature sort that comes complete with a 16-inch G.I. Joe. Simulation of shooting at something or someone with one's finger will result in paternal rage, and or the gripping and lowering of said weapon.*

It's the G-Zap Lazer Fazer. I've only seen them on TV commercials. Battery-charged laser sighting, adjustable on-off stun ray, quick trigger release, laser decals, removable scope, the works. I take it in my hand. I slowly turn it over and place my finger on the trigger. "It's the G-Zap."

Mirium nods with her eyes closed.

"Hey," says Noah, trying to see over the seat back. "That's mine."

"Relax, Noah," she says, "I'll get you another one."

"That's *mine*," he screams, and begins to wail.

"He'll get over it," she says, pushing the top of his head back down. "It takes three double A's."

"*Miiiiiirium,*" Noah sings in agony.

"Let me get this straight," Asher says. "You wrapped one of your brother's toys?"

"I didn't have time to shop."

"It's *miiiiiiiine!*"

"Here, Noah," I say, handing it to him. He takes it and sits back down, his bottom lip still trembling.

"Say thank you," Mirium tells her brother.

"*No!*"

I lean forward in my seat. "Um . . . Noah? You wouldn't have an extra tzitzit, would you?"

"*No!*"

"Where's your tzitzit?" Mirium says, peering over the chair at my waist.

"It'll be fine," Asher says. "It's not as bad as it sounds."

She glances at him. "It's a *chilul* Hashem."

"We know, we know. He'll be fine. These things happen."

"I don't think you get it," I say to him.

"Shut up for a second, okay? I know what a goddamn *chilul* Hashem is, remember? I've had four since August."

Mirium giggles and puts her feet on the back of the seat in front of her.

"Here's what you do," he says. "Are you listening? Tell Rabbi Belahsan or Mizrahe or whoever comes near you, that in seven days, you'll *never* need a fuckin' tzitzit again in your life."

"Amen," says Mirium, her Blow Pop in the air.

Asher looks at her, then back to me. "Tell him you're going to public school where you'll be eating ham sandwiches and singin' 'Jingle Bells' till Easter."

Seth roars at this. Mirium whistles with her fingers. Noah fires the G-Zap. *Zwaaazwaaaazwaaaa.*

"Ham sandwiches," says Seth, still laughing.

"That doesn't mean anything," I say.

"What are they gonna do? Call Dad? So you forgot the thing, so what?"

"So what?" I say. "So *what?*"

"Look how afraid you are," Asher says. "They've got you *so* afraid. None of this will ever, *ever* matter."

"Maybe you'll get lucky and they'll call your mother instead," Mirium says, biting a thread off her skirt.

"Fuckin' yarmulkes and Torah songs and rituals up the ying-yang," says Asher. "You're not a chimp, are you?"

"Your mom won't care," Mirium adds. "She's not even a real Jew."

Asher and I look at each other before slowly facing her. She bites through the thread and looks up at us. "What?"

### Rule Number 2 of the Green House Rules

*When faced with the question of your mother's religion, please refer to the following explanation: Yes, before she met our father she was a New England–born Protestant who was in no way associated with Christ or any church. But before our births she converted to Judaism in the presence of one Rabbi Ben Perlstein, one Rabbi Hyman Roth, and one Rabbi Avraham Schulman, and thusly, she is, and will always be, a Jew. We do not celebrate any non-Jewish holidays although we do receive gifts from the non-Chosen relatives on our mother's side who keep forgetting to call these offerings Chanukah presents.*

I pull my lunch box up on my lap and watch the school approach through the front windshield. "I think I'm gonna be sick," I say, and Mirium ducks behind her seat. "I just want to come home on the van."

Asher lifts one of his ass cheeks and pulls a crinkled yarmulke out of his back pocket. "You will," he says, putting it on.

I shoot my hand up to see if there's a yarmulke on my head. There is. My brother chuckles at my fear and gives my shoulder a shove. "Hey," he says.

I look up at him.

"Breathe, dickhead, okay? Breathe."

Because Asher is three years older, his tzitzit lineup is in another room and on another floor. I watch him climb the upper school staircase until he's gone and then walk with Noah toward the elementary wing. On our way I put my hand on his shoulder and carefully explain that I might not make it to the van that afternoon, that I "might not make it back." He takes it quite well. He points the G-Zap at my crotch and says, "Got ya," before disappearing into the kindergarten—tough little trouper. When I get to my classroom, my stomach begins to clench. I put my books and lunch box by my desk and move slowly into the inspection line behind Ari Feiger. Ari has a glandular issue that gives him breasts and makes him smell like wet skin. He also has striped pajama bottoms that creep out the back of his pants and a dirty blond afro that can actually hold pencils. When I ask him if he has an extra tzitzit he says, "Yes, but not for you," and walks away from me.

"Ari," I say, following him, "I'll pay you for it."

"I put on a clean one after lunch," he says. "It's not for sale."

"But I forgot mine," I whisper.

When he hears this he turns to the other six boys in my class and starts singing the word tzitzit to the tune of *The Flintstones*. "Tzitzit, meet the tzitzit, have a yabba-dabba tzitzit, a yabba tzitzit, you're gonna be so screwed. Ya'akov's *got no* tzitzit!" he yells and points at me.

"*Shhhh!* Shut up, Ari. The rabbi will hear you."

"You shut up."

I shove him backward and he stumbles into a desk. With a running start he comes toward me and punches my arm. I punch him back. He calls me a "pussy" so I grab his fat neck and shove him into the wall of cubbyholes by the door. The other boys gather around us. Ari runs at me and dives at my knees. We both go down to the floor and one of his chubby thumbnails scratches my top gum. Andrew Friedberg yells, "Kick his ass!" and drops to one knee like a ref.

"Mizrahe!" says Gary Kaplan from his lookout station near the door and we freeze and run to line up. When I get there I taste some blood on my tongue and my right knee throbs. Ari breathes heavily in front of me, fumbling to bobby-pin his rainbow yarmulke. I slide my hand down my leg to my knee and my finger touches skin. The hole is tiny and already frayed, the size of a dime. I stand up straight.

### Rule Number 3 of the Green House Rules

*The wearing of torn or tattered clothing including dress pants, jeans, pajamas, T-shirts, sweaters, or dress shirts at any time will result in the following act: Abram R. Green, C.P.A., will place two fingers inside the hole and tear the garment from your body. The child will then go to his room to dress again, his destroyed garment flapping as he goes.*

  a. *Tattered clothing = disrespect of self and parents who purchased clothing.*
  b. *The decision to don torn garments evokes a failure to comprehend one's good fortune.*
  c. *Failure to comprehend one's good fortune = an inability to be grateful.*
  d. *Being frightened and humiliated is an absolute way to learn that damaged clothing sends a blatant message about one's self and family to one's neighbors, friends, and school peers.*

The rabbi enters the room singing in Hebrew. "Torah, Torah, Torah, Torah, Torah, Torah, To-rah, tziva lanu Moshe—Line up, line up, we're late—Torah, Torah, Torah . . ." Rabbi Mizrahe's one of the younger teachers at Eliahu but no less pompous and pasty. Squat and balding with absurd physical strength, he's five foot two-ish but has the calves and forearms of a carnival freak. He's got the long beard, the dark velvet yarmulke, the ribboned *peyos* and the longest, yellowed tzitzit on this

God's earth. I have him every day for Talmud and Hebrew, and on Tuesdays and Fridays he's my math and English teacher. He seems to truly despise school-aged children but because I read Hebrew better than most he saves his sharpest belittling for my classmates. He could care less that I haven't done a math assignment all year or that I spell like a chimpanzee. He calls me up to the front of the room when he's tired of his "lesson plans" and has me read in Hebrew from random spots in my siddur. He'll let me go a half hour or more, his feet up and crossed, his eyelids fluttering shut. From that close to him I can smell tobacco in his greasy hair and muddy coffee on his breath. And nose hairs. My God. A few come out of one nostril and curl into the other. No really.

". . . tziva lanu Moshe!" Rabbi Mizrahe tosses his books and cigarettes on his desk and exposes every filling he's ever had with an endless yawn. No tooth is spared. In nine seconds the song will begin again from the top. It's like being stuck on an orthodox carousel. "Torah, Torah, Torah, Torah, Torah, Torah, Tor-ah, tziva lanu Moshe."

Rabbi Mizrahe moves toward the lineup and touches each of Gary Kaplan's tassels. Gary sings along to "Torah Torah" but stops completely when the rabbi steps past him. I feel a sour and tingly stomach-burning climb up my throat. I try to swallow but I have no spit. Michael Bornstein is next. His yarmulke needs centering but his tzitzit has never hung better. And then I see him. I see my brother. He's hopping in the hallway, trying to find me. I shake my head. "Too late," I say without sound. Too late.

As the rabbi moves closer, our eyes meet. I sing with him, ". . . tziva lanu Moshe." I watch his fingers touch Ari's tassels. I watch him finish and step up to me.

"Excuse me, Rabbi Mizrahe," says Asher.

The rabbi stops his song and turns to the door. Asher keeps his eyes from me and takes a step closer.

"I need to tell my brother something. May I see him for a second, please?"

Rabbi Mizrahe faces me and nods his head. Asher steps up and grabs me by the elbow. He leads me back toward the door.

"Do *not* . . . leave this classroom," the rabbi says. "Torah, Torah, Torah . . ."

Asher holds my shoulders and turns my back to my classmates. He reaches in his pocket for his balled-up tzitzit and crams it down the front of my pants.

"No time to put it on," he whispers. "Untuck your shirt and let the fringes just hang over your belt."

"No, no way."

"You either try it or you *don't*. I'm not gonna stand here all day."

"Wait," I say, but he yanks up my shirttails.

Asher grabs the tzitzit and slides it around the waist of my pants. He then adjusts the tassels so they droop from all four sides.

"It's crooked," I say.

His eyes slowly shut. "I'm gonna *kill* you. It's *fine*. I'm leaving you now." Asher turns for the door and stops. "Thank you so much, Rabbi."

The rabbi glances over his shoulder, the song still flowing from his nearly closed lips. "Wait," he says, and approaches us.

"I . . . really have to get back," Asher says, his thumb toward the hall.

"What is happening over there?" he says, his head on a tilt. Asher moves for the door.

The rabbi steps up to me and reaches for my two front tassels. Asher steps into the hall. "I'll see you later, J." Rabbi

Mizrahe reaches for the two rear tassels. He gives them each a squeeze and walks to the door.

"Asher!" the rabbi says, and motions my brother back into the room with his finger. Asher taps his watch and moves toward the staircase.

"I'm *so* late. I'll come back when—"

"Come here, please."

Asher folds his arms and walks slowly back into the room. Mizrahe steps up to him and reaches under his shirttails. "Where are your tzitzit?"

My brother puts both hands in his pockets and shrugs. "I don't know," he says.

The rabbi grabs the back of Asher's neck with his small right hand and playfully jostles his head around. He presses his forehead against Asher's and smiles. "Where are your tzitzit?" he says softly.

Asher glances up at him, their heads still pinned.

"I think I . . . must have packed it," he says with his own chuckle. "We're moving, you know? To Piedmont."

Rabbi Mizrahe laughs. "Today? You move today?"

"No . . . ," Asher says.

"No," the rabbi says, shaking Asher's neck. "You love your brother. You will take risks for your little brother, yes?"

Asher tries to pull away but the rabbi doesn't allow it. He gets more of a grip, keeping their foreheads locked.

"Would you let go of me, please?" Asher says, and puts his hand on the rabbi's shoulder. He begins to push him away but he can't get free. Mizrahe's face turns pink and his feet shift for more leverage. He seems to think it's a game, his cheeks rattling from the force. Ari turns to me in disbelief.

"Rabbi Mizrahe," Asher says, his head shivering to pull away. "Get *off* me."

I take a step toward them. "Rabbi," I say. He is holding his breath, struggling to keep Asher locked in his grip. "Rabbi Mizrahe," I say again, and reach for his elbow. Asher jolts to get out but is pinched in the vice. "Get *off* him," I yell. The rabbi widens his legs and moans, bumping his desk into a screech.

"You're nuts," Asher says with a forced grin as his eyes turn serious and widen. I watch his back stiffen, trying anything to break out. I am helpless as he peeks out at me, locked in this embarrassment, this absurd and abusive game.

"What should I do?" I say to him, and he laughs and tries again to jar himself loose. "*Stop!*" I yell at Mizrahe. "*Stop it!*" And then it happens. I'm on my way, my hands out and on him, yanking at whatever I can grab. I feel the buttons of his shirt against my fingernails, the mush in his belly, his breath. And a second before I no longer touch him, I hear the give of something sewed, the severing of cloth. Asher spins out of the hold, sliding backward to the ground, his head nearly banging the floor. I stand next to Rabbi Mizrahe who stares down at his waist, lifting the remaining fringes of his weathered tzitzit. In my palm is a handful of the woolen and woven. I see them there, a part of me now, like a gash in my skin too wide to hold closed. I drop them, letting them rain near my shoes, the tiled floor. And then I run. Past my brother, down the hall. I run from that room.

## Son of Abraham

They haven't found me when the office calls my house. My mother is told she must come to Perth Amboy to pick up Asher. A "desecration of God" is what they call it and he's given a rest-of-day suspension. "Jacob too has been charged," she learns, "but is hiding somewhere in the building." When they're unable to find me by the time she arrives, my mother calls my father with fear in her voice. He tells her to calm down, to bring Asher home. He assures her I'm there, says he'll call when they find me. "I'll take it from here."

As a fugitive I've never been that strong. In a hide-and-seek game when I was six my father found me underneath an afghan in the middle of the living-room floor—a story he just loves to retell to friends. My brother had taken my new spot behind the drapes in the den and my mother and sister were both crouching in the nook beneath the basement stairs. The countdown was loud and hurried I remember, and there was just nowhere else to go. When my dad performs the memory he usually stands and goes through all the motions. He says he leaned an elbow on my covered head and asked the empty room where his son could have gone. The skit always draws a laugh and that's why he does it, but now, as I play the game in the halls of Eliahu Academy, I can only wish we were the family he loves to portray. I could see him through the square holes of yarn that day, his hands on his hips, these forlorn eyes. And I knew what grade I'd been given for my lame attempt to vanish. He circled me twice before gripping the afghan near my ear and flung the thing high with all the strength he could muster.

In a way I'm relieved when Rabbi Belahsan finds me on the second floor, standing on a toilet seat like a wide-eyed cave boy. It's past eleven by then and I'm drained and teary from my flight and capture. I sit in the office next to Rabbi Mizrahe as he dials my father's number. "We found him," he says into the phone, and begins a diatribe on the pure size of this unprecedented *chilul* Hashem.

"The numerical value, Mr. Green, of the Hebrew word tzitzit, is six hundred. The eight threads and five knots make a total of 613, the exact number of precepts in the Torah. The Torah is a grid for conduct, Mr. Green, the conduct of how we as Jews should behave under God. The Talmud tells us . . ."

I stare down at my clasped hands, trying to picture my father's face, his thoughts. He is humiliated for the family, ashamed of me, infuriated by this murky lecture.

". . . where each fringe represents the numerical value of Hashem *echad*. This means, The Lord is one. The Lord, Mr. Green . . . is one."

There is a small pause in which the rabbi looks up at me and switches the phone to his right ear. I can hear my father speaking but I cannot hear his words. Rabbi Mizrahe interrupts him. "When a child fully honors his father and his mother, Mr. Green, the Lord says, 'I account it to them as though I were dwelling among them and they were honoring me.' So, my final question to you is this. Do your sons fully honor you, Mr. Green? And do they honor God? Please, now come. Retrieve your son."

We sit in the parking lot of a Burger King three blocks from the yeshiva. My father pokes the inside of his cheek with his tongue and stares straight ahead, out the windshield of his Cadillac. I keep my head turned away from him, trying not to move, then bump the power-window button with my elbow.

"*Leave* it!"

"Sorry."

"You can't just sit there?"

"I can."

"Can't behave."

"I can."

"Is that how you sit in class?"

"No."

"Fidgeting?" He bangs the steering wheel with his palm and uses the pain to taste his rage. He peers at me with thinned eyes as if I'd bit him, waiting for me to cower, to look away.

My mother once told me that my father never stops loving us, even when he's lost his mind. A difficult thing to believe for sure, although every tantrum, however potent and lengthy, ends with a flurry of uninhibited affection, as if he's sorry it all had to come to this. My parents got married five months after they met at a party in Belmar, New Jersey. The irony that it was the annual clam bake for my father's accounting firm has always added flavor to the story. "Shellfish brought us together," he always says when telling the tale. My mom says before Asher was born she had no idea her husband even had a bad temper. It began soon after they brought him home, when my father learned that parenting was in fact a task of selflessness and that the beautiful girl he'd seen at the party was now someone to be shared.

My father reaches into the pocket of his overcoat and pulls out the suspension notice. He unfolds it onto the steering wheel and stares down at the words. Six and a half days left of yeshiva and it's my first official pink slip. Asher has them wall-papering the back of his closet. I've seen him give tours to his friends.

NAME: Asher Green
GRADE: 5
DATE: May 3, 1975
TEACHER: Belahsan
REQUEST: 1-day suspension
REASON: Called Rabbi Belahsan a "cock smoker" after rabbi tore front cover off his copy of *Beneath the Planet of the Apes*. Disrespect of teacher and minyan.
OUTCOME: Suspension accepted—called mother.

(Laloosh claimed Asher had it hidden behind his prayer book during the morning minyan service. Asher vehemently denied this charge but later claimed to have read the entire Apes series while davening.)

NAME: Asher Green
GRADE: 6
DATE: October 16, 1975

TEACHER: Hadad
REQUEST: 1-day suspension
REASON: Asher wore a belt buckle to school that spelled out the word *bullshit*. Dress-code violation.
OUTCOME: Suspension accepted—called father.

(The belt buckle was huge and brass and had been stuffed in his pants until he got to school. He lasted until lunchtime when Rabbi Hadad led him to the office by the actual buckle itself. The story became legend at Eliahu Academy.)

NAME: Asher Green
GRADE: 8
DATE: September 5, 1977
TEACHER: Cohen
REQUEST: Expulsion
REASON: Vandalism
OUTCOME: Impossible to link drawing to the accused student, Asher Green: Expulsion denied.

(A disturbingly accurate pencil drawing of Rabbi Belahsan was found pinned-up in the yeshiva library. In it, the rabbi was in a consensual threesome with a lobster and an erect pig. Asher came inches from being expelled and there was serious talk of calling the police. To this day, Asher says it wasn't him. I saw the drawing. I only know one person who can draw like that. That pig belonged to Ash.)

"Name," my father says: "Jacob Green. Grade: fourth. Date: October ninth, 1977. Request: Su*spension*, one . . . full . . . week. Reason—this is my favorite part: Destroying—let me read that again—*destroying* Rabbi Mizrahe's tzitzit." He folds the paper and places it back into his pocket. "I'm *trying* Jacob . . . to recall a time in my life where I have felt this *level* of humiliation, so I'm going to need some more time to try and . . . pin it down . . . if it exists at all. Do you have time for me to do this, this kind of search?"

I keep my head resting on the window.

"*Hello?*" he barks.

"Yes, yes."

"You're not too busy, too *booked?* Gotta be somewhere?"

I shake my head.

"Answer me with words."

"No."

"No, what?"

"I'm not too busy," I say, covering the hole in my pants with my hand.

He puts his glasses on the dashboard and leans his forehead onto the steering wheel. He then slowly begins to thump his head against it, banging the ridge above his eyes harder and harder.

"Dad?"

"Still *thinking!*" he hollers, his dark hair jolting forward with each smack.

"Stop."

"Stop, *what?*" he says, lifting his head off the wheel.

"Stop doing that."

"Stop making a fool of myself, stop making a fool of *you?* What? Tell me what I'm supposed to say to a son who *destroys* a rabbi's tzitzit. Tell me!"

"He was hurting, A*aaaasher,*" I say, and drop like a rock into tears.

"Oh, tears, right, great, I *love* tears," he says, putting his glasses back on. "I don't even know you. *God!* Where's my son?" he yells, craning his neck to the backseat. "Are you back there? *Is* he? I don't see him. Do you see him? Maybe he's in the goddamn *trunk*."

I wipe my face.

"Does this em*barrass* you, Jacob? It should. Do you feel it? Do you feel what I feel inside me?"

"Soooorry."

"Do you?"

"Noooo."

"No?"

"I mean yeeees."

"*Not* good enough!" he says, and jumps out of the car.

I watch him hustle across the parking lot to the door of the Burger King and stop. He takes his glasses off and motions to throw them with a jolt of his arm but doesn't let go. He suddenly looks up at me in the passenger seat and begins to jog back. I try to sit taller but slide on the interior. I can see the entire bottom row of his teeth. He swings the door open. "Get *out! Follow* me!" He walks back to the Burger King.

## Rule Number 4 of the Green House Rules

*I. As of July 1975: After consuming meat products, all family members must wait one full hour before eating any dairy products. Meat and milk will never, under any circumstance, be eaten together.*

   *a. Nonkosher meat (Allowed, outside of house.)*

   *b. Swine (Never.)*

   *c. Shellfish (Never.)*

   *d. Cheeseburger (Never.)*

   *e. Bacon cheeseburger ( Never, never.)*

   *f. A Whopper without cheese (Allowed but not in house.)*

   *g. A Whopper with cheese at a friend's house (Never.)*

> h. A Whopper without cheese at Grandma's house (Allowed.)
>
> i. A Whopper without cheese in the garage (Why would you want to eat a Whopper in the garage?)

II. *The family will have two sets of dishes and two sets of silverware for meat and dairy meals. If a meat spoon touches a dairy spoon it must be boiled or buried in the garden.*

> a. Really? (Really.)
>
> b. Do we do that? (We boil.)
>
> c. Why? (We're kosher.)
>
> d. Why? (We're Jews.)
>
> e. Why do Jews . . . ? (Because we're Chosen.)
>
> f. What? (The animals are killed in a less painful way.)
>
> g. What does that have to do with eating ice cream after dinner? (It's tradition.)
>
> h. What happens if I forget? (Your father will go ballistic.)
>
> i. What's ballistic? (In this case it's a rotating column of fury, usually accompanied by a funnel-shaped downward extension of a cumulonimbus cloud which moves destructively over a narrow path.)
>
> j. Oh . . . that.

"A Whopper with*out* cheese. I do not want cheese on it. Ze-*ro* cheese, please . . . thank you. And a Coke, medium."

"You want fries with that?"

"Fries, sure. But I do *not* want cheese on—"

"I understand."

"Thank you. I don't eat cheese with meat," my father says with a slight bounce on his toes, and turns to the woman behind us in line. He smiles at her. In his perfect dream the woman would grip the tip of her chin and blink before speaking. "So you don't eat meat with cheese. How interesting. Are you a Jewish man?"

"Yes," my father would say. "I am. We are. This is my Jewish son, Jacob. His Hebrew name is Ya'akov. I don't allow him to eat meat with cheese either because he is my son. We don't eat meat and cheese together in our Jewish home."

"I see," says the woman. "But I thought kosher Jews weren't permitted to eat nonkosher meat."

"Nice meeting you," my father says, lifting his tray of food. "Shalom to you and the people you love."

"What a kind Jewish man you are."

He nods with a grin then turns to the cashier. "Can I get some more ketchups?"

During the week of Passover we always go to restaurants. My father waits with bated breath for the waiter to ask if we'd like any bread. No, no we would not like any bread. We are Jews and it's the week of Passover and Jews stay clear of yeast of any kind during the week of Passover. So please bring us some matzo. You do have matzo, don't you? And please look for the largest box of matzo you can find. Not the tiny, normal-size box but something that will take up most of the table, perhaps knock some of these less useful items over like water glasses and silverware. And when the waiter brings the box out, my father places it in the middle of the table as a billboard for all to see. FOR THOSE OF YOU STARING AT THIS ENORMOUS BOX OF SPECIAL "BREAD" LET ME EXPLAIN. WE ARE JEWS AND AS JEWS WE DO NOT EAT BREAD ON THE WEEK OF PASSOVER AND WE NEVER, EVER EAT MEAT WITH CHEESE.

I sit across from him in a booth at the Burger King as his focus shifts to meat. Our table is clown-nose red with yellow trim. There's a sun-wrinkled poster of two jousting unicorns in a thin gold frame to our right. Someone left a stack of napkins pinned to the table with mustard. My father smears the mess away onto a booster chair to his side. "Pigs."

"Dad?"

"Do not talk," he says, tearing a ketchup packet with his teeth. "You hear me? I don't want to hear any of it. I just want to eat my lunch. In a week we're moving away and leaving this . . . hor*rendous* event behind and . . . I won't have to see or talk to any of these people again. You'll go to public school and you'll attend Hebrew school at the temple afterward. That's *it!* Not a soul will know that you *ripped* Rabbi Mizrahe's tzitzit in two and we'll just move on with our lives. Pass me the napkins."

"Hebrew school?" I say.

"Yes. It's through the synagogue. Three days a week. I paid the tuition yesterday."

"What time will I get home?"

"You'll be home for dinner. You are *not*, I repeat *not*, to give me a hard time about this."

"But that's not—"

"What? I can't wait to hear this. That's not, *what?*"

"That's not what other kids do in public school."

"Too bad. You're going."

"Eric, Brian Cohen. All the kids from temple. They all go to public school and don't have to go to Hebrew school after."

"So what's your point? You want to be like everyone else? You're a Jew who's learning about his history, his people. And you'll *continue* to learn about them whether you like it or not. The struggles, the triumphs, the sacrifices." My father lifts his Whopper with both hands and takes a bite.

"But you said we were done with Hebrew school."

"*Yeshiva.* You're done with yeshiva. Your mother begged me to get you out and you're out."

"Three days a week?" I ask.

"Tuesday, Thursday, Sunday."

"Sunday?"

"*Zip* it!"

I snag the yarmulke off my head and squeeze it, my face lowered.

"Sulking now," he says, leaning over the table. "One day I'll be *dead* and you can live your own life. Is that what you want?"

"No . . ."

"Understand something, right this second. Look up at me. When my father died," he says, and lifts his index finger. He takes about nine gulps of Coke from the straw. I watch his Adam's apple churn beneath his beard. He lowers the cup and lifts the burger. "I was twenty-one years old. Did you know that?"

I nod.

"Words."

"Yes."

"I was in Michigan, at school. And my mother called to tell me that he was very sick." He takes another bite. He chews. And chews. "But he was already dead." The index finger. The sip. "She lied to protect me," he says through a hurried swallow.

"She lied?"

"To protect me."

"From what?"

"From . . . worrying about him. She was trying to . . . ease me in . . . but the point of the story is this. I wasn't involved in Judaism at all before my father died. He didn't—"

"You didn't go to Hebrew school?"

He shakes his head and takes a bite, chewing quickly so he can speak.

"Nobody made you go?"

"I would have liked Hebrew school."

"How do you know?"

"The point is this," he says, swallowing the rest. "At my father's funeral I met some men who invited me to join them in prayer, to join their minyan. And it was then I learned of an absolutely incredible man named Abraham. I hope to God you've heard of Abraham. Have you?" He takes a bite, awaiting my answer.

"I think so. Yes. Abraham, yes."

"You think so. He's the goddamn *father* of the Hebrew people. A crucial character in the history of the Jews."

"I know him, I know him. He's friends with Moses, right?"

My father stares at me for a moment. "Just listen. Can you do that?"

"Yes."

"Super. Abraham lived to be 175 years old. And came from the Sumerian town of Ur in Iraq."

"He was 175?"

"Yes. He was an incredible—"

"How come no one lives that long now?"

"Well . . . he's Abraham and he had a very special relationship with God and if you let me tell you—"

"How old was your father when he died?"

"He was fifty."

"That's young."

My father shuts his eyes and lets his head dangle from his neck. "Abraham had a son named Isaac with his wife, Sarah. And what God asked Abraham to do was to sacrifice this son, okay? To *sacrifice* him in the name of God."

"Like a sacrifice fly?"

"*Jacob!*" he yells, his jaw jetting forward. "*Listen* to me! I'm teaching you something important."

"Sorry."

"You asked me why I'm *sticking* you in a Hebrew school and I'm telling you. Now listen."

"Sorry."

"This is exactly why your grades are an embarrassment. You don't *think*," he says tapping his head, "up here. Can I continue now?"

I nod.

He slaps the table with his palm and his glasses slide down his nose.

"Yes," I say. "Yes."

"God *damn* it," he says, shaking his head. He takes a bite and chews. "Gob ast Abraham—" He sips. I watch his Adam's apple. "God asked him . . . to take his son to Moriah and offer him as a burnt offering. He was going to sacrifice his son to prove to God how much he . . . honored God."

I slowly raise my hand.

"What are you doing?"

I bring my hand down. "Is a sacrifice when—?"

"A sacrifice is when someone gives up something they love for the good of something else."

"He was going to give up his son?"

"Yes."

"Where would his son go?"

"Nowhere. He'd be dead."

"He would?"

"Yes. Abraham felt that if God told him to . . . sacrifice his son, then he'd be proving to God that he was there for him . . . okay? Loyal."

I begin to raise my hand again.

"Just *ask*."

"Why . . . um . . . would he kill his son for God?"

"Because. God is the Almighty."

"But why would God want Isaac to be dead?"

"He doesn't. He just wants Abraham to prove his loyalty. So, the point is that Abraham is one of my favorite characters in Judaism because he shows his loyalty to God in the most intense and powerful way possible. He was willing to slay his beloved son in the name of his ruler, his God. Do you understand the power, the immensity of this decision of Abraham's?"

I nod.

"Good. Slide me some more napkins."

I hand them to him.

"So, we, as Jews, make certain sacrifices as well. We don't eat cheeseburgers, we don't eat pig products, we fast on Yom Kippur, we avoid bread on the week of Passover, we cover our heads in synagogue, we—"

"Can't play with guns."

"That's not because of Judaism."

"It isn't?"

"No. It's because of death. War." My father takes a last bite of his hamburger and drains his Coke.

"So, how did Isaac get killed?"

"He *doesn't*. Four years of that *pit*. I want you to read this when we get home. *Tonight!* God sees that Abraham would have killed his son, so he stops him from doing it. Abraham passes the test. He passes. He wins. Let's get out of here," he says sliding out of the booth with his tray.

I follow my father to the door. Outside the Burger King it begins to rain again. We jog to our parking spot and I wait for him to unlock the car.

"Dad?"

"What?" he says, and looks over at me.

I rest my forehead against the window and squint inside the car. "Would you kill something for God?"

"What? I couldn't hear you."

I look up at him, covering my head with my coat. "Would you kill something if God told you to?"

He shakes his head and looks down to turn the key. "No."

"What if God said you could live to 175 years old?"

"No," he says and opens his door.

I open mine and get inside next to him. I reach to pull my seat belt on. "What about two hundred years old?"

"The story is a metaphor."

"A met—?"

"There are more realistic ways of sacrificing than taking another's life," he says. "More realistic ways of proving loyalty to God."

"Like being kosher?"

"Exactly."

"Like going to Hebrew school?"

"That's not a sacrifice. That's education. Education is a gift." He starts the car and pulls out onto the street. We ride in silence for a while and my father drapes his hand over the hole in my pants.

I look down at his long fingers, strumming casually against my knee. "Who tore your slacks?"

"No one. I fell. I fell today."

"At home?"

"No. No. I fell at school."

"Before or after you—?"

"Before. Way before."

He slides his hand off my leg and pulls the car over to the side of the road. He puts it in park and faces me. "Will you wear them again?"

"No. No way. I won't. I'm sorry, Dad. I know they're expensive."

"You do. Really? How much, how much you think they cost? Mr. Mathematics, here. Take a guess."

I put my hand over the hole. "Fifty."

"Fifty, what? Cents?"

"No . . . Dollars?"

He leans over my legs with all his weight and puts his index fingers inside the hole. He jerks his arms apart with a grunt and sits up straight. The tear runs the length of my shin but stops at the ankle. I hold the fabric closed with my fingers and turn my shoulder from my father. He sits for a moment, as silent as I, and puts the car back in drive. "Your brother's bar mitzvah is in less than a week," he says, pulling onto the road. "Let's talk about what you're wearing."

## Going Public

Asher and I stand in our new driveway wearing matching Adidas and cuffed Levi's jeans. In seconds we'll be off to school, yarmulkeless and apart from one another for the first time in our lives. Piedmont Junior High is down Saber Street and sits along the reservoir by the train tracks in town. Fillmore Elementary is at the top of Bristle, closer to our house, behind Knole Park. My mother kisses our faces a thousand times and writes "I love you" in bubble letters on the top of my lunch bag. Asher crumples it into a ball as soon as we get outside. He sticks my sandwich and banana into my book bag and tells me they murder people for less in public school. My father opens the front door a crack and bends to get the newspaper. "Good luck today, boys."

"Okay," Asher says.

"Thanks."

"D'you get it done, Asher? Hy and Molly?"

He nods.

"D'you send it?"

"On my way. I'll do it on my way."

"It should really go today."

"I said I'd do it."

"There's a mailbox just down—"

"I know, Dad. I'll do it."

"Okay then. Love you guys. Go make me proud. The brothers Green," he says with a lightly pumped fist, and closes the door.

Asher grabs a pen from his bag but it's dead. He furiously tries to shake the life back into it but fires it over the Sinkovitz's garage when it fails him. I hand him one of mine and he pulls a blank thank-you card from his book bag. He then spins me around to use my back as a desk.

During the housewarming party Hy Weiner eats an onion bagel with tuna and tells my father he's *not* received a thank-you card from Asher. That's twelve days since the bar mitzvah in which the Weiner mailbox in Livingston has been empty of thanks from Asher Green. My father hunts down my brother at the party. Asher says he wrote the Weiners. My dad says prove it. They check the list:

Hy and Molly Weiner:
Cross pen/pencil set + Zero Mostel album entitled *Tevye & Friends—Live from the Wailing Wall.*

Asher's right. The Weiners are crossed off. "You'd better rewrite it," my father says. I already wrote it—So write it again—There's two hundred upstairs, Dad.—Then you better start now—I'm not gonna do it—What did you say?—I *thanked* the Weiners—Why would Hy lie?—I have no idea—You're saying Hy lies—I'm saying I wrote it—I'm *saying re*write it—It's already sent—But not to them—I wrote *this* address—Then it would've arrived—Fine, okay—They gave you a *gift*—And I thanked them for that—You'll *write* it right now—I'll write it tomorrow—Am I speaking in *French?*—It's too late to mail it—I'll get you a pen—I have one right here—Write Herman, not Hy—I'll do it upstairs—What did they give you?—Music and pens. "One day you'll make a friend as giving and as kind as Hy Weiner, Asher. I don't think you even know what it means to have friendship like his. I really don't."

**Rule Number 5 of the Green House Rules**
*Failure to sufficiently acknowledge the generosity of any gift or offering, however unsubstantial it may be deemed, will result in the repossession of the aforementioned offering. Depending on the severity of the child's apathy, punishments may exceed the retraction of the ignored gift and focus more keenly on the removal of privileges, allowances, expressed desires, and any and all previously acquired generosities. Yours is a family whose blunders—be they failures of youthful indifference, failures of judgment, failures of academia, failures of faith, or other—reflect each of the members of this family. As a result, if one of us must wear the humiliation of another's error, then the culprit of said error, will need to relearn the repercussions of failure.*

"Hunch your shoulders a little," Asher says as he writes. ". . . for . . . the . . . gen . . . er . . . ous . . . gift . . . which . . . you . . ."
"Asher?"
"Hunch more . . . like, bend. Good."

"Are you nervous?" I ask him.

". . . am . . . using . . . the . . . act . . . ual . . . pen . . . to . . . write . . . this. Nervous about what?"

"About today."

"What, school? I don't know."

"You are."

"It'll be fine. Sin . . . cere . . . ly."

"I think I miss yeshiva. I miss Eliahu."

"Are you outta your fuckin' mind? Miss *Eliahu?* Don't even say that around me, okay? The address and we're out of here. Hy . . . and . . . Molly . . . *Weiner,*" he says with nasally exaggeration. "Livingston, New Jaaazy. Home-udda blintz and the giant schnaaaz. I should write Hy and Molly *Penis* instead. You think your dear old dad would like that?"

I laugh.

"Stop shaking, I got to write the zip."

"Hy and Molly Schlong," I say over my shoulder.

Asher takes the envelope off my back and we walk out to the sidewalk. "Hy and Molly Love-sausage," he says.

"Hy and Molly Stiffy."

"Hy and Molly Dork . . . pud, putz, poker, pecker, peenie, twanger . . ."

We both crack up and Asher drops the letter in the mailbox on the corner.

"Hy and Molly . . . um . . . *bean* pole," I say.

"Bean pole? That's not one."

"Yes, I think it is."

"No."

"Hy and Molly *Dong,*" I try.

"Better," he says. Asher stops at the corner of Saber and looks down the hill. "Well, I'm outta here," he says with a quick salute.

"Wait," I say, and step closer to him.

"What?"

I turn to see the front of my school through the trees in Knole Park. It's got red bricks and smokestacks, looks like a crematorium.

"You're stepping on my foot, man. Get off me."

"Sorry."

"What's wrong with you?" he says.

I turn back to the school. "I don't think I . . . like this place."

"You like it fine."

"No."

"You *like* it."

"I don't."

"Then snap out of it."

"What time is it?"

"Time to get over whatever you're—"

"What time do you—?"

"Half past cow's ass, all right?" he says and rubs the back of my head with his palm. "First day's . . . shitty and . . . then it's just . . . ya know . . ."

"Just what?"

"*School.* Fuckin' school," he says, walking away. "See ya later."

"Wait."

He stops with his back to me and stares up at the clouds. "For what, man?"

I walk around him and look up at his face. "Let's not go."

Asher brings his chin down from the sky and squints at my hair. "You're bein' a puss."

"No I'm not."

"You should comb this," he says, and licks his palm.

"What are you doing?"

"I just want to wet it."

"Go away."

"It's sticking straight up in the back."

"Don't."

"Let me just flatten it. You didn't shower, did you?"

"Get off. I'll fix it. Stop."

"Fine," he says. "Go to school like that. Alfalfa. The kids'll call you Alfalfa for the rest of the year. Look at the new kid and his fucked-up hair."

"I'll fix it," I say, pressing it down.

"Good. You should. Looks ridiculous."

Asher lifts his book bag higher on his shoulder and exhales the autumn air. He glances at his new route to school and then down at me. I don't know how he stays so calm. We're just a couple of Heebs who can all of a sudden wear our "play clothes" to school. Hi, my name is Jacob. I can recite the book of Esther and say the Hebrew blessings over bread, wine, and macaroons. Want to come over?

"Okay, Alfalfa," Asher says, and walks away from me across the street. "Poor Alfalfa . . . poor, poor Alfalfa. Remember that episode? With the fish?"

I step to the curb and watch him go.

He stops when he gets to the other side and faces me. "Good luck," he says under his breath, and heads down the sidewalk.

"What'd you say?"

"I said good luck."

I watch him go a few more steps. "Good luck too . . . to you. What time does the junior high let out?" I yell at his back.

"Same as yours, I guess." He cuts through some hedges and walks down Bristle Street. He looks back at me just before he turns the corner and I wave on my toes but don't think he sees.

I glance down at my new white sneakers and feel homesick for the yeshiva I hate. I think of the long bus ride, my brother's shoulder against mine and how greedy and blind I was for not seeing what I had. I tell myself I'll see him later, in a few hours, not that long. A group of boys my age walk across the street toward the school. They're shoving each other and hurling acorns at mailboxes. I step slowly down the sidewalk, giving them a chance to get ahead. And then I follow them. All the way to class.

THE THING I notice first about the fourth grade at Fillmore Elementary is death and God—or the amazing lack of them. A whole morning goes by and there's no talk of plagues or slavery or the smiting of anyone, and not as much as a peep on sacrificial slaughters or pestilence. By lunchtime we do some vocabulary flash cards, learn how the Sioux liked to dance, and watch a cartoon filmstrip on magnets. The magnets have googly eyes and giant ears and wear top hats with daisies on them. And they really like to dance. Just days earlier, Rabbi Hadad, a nearly seven-foot Moroccan Torah teacher with a limp and special shoes was quizzing us on the lessons of the Tanakh. Pointing like a game-show host, the rabbi would give us the opening line and place his hand behind his ear for us to finish it in unison.

"He who fatally strikes a man shall be . . ."

"Put to death!"

"When a man schemes against another and kills him treacherously, the man shall be . . ."

"Put to death!"

"He who insults his father or his mother shall be . . ."

"Put to death!"

"Whoever lies with a beast shall be . . ."

"MICHAEL THE MAGNET has a magnetic personality. Just watch how Sammy Steel and Ira Iron come running when Michael says hello." [*beep*]

"Say, Sammy and Ira. What do you say we make a connection? A *magnetic* connection that is."

"Sounds *magn*ificent, Michael." [*beep*]

"Great. Let's dance!"

THE CLASSROOM IS huge and bright and has a living gerbil named Rerun in the science corner. The floor is carpeted and there's a locker in the coatroom that has my name on it in glitter. My teacher, Mrs. Carnegie, is a lanky redhead with freckles on her lips and earlobes. When she smiles her top lip disappears and you can see her tan gums way up high in her mouth. It makes her teeth look enormous but she seems really happy. She has me come to the front of the room when I first arrive and asks each of the students to say their names. There's Kristen, Barry, Jackie, Paul, Kara, Glenn, Cecil, Andre, Tara, Andy, Gary, Kyle, Dana, William, Jon, Cadence, Jill, Maggy, Thomas-not-Tommy, Rob, Nicholas, Lisa, Dee, and Patty. I wave to each as they say their name and feel Mrs. Carnegie's hands squeeze my shoulders. They all wear very bright and different-colored clothing and some of them are Chinese, I think, and some black. The kid named Jon says, "Hi, I'm Jonny, Mets or Yankees?" Everyone laughs. I say "Mets" and half of them cheer and boo.

"Jacob comes from a special school called a yeshiva," Mrs. Carnegie says. "It's a school where children learn Hebrew for half the day, right, Jacob? And then all the other subjects like math and English and science for the second half?"

I nod. Science?

"Maybe if we ask him nicely, Jacob would write something in Hebrew on the board for us."

My classmates applaud for this and Mrs. Carnegie leans over my shoulder from behind me. "Would you?"

I nod and face the blackboard.

"Did you know there are seven other Jewish students in this class, Jacob?"

When I look out at them, a kid in the back named Barry is waving at me. I take a piece of chalk and write Ya'akov on the board in Hebrew and then stand there like a moron, unsure of what to do next. A girl named Dana and a girl named Kristen start to tap each other and snicker in the front row. They're both prettier than most of the girls that went to Eliahu and wear something wet and clear on their lips that smells like cotton candy. Dana's hair is brown and long and slides around a lot when she turns her head. When I look at her she bumps her shoulder into Kristen's and they both laugh with their hands over their mouths. I check the zipper on my new Levi's jeans and Dana points at my crotch before bending at the waist with the giggles. I lick my hand and pat down my hair.

"And what does that word mean?" Mrs. Carnegie says, bowing toward the board.

"That's just my name."

"Oh, that's wonderful. That's the Hebrew word for Jacob, class. Would you read it for us, please?"

"Ya'akov."

"Gazoontite," says Jon, and the whole class laughs.

Mrs. Carnegie stares him down with her hands on her hips. Jon shrinks behind his desk as the seconds pass by. "Thank you," she finally says, returning to me. "It sounds a little like Jacob, doesn't it?"

I nod.

"Well, welcome to Fillmore, Jacob. It's wonderful to have you in our class. Isn't it students?"

They applaud again.

"Okay, now. We have a big day as usual. You all know what time it is. So let's get started."

The class lets out a moan and each kid reaches for a textbook. Mrs. Carnegie walks to her desk and lifts a booklet from her center drawer. She guides me by the shoulders to a desk right next to Jon and lays the papers on top, facedown.

"I need you to take this small quiz," she says. "What kind of math were you doing at your old school?"

"What kind of math?"

"Yes, were you doing any division or long division?"

"Division . . . no."

"None of that yet, huh? How 'bout word problems, any of those?"

"Yes . . . like . . . spelling?"

She blinks a few times and hands me a pencil. "Do your best. Let me know when you're done, all right?"

"Okay."

"Chop, chop, class, everyone should be working. Can't talk to your neighbor if you're working. Just can't. Jonny, let's go." Jon sits on his knees, bending over his desk. He waits for her to walk away before putting his pencil in his mouth and offering his hand. "Did I embarrass you?" he whispers.

"What?"

"Did I embarrass you? When I said gazoontite?"

"No," I say, shaking his hand.

"Your Hebrew name sounds a little like a sneeze, doesn't it? Ya'akov," he says, covering his nose.

I smile at him. "I guess."

Jonny is tiny with jet black hair that falls past his shoulders. He also has very tan skin, as if he just got off the beach.

"I'm Jewish," he says. "Gruber. So don't be offended, okay?"

"Okay."

"So the Mets, huh?"

"*Jon!*" says Mrs. Carnegie, and he flops off his knees and opens his book.

I pull my chair in closer and pick up the pencil she gave me. Rerun is in a tank right behind me. He's sucking from his water bottle, making it rattle, his tiny paws gripping the sides. It's really funny to watch. He drinks like a person. I smile at him and look to see if Jon notices. He's back on his knees with his head dipped, scribbling away. This is a good school. There's a decorated Christmas tree in the corner by the flag and a huge map of the world painted on the wall near the encyclopedias. That kid Barry says there's pizza for lunch today, and you can get a Coca-Cola from a can if you have a quarter. The girl named Dana keeps putting on that lip stuff and turning around to see me. Her sweater is pink and fuzzy and the hairs look like they're floating.

"I hear talking," says Mrs. Carnegie.

I look down at the booklet. I flip to page 1.

1. *Amy watched 8 hours of TV on Sunday, 8 hours of TV on Monday, 9 hours of TV on Tuesday, 3 hours of TV on Wednesday, 5 hours of TV on Thursday, 3 hours of TV on Friday, and 8 hours of TV on Saturday. How many more hours of TV did Amy watch from Monday to Saturday than from Tuesday to Saturday?*

"Pssst."

I glance over at Jon. He points with his chin to a piece of notebook paper taped to his knee. It says *The Mets? What about Reggie, Guidry, Nettles?*

He peeks at me under his armpit and raises his eyebrows. I go back to my quiz.

*2. Jane practices the piano for 3 hours during every prac-
tice session. Jane has 3 practice sessions each week. During
a 17-week period, how many hours will Jane practice the
piano?*

I rub my eyes with the heel of my palm and look up at Mrs.
Carnegie. She stands from her desk and walks to the back of
the room.

*3. If Brad drives at 46 mph, how many hours will it take to
drive 414 miles?*

"Psssst."

*4. A crate of apples weighs 225 pounds. A crate of plums
weighs 130 pounds. How many pounds would they weigh
if . . .*

"Psssst!"
I turn to Jon. "The first one is eight," he says, glancing be-
hind him at Mrs. C. "Eight more hours. The TV girl, right? It's
eight. Write it."
I press the pencil tip to the paper. I press it until it snaps off.
I can't do these. I'm not smart enough. *Jane practices the piano
for 3 hours during every . . .*
Mrs. Carnegie taps my shoulder and I flinch. "How's it go-
ing?" she says, and kneels at my side. "Did I scare you?"
"I'll help him," says Jonny, way too loud, and I see all these
heads pop up and stare. He closes his book and stands.
"Sit . . . down . . . now."
"But he's—"
"One more chance. Sit . . . down . . . now."

Jon lowers himself back down.

"Concentrate on your own work, Mr. Gruber. Understood? Let's go. Open that book back up."

"Just trying to help."

"How's it going over here, Jacob?"

"My pencil broke. It just—"

"Here's another one," she says, and gives me hers. "Are these confusing to you?"

I look down at the words, the numbers, the names Jane and Brad. When I hear the girls laugh I glance up and see Dana. She moves Kristen's blond hair behind her ear and leans in to whisper.

"Let's try this second page together, and we'll go from there, sound good? Jacob?"

"Yeah."

"Are you ready?"

I nod.

"This is straight-up multiplication, all right?" Let's try a few," she says. "Ready?" She flips the page over. "Okay, number one. "Seven times eight."

Seven rows of eight things or . . . eight rows of seven things. Like cars or . . . oranges. Seven rows of eight oranges is . . . like . . . a lot. It's like . . . a wall of oranges.

"Would you *please* turn around, Dana, Kristen, Jackie, all of you, *right* now. I'm coming over there next. In two minutes I want to see what you've accomplished today. Will you be ready for me?"

Twenty-six, twenty-seven, twenty-eight, twenty-nine, thirty, thirty-one . . .

Mrs. Carnegie kneels back down and stares at my work. "What are you—tell me what you're doing right now," she says, blocking the girls with her back.

"I'm drawing seven rows of eight things. These are oranges."

"I see. Okay. Did you learn any multiplication at your old school?"

I nod.

"Can you tell me what two times two is?" she whispers.

"Four?"

"Good. Can you tell me what four times four is?"

Not without drawing more oranges, but ya know what I can do? I can sing the "Four Questions." You know, from Passover. "'Ma nishtana halila hazeh mikol halelot—mikol halelot. Sheb'chol halelot . . .'"

"I'll be right back," I hear her say, and she storms off to scold the girls up front.

I watch her go and then look down at the page. My cheeks and neck tingle with fearful embarrassment. I'm going to be in the third grade before this day is over. My father will die. And then he'll kill me. I'm the stupidest person in this class. I just got here and everyone in this room is going to know.

"Pssst."

When I look at Jon he's got the same piece of paper taped to his knee. His first message is crossed out and underneath it just says *Jane practiced 153 hours.*

"One fifty-three," he says without sound. "Write it."

# The Sabbath

One's "thing"—(1) A point of personal interest; a hobby, sport, or avocation that succinctly defines a person. (2) A brief coupling of words used to evoke someone's personality in a small-talk setting: *Billy's thing used to be soccer; now it's masturbation.* (3) A laconic summation of one's character and interests used for the purpose of categorization and judgment. See also "What do you do?"

I choose to lie when my father asks about school. I'd be stupid if I didn't. Like in class, there are right and wrong answers to every question he has. But unlike class, I know the answers he wants: (1) Yes, Dad; (2) Very; (3) Always; (4) All of them; (5) Every day; (6) Constantly; (7) Oh, yes; (8) A *lot.* (9) Yup;

(10) Of course me. The answer to that is . . . me. As he and I join the family in the dining room for Shabbat, he flattens a yarmulke on my head, and kisses the corner of my eye. "Now that," he says, "is what I like to hear."

When the first blessing comes to an end, both candles are lit. My mother stares at them before sitting, a hint of a smile. My father lifts his cracked leather prayer book and opens to a page marked by a frayed violet tassel.

"Thank you, Claire," he says, his voice softened, lethargic. "Lovely as always." He places his glasses back on his face and smooths the page with his palm. "You shall love the Lord your God, with all your mind, with all your strength and with all your being. Take these words which I command you this day upon your heart. Teach them faithfully to your children, speak of them in your home and on your way, when you lie down and when you—"

"Aaaafffffflllooo" is the sound that leaps from Asher's mouth. He sits frozen before facing my father, his head still lowered in a cave of brown hair. My father slowly closes his book and removes his glasses.

"Sorry," Asher says, straightening his yarmulke, and sneezes a second time. "Affffloooo."

My father rests his chin on his fist and glares at the top of Asher's head.

"Just . . . continue," Asher says, and sniffs. "Keep reading. I sneezed."

"Abram," says my mom. "He said he was sorry. Come on now."

"Asher interrupted," Dara announces, chewing on the tip of her ponytail.

"Mind your own business," Asher says to her.

"Mommy, I'm hungry," Gabe says from his booster chair, rubbing his eyes.

And the silence resumes. I look down, can see my face in the reflection of my large white plate. I tap the handle of my spoon, counting each of the seconds of this poisonous silence. Fourteen . . . fifteen . . . sixteen . . . and my father reopens the book.

"You shall love your God . . . with *all* your mind . . . with *all* your strength . . . and with *all* your being. Take these words which I command you this day . . ."

I swallow a yawn through my ears and stare at the braided challah I will bless when the time comes. It's been my role on Fridays nights for as long as I can remember; the *hamotzi* is what they call it. My dad says I read Hebrew better than most of his friends. He likes to have them over so he can watch their faces as the words roll from my trained tongue. There is nothing else I do in life that is so assured to please him, no other triumph so rewarded. He calls it my gift, my "thing." As he reads the prayer he runs his hand through his pitch-black hair and scratches his scalp. Shabbat has always seemed to exhaust him or remind him of the workweek he's somehow escaped. His sluggish movement and melancholy tone may also be an offering to the plight of his religion, an homage to perpetual atonement and unceasing pogroms. Any deviance from the respectful pace he seeks is a blatant declaration of our lack of historic empathy. Our advantage is that we've been trained since birth to sit as statues at this table. Our disadvantage is that we are children. The penalty for religious indifference in our home has forever been clear. It is rage.

As he finishes he slides his prayer book over to Asher without looking at him and leans back in his chair with folded arms. Asher brings the book into his lap and begins. "Shma Yisroel—"

"Clarity . . . please."

"Adonai Eloheynu, Adonai Echad. Here oh Israel, the Lord is our God, the Lord is one. *Ve-ahavta et Adonai Elohecha . . . bechol levavcha . . .*"

Five days into public school and Asher has a circular cut on each of his four right knuckles. The gauzy bandage my mother uses goes halfway up his wrist and makes it look worse than it is. He says some "freckled fat fuck" with braces kept mumbling "faggot" as he passed him in the hall. He couldn't even hear the kid the first few times and thought he was saying "bag it" under his breath as he passed him. But then the kid enunciates better so Asher throws a punch and the kid's mouth explodes and there's blood everywhere and this sniveling freckled fat fuck tries to get him expelled. Asher comes an inch from getting booted but squeaks out a suspension with probation and five hours with a social worker named Don. My father almost breaks his own foot, kicking Asher's bed frame. He threatens boarding school and even makes some calls but says he can't find any that are run by Yids. The day after all this happens, Asher convinces me to ditch our very first day of Hebrew school at Temple Beth Tikvah. We ride our bikes to a 7-Eleven instead and he buys us both Slurpees and a magazine called *Twat*.

"*. . . Ochtovtom al mizuzote beytecha uvisharecha.*"

My father takes the book back and flips to another marked page. "Do not. Do . . . not imagine that character is determined at birth," he reads. "We have been given free will. Any person can become as righteous as Moses, or as wicked as Jereboam. We ourselves decide whether to make ourselves learned or ignorant, compassionate or cruel, generous or miserly. No one forces us, no one decides for us, no one drags us along one path or another; we ourselves, by our own volition, choose our own way."

I'm still ten good minutes away from blessing the challah and I decide to play a game I call "the Unthinkable." If I were to lift the bread as I utter the blessing and hurl it in a tight spiral at the refrigerator. If I were to ram my nose into the braided loaf or sit on it or have it drop from my butt like an enormous turd. If I put it in my mouth and thrashed my head back and forth like a Doberman, leaving nibbled bits of challah bread in our soup bowls and the creases of our laps. Or if I molded it into a big breaded schlong and bumped it repeatedly against Asher's forehead.

And my father sings, "The sun on the rooftops no longer is seen. We come now to welcome the Sabbath, our queen. Behold her descending . . ."

Just before I do the hamotzi, my father will ask each of us what we're grateful for this week. In the past it's been easy to say the right thing: I'm grateful for Mom, for Dad, for the weekend, for the food Mom made for dinner. But lately he's been disappointed if our answers are what he deems "thoughtless." Asher says he's grateful for his skateboard for three straight weeks in October. My father calls him into his bedroom after dinner. He explains how ridiculous it is for someone to be grateful for a piece of fiberglass on wheels. "I'm grateful for my *skate*board," my father mimics as he removes his cuff links. "I'm grateful for the little wheels and the little stickers I put on it. I got a question for ya," he says. "What do you think Anne Frank would be grateful for?"

"Anne Frank?"

"Yes, Anne Frank. If she didn't die of typhus in Bergen-Belsen and had the chance to be grateful?"

"I have no idea."

"Well, try."

"I don't know."

"You think she'd say something as moronic as a skateboard? Do you? You think she'd take the time to acknowledge the . . . the . . . *wheels* and . . . all the new stickers. Somehow I don't. I just don't see it."

I begin thinking of what I might say from the time school lets out on Fridays. I'm grateful for Anne Frank. I'm grateful for Jerusalem and Israel Bonds. I'm grateful for synagogues and shank bones and the chills I get when Jews win Oscars. But I'm most grateful that neither of you know that I'm the stupidest person in the fourth grade. You see, Mom and Dad, if Moishe eats 4 pieces of bacon on Monday and 12 shrimp on Tuesday and 48 links of sausage on Wednesday and 612 oysters on Thursday and 8,000 Christ wafers on Friday and—

"Jacob?"

"Yes?"

"It's your turn," my father says, resting his chin in his palm. "Tell us what made you grateful this week."

"I'm grateful it's the weekend . . . and . . . for you and Mom."

"Thank you for that. What else?"

"And, I'm grateful that I made a new friend so fast. In Piedmont."

"Jonny, right?" my mom says.

"Yeah."

"He's a sweetie."

"Okay," my Dad says. "Anything else?"

"No. That's it."

"Asher?" my father says.

My brother shifts in his chair but says nothing.

"Asher," he repeats.

I glance over at him. He's got his cloth napkin wrapped around his hand.

"Uh," he says. "Let's see."

How about the Unthinkable? I ask him in my mind. He'd have so much to say: Um. Right. Hi. I'm supergrateful that neither of you know that I store about twenty mock firearms in the tunnels of our new air-conditioning system. In Rockridge I had to keep them buried in a box in the yard so this is really lucky. If you were to remove the grate in the floor of my room and reach your arm down and to the right, you'd feel the handle of a fake 357 Magnum with laser sighting. I also own three pump rifles, a BB gun with an attachable scope and over ten high-powered water pistols that can shoot up to thirty-five feet if it's not too windy. And Jesus fucking Christ I'm grateful neither of you know how many porno mags I keep in the removable headboard of my bed frame. I'm also grateful you don't know that I let Jacob look at them and that we read the filthy articles out loud to each other and laugh our asses off at all the variations of the words *penis, breast,* and *vagina.* Did you know that breasts are also known as fun-bags, honkers, headlights, and bezongas? So, I'm grateful I found a way to own the weapons I'm forbidden and I'm supergrateful for the publishers that print *Skank, Beaver Hunt, Cans,* and *Coozey Digest.*

"I guess . . . I'm grateful it's the weekend," he says with his head lowered, nudging his fork.

My father reaches for Asher's wrist and lifts his hand away from the silverware. "Can you just *leave* it?" he says with a hint of fury, and nods to show he's still listening.

"Mommy, I'm hungry," Gabe says, his forehead touching the table.

"It's almost time to eat, sweetie."

"Patience, Gabriel, please," my father says. "Go ahead, Asher."

"I'm done."

"You're done. He's *done*, Claire. He's grateful it's the weekend," he says, clapping once and turning his palms up.

Asher sighs and brushes the hair from his eyes. My father stares at him for a few seconds, attempting to spend his rage through his jaw. It makes his entire cranium vibrate. I feel for my brother right now. My dad's all over him. It becomes increasingly tricky to keep from infuriating our father when he's decided it's you who grinds him. If this edging leads to a tantrum, depending on the severity, all will be wiped clean by the time the morning arrives—but never sooner. It's then that my dad will apologize for despising our very presence in his home and quickly begin to douse us with a giddy and sort of hurried affection. We will often receive gifts in the wake of these apologies: impromptu matinees, trips to Toys "Я" Us, movies, clothes, and rapid-fire tickling that takes your breath away.

"Baruch ata Adonai, Eloheynu melech haolem, hamotzi lechem min haaretz," I say, lifting the challah.

And my father says, "Amen."

With the blessing for the bread complete, it is time to eat. On nights like this, where one of us is in the hot seat, the boundary of silence is softened but still demands control. My mother speaks of her return to school and being a freshman at Rutgers at the age of thirty-seven. She's a certified physical therapist but chose to go back to college last spring; a degree in psychology is her goal. She addresses the top of my father's head, his soup spoon churning from wrist to mouth. Asher bumps his pot roast with his fork and lines his carrots up like he's building a raft. I peek over at him but he doesn't look my way.

"So with night school and the summer seminars they offer,

I could feasibly have a private practice somewhere in the . . . let's see . . . mid-1990s."

"Nineteen ninety!" I say. "Are you gonna drive a Millennium Falcon to your office, Mom?"

"A what?"

"Can I go to your office, Mommy?" says Dara.

"Not yet, baby."

"I want to go," says Gabe.

"We'll all go," my father says. "If Mommy doesn't change her mind that is. Long road, a Ph.D. You may decide to jump off at some point."

"I doubt it," she says, smiling.

"It's not as if you're not busy with . . . or . . . ful*filled* by your family."

"I can do both," she says, reaching to touch my cheek. "No one here is losing me."

"A Ph.D. is a haul," my father says. "When are you gonna study? In the middle of the night?"

She looks up at him and then down at her food. "I'll find a way."

He laughs and lifts his spoon to his mouth. "If you make it, do we all get free therapy?"

She dips her spoon into her bowl. "You refuse to go, remember?" She brings the soup to her mouth.

My father leans back in his chair and blinks at her. "I was making a joke."

"Gabe!" Dara screams. "Stop touching my carrots."

Gabriel is leaning halfway out of his booster chair with his hands in Dara's plate.

"Gabriel, keep your hands on your own food," my mother says.

My father lifts a bored gaze to both of them. He then glances at Asher just in case he missed something to scowl at. Asher takes a bite at just the right time. My father looks back at my mother. "You don't know a joke when you hear one, huh?"

"I . . . need to buy a few more books on Monday," she says, avoiding his stare. "One of them is forty-five dollars. Should I just use the credit card, or do you want to give me some cash?"

He sits forward shaking his head and lifts his spoon. "You said someone named Judith called."

"So you'd rather I use the credit card then."

"Fine, sure, *do* it. Who's this Judith person?"

My mother looks up at my father for a second and lays her spoon on her napkin. "Judith Cohen. From the temple. Steven, her son, is selling raffle tickets or something . . . for a carnival at the Hebrew school. She just wanted to know if we were interested."

"The boys' Hebrew school?"

My mother nods.

"Wonderful. So you have them to sell as well?" he asks me.

This could be bad. Neither of us has been to Hebrew school quite yet. "I have them," I say.

"What are you waiting for? How many do you have to sell?"

"Twenty. I think . . . twenty."

"You think? How many'd *you* get?" he says to Asher.

"About that. Twenty. Twenty-ish."

"Have you tried to sell any?"

"No," Asher says. "There's still a lot of time."

"Have *you* tried yet?" he says to me.

"I'm . . . tomorrow I was going to—"

"You'll call the Litvins, the Brotts, the Kafins. Everyone at my office. I'll give you the temple registry. You'll have 'em sold by Friday."

"Thanks, Dad," I say.

"What are they, a buck apiece?"

"I think, yeah."

"Yes, not *yeah*. Yes."

"Yes."

"I'll buy five," he says to me.

"Great," I say, smiling and nodding. Asher gives me a death glance, and I pull back on the joy.

"And I'll buy five of yours, Asher," my mother says.

My father looks up at her. "Let him do his own legwork, would you, please?"

"You can't offer to buy some from J and not—"

"Asher doesn't have a learning disability, Claire."

In the pause that follows, I wait before looking at my mother. She shuts her eyes and lets her head fall sideways on her shoulder.

"I've asked you not to do that," she says. "I've asked you not to say that in front of the others. To label him."

My father brings a spoonful of soup to his mouth and dabs his lips with his napkin. "The point is this: With the grades Jacob gets in school, he should be studying, not selling. This one can sell his own raffle tickets. Maybe the kid you punched will take a few. His parents too."

"Who did Asher punch?" Dara says.

"I want puuuunch," Gabe says to my mother.

"You have juice right there."

"No, Mommy."

"Gabriel," she says. "Sit back down and eat your dinner. We don't have any punch in the house."

I see my father look my way as he reaches for more challah. "Besides, Jacob tells me he's doing wonderfully at his new school." He peeks at my brother. "The kids like him, the teacher likes him. Not a scuffle for miles. Says he's gonna change things around, right? Start anew."

I put a carrot in my mouth and stare down at my plate.

"Sometimes," my mother says, with her hand on mine, "change is the perfect medicine for—"

"You want to go to a real college someday, right?"

"Yes."

"Like where?"

"Michigan."

"I want to go to Michigan too," Dara says.

A laugh seeps from Asher's lips. "It's the only college he's ever heard of."

"No it isn't," I tell him.

"This one," he says, pointing at Asher with his thumb, "an *adult* in the eyes of the Lord and he can't think of anything to be grateful for in life."

"I told you what I was grateful for. You just didn't like it."

"The doodler. Doodles all day long and rides his skateboard. 'How's your bar mitzvah boy doing, Abram?' 'Well, today he drew a cow skull in one of his fifty notebooks. How's *your* son, Irv?' 'Well, he's in all AP classes and he's going to Israel this summer.'"

"That's what you want from me?" Asher says.

"Enough," he says, waving his hand.

"You want me in *Israel*, Dad?"

"Asher drew something beautiful today," my mother says. "All in pencil, it's this montage of—"

"Oh, that's just . . . my son the doodler. He can take over for Charles M. Schulz. Draw . . . Snoopys and things for a living."

"Abram. I really don't like that."

"You really don't like *what*, Claire?"

My father tosses his fork on his plate. Everyone but Gabriel looks down at their food.

My father waits.

Three . . . four . . . five . . . six . . .

"Not now," she says gently, and resumes eating.

My father nods his head, his eyes still pinned on my mother.

"Did you ever get back to that fella at the dry cleaners?" he asks.

"Yes. They said they're still looking. The vest, right? The blue?"

My father slowly blinks his eyes. "The vest that goes with the *suit*, Claire. I told you eight times which vest."

"They said they're still looking."

"If you can't remember something as simple as a color, I'll help you. I'll get the jacket right now."

"Don't go now, Abram. Eat your food."

My father stands and walks quickly from the room. My mother touches the corners of her mouth with her napkin and follows him. We all stop eating to watch her leave.

"Mom?" I say.

"I'll be right back," she says from the door.

"He's gonna rip her in two," Asher mumbles.

"Don't say that," I say.

"Don't tell me what to say."

I point at Gabe and Dara. "You're gonna teach them that."

"Mind your own fuckin' business."

"I'm telling Dad you said 'fuckin','" Dara says, and slaps Gabriel's hand away from her food. "Get *away*, Gabe."

"I don't give two shits what you do," Asher says.

"I'm telling Dad you said 'two shits,'" she says.

"Great. Throw this in while you're at it." He stands and begins to unbuckle his pants.

"Asher, don't." I say.

"Look who's scared."

"I'm not scared."

"Yes, you are. You're fuckin' scared. You're scared to death."

"Why are you trying to make him mad?" I ask.

"Why are you trying to make him *proud?* Michigan. You know he wants to hear that."

We stop as we hear him holler upstairs. I turn that way and stare at the door. It's a thunderous and sudden bark, as familiar as any learned prayer. "I'm not trying to make him proud," I say.

"Oh, you're not? Mr. Michigan. You tell him what he wants to hear."

"You're no different. You don't stand up to him."

We hear them coming down the stairs. Asher buckles his belt and sits down.

My father walks back in the room, his napkin flapping from his collar. My mother follows slowly behind, her face a pallid stone. She smiles at me as she passes, mostly with her eyes, and I think to touch her, but know it's a mistake. She lifts her fork and brings a carrot into her mouth to chew but not taste. Underneath the table, I rest my finger on her knee.

"I have an announcement," my father says, pulling his chair close to his plate. "Tomorrow morning I want to clean this entire house. Every inch. There is *so* much crap lying around it's making me *sick!* I want to be unpacked. I mean every single box and every single thing put away. If I even *see* a box tomorrow night there's gonna be trouble. We'll sort out the attic, the closets, the garage, all your rooms, and take everything we don't need to the dump. Jacob and Dara, your job is to bag all the clothes and toys you no longer use and make your rooms spotless. Asher, you are to begin the day by cleaning every bathroom in the house. Got it? Hello? You in there? If I see a single hair on the toilet seat I'll know exactly who to contact. We'll do it as a team, we'll do it as a family. No one leaves or makes plans before this place shines, yes? Help me write my gratefuls for next week's Shabbat. I'm grateful we're finally un-packed and there's some order around here. Who in God's name put those wet towels in the laundry room? They smell like one of Aunt Ida's wigs dipped in piss."

A laugh seeps from my lips. Asher tries to prevent it too, but he can't; he lowers his head. My father's eyes light up from the reaction. He smiles from ear to ear. He grips the back of Asher's neck, then ruffles his hair. "Okay, Greens? If cleanliness is next to godliness, then tomorrow we meet the Lord!"

"Yeaaaah," says Gabriel, and claps his sticky hands.

# II

## 1980

## Thirteen Years Old

*With the textured tradition of his ancestors
and with the great and overflowing pride of his parents,
Jacob Philip Green will be called to the Torah
to become a Bar Mitzvah.
Please share with us in our unfettered delight
as we celebrate the manhood of our beautiful
blond boy. November the first,
nineteen hundred and eighty at nine o'clock.
Temple Beth Tikvah
in Piedmont, New Jersey.*

## Meg

Three years later and just like that, my brother is finished with me. He's done sharing his time, his porn, his tunes, his angst, his friends, his room, and his filthy language with me. I can hear his music every day from outside his locked bedroom door. The Boomtown Rats, UFO, the Surf Punks, Squeeze, the Plasmatics, Missing Persons, Jethro Tull, the Cars, Devo, Sex Pistols, AC/DC, Judas Priest, and a fat and sweaty rocker named Meatloaf. I get glimpses of him. "Sightings" are what I call them. Running down the stairs, kneeling into the refrigerator, hunkering down behind a tall box of Lucky Charms with shoulders slumped, slurping like a banshee. I sometimes see him with all his skate-punk friends or this girl he likes who my father calls a shiksa. Her name is Brigitte and

Asher's friend Nicky tells me, "She's a slutty Catholic chick that can suck the chrome off a trailer hitch." When I ask Jonny what the hell this means he says, "A slut is a hooker and a hooker's a whore." Asher keeps her as far from the family as possible.

## Rule Number 6 of the Green House Rules

*As it states in the Torah, Deuteronomy 7:1–5, "You shall not intermarry with any Hittittes, Girgashites, Amorites, Canaanites, Perizzites, Hivites, or Jebisites. Do not give your daughters to their sons or take their daughters for your sons, for they will turn your children away from me in order to worship other gods—and the Lord's anger will blaze forth against you and he will promptly wipe you out."*

*a. What's a Girgashite? (Just don't date Gentiles.)*

*b. Don't date what? (Goyim, non-Jews.)*

*c. Why? (Because you're a Jew and Jews should not marry non-Jews.)*

*d. Why not? (Because love, on it's own, is never enough.)*

*e. It's not? (No.)*

*f. Was Mom a Girgashite? (Your mother was Protestant but she was always searching for more.)*

*g. More what? (More faith.)*

*h. Did she find it? (Of course. Faith is the only thing more durable than love. It's a massive and complex concoction of shared vision, common values, the awareness of one's rooted history, and perhaps most important, love itself. But love cannot do it alone. It cannot. The road is too long. What an all-Jewish union provides is tantamount to the foundation of a healthy, lifelong marriage and the offspring it produces. Dating non-Jews is simply bad practice and*

*often leads to the diluting of our ever-dispersing reli-*
*gion. Do you understand what I'm saying to you?)*
i. *Yeah. Dad? (What?)*
j. *What's a trailer hitch?*

Brigitte's sensual and curvy and Nordic-like with big Jersey hair and very high cheekbones. Like Asher, she fits into the bohemian/skater/metal crowd, but because she worships Black Flag and wears knee-high combat boots she can also mingle with the punkers and the marginally insane. I always come out of my room when I hear her voice and then pretend I didn't know she was there. She smiles as she passes me and stops, hands on knees, as if she's spotted something furry in the brush. Asher tells her to ignore it, to keep away; he wings a rock at it. He then grabs her by the elbow and into his room — the mecca of all that's hip and retro and evil and artistic and dangerous and sexy and dark and zebra-skinned. And the only place in the world I want to be. It's where he paints, hides, broods, reads up on the great anarchists of our time, and humps this forbidden girl from Hayward through the floorboards. I blow-dry wings into my hair, listen to Journey, pretend I hate *The Muppet Show,* and deny having any idea how the LEGO firehouse got under my bed. He's cool, I'm not; he's rock, I suck; he drives, I can't; he drinks, I can't; he fucks, I wish. I'm a bar mitzvahed junior high student with braces, a bedtime, and a father so far up my ass you can see him performing in my pupils. I want to hate stuff like Asher and have punched holes in the walls behind my posters. I want a girlfriend with stone-washed jeans and tobacco breath and the gumption to give blow jobs. I want someone to paint the *Highway to Hell* album cover on the back of *my* jean jacket and smoke weed and go to concerts and screech tires and swig Stroh's and flip off cops when they're not looking. Instead I'm in fuckin' temple again at 6:30 A.M., waiting to wrap tefillin on the anniversary of my grandfather's death, listening to my father pontificate on the downfall of my brother's faith. Who, by the way, should be standing right next to me, strapping his tefillin onto his ass too. But isn't. "Why?" I ask. "Because Brigitte's a goy, because Dad's a dick, because I don't give a fuck, and because I feel like Kunta Kin Kike, when I'm bound up in tefillin straps," he answers. "That's why."

Just inside the sanctuary I pull the thing out of its velvet bag. Tefillin are two black boxes that contain verses from Scripture that bar mitvahed males affix to their foreheads and arms with leather straps. Forever my vote for most bizarre Judaic ritual, the impetus comes from Deuteronomy in which God says, "You shall bind [the verses] for a sign on your hand, and they shall be for frontlets between your eyes." A less popular and figurative interpretation suggests that God wanted these crucial writings to be kept at hand and in sight. But I guess some early rabbi decided to take this literally and one thing led to another and now I'm strapping a black leather box to my face while listening to my father lambaste his son.

"*I'm* here. *You're* here. Is *he* here? No! No, he's not."

To my left bicep I'll moor the other box, which is attached to a long strand of the inch-wide leather strap. And after a quick prayer I'll wrap it tightly all the way down my elbow, forearm, wrist, and fingers in this extremely precise coiling process that can only be learned with practice. For weeks before my bar mitzvah I was absurdly lost in the specifics of wrapping tefillin. But it was Asher, believe it or not, who helped get me through it.

"And now he's punishing *me*," my father says, lifting his "for frontlets" box on his forehead, "and his grandfather's memory.

Just . . . flat-out ignoring this crucial day in my life and why? Why Jacob? Why isn't *this* day, the day of my father's death, a crucial day in your brother's life? Easy. Selfishness. Self-indulgence. Self-interest. Well, you know something? I can be selfish too. How's he goin' to college without money? Ask him! Who does he think's paying for it? Who?" He centers the *shel rosh* box above his brow ridge and looks at me for a reaction.

"I don't know."

My father shakes his head and tosses his *talit* around his shoulders. "If all you do is take and take and take, then you're a *fool* to extend your hand. What goes around, Jacob, will for-*ever* come around. Trust me," he says pointing at the ceiling. "He's watching. Always."

ON THE WAY home from synagogue my father says I have to write twenty thank-you notes per night for my bar mitzvah gifts. There are hundreds of them and he feels I'm way behind. Each note will be individually checked for proper spelling, grammar, syntax, and word choice, and I'm told over and over that each syllable should be considered "a jewel, a cut and cleaned jewel." He asks if I understand this. I tell him I do.

He tears the first ten I write into tiny tan bits and lets the pieces rain onto my hair. He then pounds my desk so hard he has to grip his hand and hop around like the maniac he is, bending over his pain. He's in my face the next night again. I'm a "shitty speller," I can't remember to mention the gift, I write "to" instead of "too," I write "your" instead of "you're," I write "Shwartz" instead of "Schwartz," I write "love" instead of "Love." He then tells me to get thirty done by the time he gets home from work. I blow it off and use some bar mitzvah cash to buy albums Asher wants but doesn't yet own. I buy a treasure, a pure beauty of a Jethro Tull album. It's got Japanese writing on the front and a sticker that says "A Must-Have" with three exclamation points in the shape of electric flutes. When I get home from the store I run up the stairs with the bag swinging in my hand. I knock on his door.

"What?" he yells from inside, the music blaring.

I wait. I hear him coming.

He unlocks the door and opens it a crack. "What?"

"Oh, you're home," I say, trying to catch my breath.

"You didn't hear the music?"

"I did but—"

"What do you want? I'm really busy." Asher's got no shirt on and he's wearing his black pith helmet. There's a streak of red paint on his cheek and chin, and his hair is tied back with a gray rubber band.

"I was wondering . . . if you've ever seen *this*," I say, and reveal the album from the bag. "It's a live, double album with acoustic 'Aqualung' and four encores including 'Thick as a Brick,' 'Skating Away,' and 'Bungle in the Jungle.' These are Japanese letters," I say pointing. "It's an inport."

"A what?"

"It was made in Japan. Live. It's inported."

"*Im*ported, schmuck-o. Not *in*ported."

"That's what I said."

"You said *in*ported."

"Imported. It doesn't matter. It's a must-have. See? These are flutes."

"Yeah. I see, I see."

"Have you ever heard of it?"

"No," he says, taking the album from my hand. He flips it over and reads the back. I look over his shoulder into his room while he allows me the time. I can see his "Never Mind the

Bollocks" poster over his bed and a long, tin box of colored pencils on his drawing table. There are paintings all over the carpet, some leaning on the wall—charcoal cityscapes with anvils that float and shadowy nudes that grasp behind Dumpsters and this bald and creamy guy with an eggbeater for a brain who appears hog-tied with some type of cord. I see his latest skateboard with the Charles Manson sticker on the nose and above his stereo there's a poster of Wendy O. Williams cutting a Cadillac in half with a chain saw. Dr. Zeus, G.I. Joe, and a topless Farrah Fawcett doll all sit on round blocks of Sex Wax on the shelf. It smells like paint and farts.

"Nicky has this," he says. "It's a bootleg, I've heard it. Sounds like whoever recorded it had the tape recorder mashed against their colon. Enjoy." And the door slams closed. Dick.

On the way to my room I see my mother jogging up the stairs. She's been out of the house every night since her grant came through and now runs everywhere she goes. She says she's on a team of psychology students and professors who got all this money from the government to interview birth mothers and the children they gave up. She's in Trenton, she's in Belmar, she's in Hackensack, she's in Nutley. And when that's done for the day she studies through the night and on weekends. My guess is she sleeps while she drives.

"Hey, babe."

"Hi."

"I need to talk to you for a second," she says, and walks toward me.

I'm still a little shocked by the "perm." She did it without warning over the weekend and now there's this woman in my house with curly brown hair. Today she's got big dangly hoop earrings on and a wide, suede belt that hangs low on her hips. She looks like Peggy Lipton in *The Mod Squad*.

"What ya got there?" she says.

"A record."

"Who?"

"Jethro Tull."

"Is he good?"

I laugh at her. "Jethro Tull's the name of the band," I say, shaking my head. "It's not a *he*."

"Don't be mean."

"I'm just telling you."

"Are *they* good? Jethro Tull?"

"Yeah."

"What's it . . . rock?"

I nod and look down at it.

"You gettin' a haircut anytime soon?" she says and forms my hair into a ponytail with her fingers. "Jethro?"

"I *just* got one."

"No. I took you. That was four months ago. Just a trim."

I ignore this.

"I'm serious. Not this week, but soon, right?"

"Right."

"Listen. Meg's making dinner tonight." Megan Reeves. A Moraga College nursing student who cleans the house in exchange for room and board. "I'll be at Rutger's with Nathaniel and won't be home until late." Dr. Nathaniel Brody, the head of the research team and a mentor of my mother's. "Dad's got rehearsal until ten." The Leiland Community Theater, he's in the chorus, some musical called *Annie Get Your Gun*. "He's taking Gabe and Dara with him." Good. "Your father wants to see at least twenty thank-you cards finished by the time he gets home tonight, okay?" He told me thirty. "No TV until you do 'em. Don't make him mad, sweetie. Use the gift list and the dictionary and be careful about the y-o-u-rs and the y-o-u-'-r-es all right? You know how crazy that makes him." Crazy? Wrong word. A kiss to the cheek, a crouch, and some eye contact. "You okay, pal? You look tired tonight." I'm dynamite, Mom. After me and the boarder eat some fish sticks, I'm gonna thank every Jew from here to La Jolla. Then, when Dad gets home with rosy makeup on his cheeks, he'll read what I've done, threaten me with his Hitler face, and shred them into confetti. "I'm fine."

"Get those thank-yous all done and mailed and I'll take you to a record store this weekend. Any two in the store." Bribery. I'll take it. Another kiss, this one on the head. And off she goes. Freud's her "thing."

Dear Irving and Selma Goldfarb,

If only there was enough space on this tiny card to evoke my unfettered joie de vivre for what you have done. The gaiety, the mirth, the heavenly bubbling of every effusive cell that sings inside me for your kind and pithy offering. The Yarmulke I wore before you came into my life was woven of a tawdry and raffish thread. But leather, my dear friends, leather is sustenance. Leather is sublime. Leather is the most laconic of elegies. Leather is carnal. Leather is life. You, Irving and Selma, are life. You, Irving and Selma Goldfarb, are *love*.

See you in Synagogue I hope.

I love and cherish you both,

Your Jacob

Dear Irving and Selma Goldfarb,

Thank you for the Yarmulke. Thank you for coming to my Bar Mitzvah and for you're genris gift to. I wear it to Hebrew school and I wear it to Shabbat to. I hope I will see you both again.

Love,

Jacob

THE FISH STICKS aren't bad. I bury mine in tartar sauce and ketchup and then stab the mush with my green beans. Megan stacks hers before cutting them in thirds with her fork. Interesting, but it's quite a mouthful. She's twenty-one, shorter than I am, and doesn't really look like your average nurse-to-be. Aside from chain-smoking Merits and "hating" exercise, her dyed hair is as black as her eyeliner and she's addicted to "all things Hershey." I think she's sexy in a female Keith Richards sort of way, but I've only told Jonny this. There's a softness to her face I like—underneath all the hair and goop. But you have to bump into her real early in the morning to see it. I watch her lift her water glass and take a long sip. Her brushed copper bracelets jingle on her wrists and her fingernails are peach and cut short for the job. I try to break the awkward silence. "Not too bad tonight, huh?"

We make eye contact and she smiles and nods. It's the third time this week we've been alone for dinner. If there weren't any fish sticks in the sea we'd both be dead.

"So . . . when's the last time you talked to Tony Danza?" I say. Always a safe topic. She also dated Sly Williams of the Knicks.

She laughs a little with food in her mouth and lowers her chin to her plate. "You like that story. Uh . . . two and a half years."

"Was he cool?"

She nods. "But . . . he lives in L.A., so . . ."

"If you marry him you could be rich."

"Marry him?"

"Yeah."

She smiles. "If he'd ask me I'd consider it."

"I can't believe he was a boxer." I used this same line earlier in the week except I said "fighter."

"Big hands," she says, and laughs with another head dip. "Great back scratcher."

I pull a green bean out of a fish stick with my mouth only. "Look, I can eat with *no* hands."

She watches me chew. "I can see that."

"You try."

She stands a green bean up in her tarter sauce and bends over it. It first bumps her in the chin which makes her smile and cover her eyes. She finally gets it. I applaud.

"How about you?" she says.

"I already did it."

"No. I mean, do you like to have your back scratched?"

"Oh, yeah. When I was younger it was kinda my thing."

"Your *thing?*"

"It was funny 'cause . . . Asher used to get jealous because I would always ask my mom to scratch my back, right? So he decided he needed his own thing too, so, he starts saying, 'Mom, push my face, push my face.'"

"He said 'push my face'?"

"Yeah. Like I'd say, 'Mom, scratch my back,' and he'd run in front of me and say, 'Mom, push my face.'"

"And did she?"

"Yeah. She'd just put her palm against his nose and give him a shove. It didn't hurt or anything. He just wanted to have a thing with her like I did."

"That's funny."

"Yeah," I say. "But that was a long time ago." And we fall into more silence. Two Mississippi, three Mississippi, four Mississippi, five . . .

"Well, I just *love* having my back scratched," she says, nudging her food. "I guess it's my thing too."

I glance at the oven clock and touch a fish stick with my

fork. "I used to have a back scratcher in the shape of Kermit the frog," I share. "You know him, right?"

She nods.

"It had Kermit's head on it. And his, ya know . . . frog hand was the scratcher."

Megan takes another bite of her double-decker fish sticks and aims her fork at me with one eye closed. "I'll scratch your back if you want."

My penis moves. A college girl with painted fingernails. I'll get a boner before my shirt comes off.

"No pressure, of course," she says, and lifts her glass.

"You mean tonight?" I ask.

"Or another time."

I close my knees together and look at my watch for some reason. Megan drinks from her glass with her eyes on me. I bend over another green bean and look up at her across the table. "Okay."

I'VE ONLY BEEN in Megan's room once since it became hers. My mom told me to bring her laundry up to her—just jeans and T-shirts and some purple, glittery socks. The tiny room is across the hall from the attic on the third floor and used to be a storage cemetery for all our old crap. At one time there was a striped, teal drum set that belonged to Asher where her bed now sits. I painted the words KISS Army on the bass drum while he was at camp one summer and surrounded the letters with horribly drawn flames. It looked like a cat threw up on it. On paper the surprise was a perfect one. He'd arrive home, pump his fist with approval, and then jump behind the kit to parallel the heavy metal flames. He punched me eleven times in the ass instead and then hung my ventriloquist dummy from a noose tied to a shower rod. I vowed to murder him that day as I tearfully unhooked the rope and held Mr. Jeeves's limp body in my arms. The drum set now sits in a wardrobe box in the attic. So does a headless Mr. Jeeves.

"Sorry it's so messy," Megan says, reaching for the light switch. "I'm in the middle of exams and I'm kinda . . . frazzled." Her room is like a jungle. There are three ceiling-high floor plants just inside the door that sprout from a soil of strewn laundry and shoes and textbooks and dried-out peach pits in bunched up paper towel. I think I might be standing on a sandwich. Coke can ashtrays sit everywhere and are gorged with mashed-out butts and soggy matches. Through the leaves I see a row of tiny cacti on her desk, and a blow-up palm tree that bends with the weight of Mardi Gras beads. Megan steps left, over a tipped-over hamper, and dives onto her bed. "This is Bonsai Sammy," she says, and tickles the body of a mini–oak tree on her bedside table. The room has changed. I recognize the TV. It used to be in the kitchen. It's a small black and white with tinfoil rabbit ears and a broken on-off button. You need needle-nose pliers to change the channel. Megan lights a Merit and exhales an enormous stream toward the closed window by her desk. She sits up on her bed with the cigarette held high and pats the mattress. "You better untuck your shirt," she says.

There's a tingle near my testicles when I hear this but I'm hoping it doesn't mean wood. I pull my shirt up and out of my pants and walk over to the bed.

"Can I turn the TV on?" I ask.

"Sure. You need the—"

"Pliers, I know."

"Channel two comes in the best," she says.

$M^*A^*S^*H$ is on. I walk back to the bed and sit down. "How should I . . . ?

"Mmmm, why don't you lie on your stomach?"

I lay down, facing the TV. Klinger and Radar are discussing something but the sound is too low to hear. Megan lifts my shirt up to my neck. I wait for her nails to touch my skin.

"I've seen this one," she says.

"Me too," I say, but I haven't.

This is not a sexual thing. This is not a sexual thing. This is not a sexual thing. It's not. Just hang out a few seconds. Watch *M*A*S*H*. It's more like I'm with someone's mother or aunt or sister. Just don't think of her as a woman who will someday wear white stockings to work and one of those starchy hats. I'm her brother. A friend. The young son of her current landlord. Megan giggles through an exhale and the bed starts to hop. "Jamie Farr," she says, still laughing. I'm sensing a pattern. She scratches vertically first, covering the middle thoroughly before getting the sides and lower half of my back. The sides tickle a little but I brave through it, clenching my stomach. I decide to think of something witty to say when she finishes. I'm down to two options: "Tony Danza doesn't know what he's missing." Or "I'd take you over Kermit any day." About five minutes later she pulls my shirt down and pats my back. I sit up. "Kermit doesn't—"

"My turn," she says and mashes her cigarette into a Coke can. She rolls over on her stomach and pulls her shirt above her bra strap. "I like it kinda hard so don't hold back."

The only bras I've ever seen besides my mom's were on mannequins. Or in magazines. Or on mannequins in magazines. This one is creamy tan and has five hooks keeping it closed. It has lots of little lint balls all over it and a silky white tag that says "Maiden Form" in pink. Megan's skin is beautiful. It's sort of fair but olive-ish with sporadic brown birthmarks, mostly near her shoulders and hips. I reach to touch her. My fingertips brush her spine.

"Harder is fine," she says. "You can't hurt me."

I sit closer to her, glancing at the length of my fingernails. I dig in a little better and she lets out a moan. "That's it." I decide to follow her pattern, up and to the sides, and begin to look forward to the seconds I'm permitted to touch her bra. The laugh track gives off a muted roar on the tiny TV. When I look up, Frank Burns is wearing a flowered shower cap and a woman's robe. It goes to commercial.

"You got a girlfriend?" Megan says.

Penis tingle. Friend, brother, son of landlord.

"Oooh, don't stop yet," she says.

I begin again. "No, I . . ."

"Why not?"

I move my hand up the side of her back, and rest my fingers on the round of her shoulder. "I don't . . . usually like the girls who like me. Maybe if I didn't hear they liked me, I might, you know, like them first."

I can't see her face but I can tell she's smiling. "It'll happen," she says. "You're a cutie. Really. Blond and so tall. You look older than you are."

"I do?"

"Oh, yeah."

"Thanks."

"Let me get this stupid thing out of the way," she mumbles, and reaches behind her to unhook her bra. In a snap it falls away from her body. I can see the sides of her large pale breasts, pressing against her sheets. My penis begins to fill with blood. I knock my knees together to slow it down and conjure up revolting stuff like Asher says to do: curdled cottage cheese with

old-lady pubes in diarrhea with . . . It's too late. I'm like blue
steel.

"Heeeey, I did you longer than that," she whines.

"Sorry."

I reach to touch the hidden skin with the tips of my fingers.
It's forbidden and smooth and I have to think to breathe. Megan
moves slightly and I get a glimpse of the dark and bumpy part
of her nipple. I think my penis might break through the pocket
of my jeans. Her face is turned away from me, toward the wall.
I scratch for a few more seconds before she flips her black hair
away from her neck. I look down at my crotch and then search
for a pillow to use when she finally sits up. She's got them both
under her chin. I decide I'll just sit on the floor when she's
through, a subtle tuck and roll. Megan says "yes" when my fingertips go near her hips. I massage the skin above her belt and
she says it again. I sit a little closer and use both my hands.

"You found my weakness. Now a little lower," she says, and
lifts her hips to undo her pants. Praised be thou oh Lord our
God, king of the universe, creator of all that is carved and
curved into female. My penis will pop like a gag cigar. No really, it aches. Megan scoots her pants down an inch and settles back in her spot. "Okay," she says. "Like, where my spine
runs out, just . . . yes, good, right there. But harder, okay? Just
jam your thumb in there." I try it. "Nice . . . perfect. Now make
circles." I will. I do. I make lots and lots of circles. Some the
size of Oreos, others more like Cherrios. I do the Olympic sign
a few times and surround it with Mallomars, and then, without much thought, I lean down and smell the back of her
head. It smells like cigarette smoke and sugary shampoo.
When I try it again I feel her hair against my chin, my lips. I
rub this long, gorgeous woman in slow circles with my palm.

"Gooood," she says in a whisper that fades. And I gently close my eyes.

"*Gooood.*"

Dear Samuel and Dot Titelbaum,

I've noticed lately that when I put soapy water on my erect penis and stroke the tip in my hand, I get an intense feeling that seems to come from both my brain and my inner thighs. I just churn the thing over and over and my knees and shoulders and even my ribs seem to tingle in a very, *very* good way. It works in the bathtub too. It's like I'm stepping higher and higher toward something kind of huge or even a little scary. I sometimes stop the motion when my breath feels sort of lost or my eyeballs lose focus, but it's usually not long before I'm right back in the saddle. Tonight I did it with Megan in my mind. I pretended she flipped over while I was scratching her back and she watched me as I touched her two breasts. I held them, squeezed them, and then kissed them really softly. Actually, first I touched the right one with both hands. Then I squeezed it and kissed the nipple softly. Then I kissed the left nipple, which I followed with some touching, some gentle squeezing, and a few light kisses. She just loved this. I then pretended she told me to lie down on top of her so I climbed on her and pressed my body against hers. She was wearing only her underwear at the time so I felt the silky fabric against my shaft (slang for "penis"). She kept her panties on but I could feel her crinkly black pubic hair against my pulsating rod (also slang for "penis"). Oh, Samuel and Dot . . . what a feeling it is to lie on the bed of a grown woman. To feel her hands on my back, scratching up and down before tickling the sides ever so gently. I really do think I've found a new "thing." I just can't wait to—

"Jacob?" My father's voice from downstairs.

Dear Samuel and Dot Titelbaum,

Thank you for the genris gift. I was telling my Dad just the other day how much I needed a subscription to *The Jewish News*.

One big knock and the door opens. "You get 'em all done?"

"No, not yet," I say, my back to him. "I'm still writing."

"I want to see 'em before you lick the envelopes. *Every* one, don't forget."

I turn and face him. "How was rehearsal?"

"Fine, slow, I'm . . . not used to such a . . . subordinate role."

"You mean—"

"Director's one of these . . . wannabe types. *Very* closed off to creative suggestions. An ego up to here, you know? A putz. So . . . call me when you're done. And Jacob?"

"Yeah.

"*Every* word a jewel, right?"

I turn back around in my chair. I look down at the card.

"I didn't hear you," he says.

"Yes. I said yes."

Dear Herb and Rachel Abromowitz-stein-berg-er-witz,

Thank you for your genorisness. I don't know if you know this but I have this friend named Jacob. I know, it's the same as my name and you think it's me but it isn't. Jacob is a boy who went to a yeshiva until the fourth grade. I know, I know, I went to a yeshiva but trust me, there's heaps of yeshiva boys named Jacob. Jacob will be told he needs to stay back in kindergarten. He is not learning well. When all the other yeshiva children cut paper plates into the shape of dreidels,

Jacob's plate looks like a swastika. He needs another year to get it right. When he arrives at school the next fall, he walks with his classmates to the first-grade classroom and sits down. He leans his new briefcase against his leg and folds his hands. "Maybe they'll forget" is his mind-set. They don't. He is escorted back to the wide, crayon-smelling room with the piano in it. Mrs. Silverstein is his teacher again, and again she is a disgusting human being with facial warts, coffee breath, and rolled down panty-hose socks. Jacob will make it through kindergarten this time (turns out you can still spin a swastika), and will never be held back again. He will, though, be diagnosed with a "learning disability" at a time when very few people know what that means. Disadvantage: Uninformed teachers think he's stupid, as opposed to challenged. Advantage: Too early for trendy medication. The disability does not effect his ability to read or write, although he's a pretty lazy speler. It does not effect speaking or memory or even learning to read Hebrew very well. But when faced with timed, standardized tests, he begins to drift. An hour into the exam the drifting becomes a sinking and not long after he begins to drown in a pool of numbers and letters and No. 2 lead. As Jacob descends he sees "all of the above" and "none of the above" bobbing idly on the surface. "Fill in every box, even if you don't know the answer," he hears a muffled voice say. "Guessing is better than leaving it blank." So he guesses: CC AB CD BB AC AA. DCDCDCBCBBDDCDACDBCDDBBAAADBCCDABB-DCBDCDBADBCDBDCAA

"Time's up," he hears. "Pencils down." When asked to stand in front of his third-grade classmates and name the months of the year, Jacob begins with "Thursday" and wraps up with "autumn." When his fourth-grade teacher lifts multiplication flash cards to the class, he decides he'll just say "six" over and over and hope for the best. He ends up being correct twice out of thirty-five times. It becomes clear that the teachers Jacob is assigned are crucial to his ability to learn. Those with very little patience for students who daydream, tap their hands and feet, or attempt to find McDonald's characters in the clouds will not only fail to get through to him, but will also humiliate him in front of his peers. He will then return to a home where his father has zero patience for a son with limitations. The man is tortured and embarrassed by this boy who stands before him, and his blatant inability to flourish as a student, a son. His father will literally hover over Jacob and wait for him to fail—dishes washed poorly, homework done sloppily, impromptu math quizzes cornering him at the dinner table—all to demonstrate how grotesque failure really looks, feels, is. So, in honor of Jacob, I was wondering if you'd mind if I just said, thank you for coming to see me get Bar Mitzvahed. Thank you for whichever gift it was you purchased and wrapped and handed to me. And most importantly, thank you for believing me when I tell you, Jacob is *not* me. Thank God. Your both to generis!

Love,

J (I rarely even go by Jacob.)

## Thank You

When my father comes in my room he's eating a peach. "You should've seen Gabe tonight at rehearsal," he says.

"Why?" I ask, with an intentionally bright smile, eyebrows high.

He takes a bite that leaves the pit exposed and sits with a bounce on the end of my bed. "*Every*one who meets him falls in love in seconds. He's just got this way about him. He's very, very good with adults. Very mature and . . . social and giving. Bright."

I nod and glance down at the stack of thank-you notes on my desk. "Maybe they'll give him a part in the play," I say, and slide them an inch to the right.

"A part?" he says, annoyed. "He's in *kinder*garten." He takes a final bite and throws it at the trash can by the door. It hits the rim and then the wall. "Damn free throws," he says, standing and rubbing his palms together.

I let out a friendly laugh and think of something to say that might unite us. "Well" —still thinking— "the Lakers would be crazy to—"

"Let's see the work," he says. He wipes the juice from his mustache, his mouth stretched wide. "How many you finish?"

"I did . . . nine or ten but I'm not done."

"Which is it?"

"Which is what?"

"Which *number*? Nine or ten?"

"I think I did nine."

"Nine," he says through a sigh, and takes the cards over to my bed. He lies down and kicks his tennis shoes off. "What were you doing all night long?"

I think of Megan's breasts. "I had a lot of other homework."

He looks up at me with a "who do you think you're fooling" gaze from over his glasses. He shuffles the cards a few times and finds a comfy groove in the pillow with the back of his head.

"Some of them are—"

He puts his hand out like a stop sign.

"Not finished."

He reads silently. I look down at his sneakers on the floor and wish I knew which card he had. I'm somehow comforted that he's not wearing dark dress shoes, as if the Nikes he wears to rehearsal bring us closer to equals. I face my desk and begin to quietly jab the cover of my dictionary with a pen tip. My stomach burns.

"This one's perfect," he says, holding it up.

I swivel toward him in my chair. "Which one?" I say, grinning. I stand.

"Edith Gruber. You spelled everything right. You mention the Israel Bonds. You said you look forward to seeing her at Shana's bat mitzvah. All good."

"I really like Edith," I say, and reach blindly for the chair below me. I sit back down. My father brings the next card to the top of the pile. Before he reads it he reaches into his pocket for his keys. He places the tip of one into his ear and twists with his eyes closed. A time-out. I stare at the cards in his hands. I know of three that don't thank people for specific gifts and maybe five that don't mention when I'll see them again. I go back to poking the dictionary but I push too hard; the whole pen rips through the cover. I hear Megan tell Gabe it's time for bed outside my room. I'm comforted by the sound as I glance at the door.

"What is *this?*" my father says. "No. *No.*"

I turn to him.

"What is this?"

The card is blocking his face. Gabriel laughs and I hear his footsteps running down the hall. "I mean it, mister," Megan says.

"Which one, Dad?"

"*Piss!*" he screams, and flings the card into the air. It floats for a second and then tail dives into my turntable on the dresser.

"What's wrong with it?"

He doesn't answer. "*No,* Jacob!" he says with the next card already in front of his face. "Look at this. You don't mention the gift, you don't have a third line to balance it out, you don't—"

"Which one do you have, Dad?" I stand and walk toward him with a look of stunned confusion.

He lowers the card from his face. "Get the hell away from me."

"Why?"

"Step back. *Just* . . . step . . . back."

"I just want to see—"

"You want to see *what*, Jacob? Your work? Your mind at work? Spell the word *generous*. Spell it. Now."

"Why are you getting so angry?" I say.

"*Spell* the word!"

"G."

"Fantastic, keep going."

"G-e-n-e-r, um . . ."

"Um, um, um," he mimics. "Dictionary! What's it for? To *stand* on? Find 'generous.' *Pick* it up!" he screams.

I lift the book and begin to thumb for the Gs. My stupid hands quiver on the pages.

"Now!"

"I'm looking."

"Is it in there? Maybe it's a dud, it's not in there."

Generate. Generation. Generator. Generic.

"I found it."

"Marvelous. Does it say, g-e-n-e-r-*i*-s?"

"No."

"So . . . when the Mendelsons read your card and see that my son spells like a *retard*, what should I tell them? Isn't my boy *super*?"

"I'll rewrite it."

"And this one. No mention of the gift, no third line to balance it out."

"Which one, Dad?"

"Which one, *Daddy*?" he barks. "Like it fuckin' *matters*."

"Why are you yelling?"

"What did you say?"

I don't answer. I place the dictionary back on my desk.

"No. What did you just say? Are you a goddamn baby?"

"No."

"How old then? Just tell me if you're an infant so I can understand. I want to. I *want* to understand." He lifts another card. "Garbage!" he says holding the stack high, his lips tightened and white. "You want to please me, is that what you want? *Is* it?"

I slowly nod.

"Answer me, you—!" My father is now sitting up on the bed, waiting for a reply, his teeth clenched. "Answer me!"

"Yes."

"Yes, *what?*"

"Yes. I want to please you."

He smiles wickedly and shakes his head. "It's . . . sad to me, Jacob. Pathetic. You became a man last week, do you even *know* that? Can you comprehend this? This is em*barrassing,* this slop. Don't you feel it? Look at these. I see nothing witty or snappy like we've talked about again and again. And you wrote, '*Your* one of my best friends," spelled y-o-u-r. Are you . . . *trying* to do these crappy? Maybe that's it. Maybe you want to prove that you're an idiot. Are you an idiot? *Are* you?"

I squeeze my eyes closed and feel tears rising.

He bunches the next card into a ball and throws it toward me. It hits my *Incredible Hulk* pencil sharpener and falls onto the carpet. When I glance at him, his face is pinched and furious, struggling. He sits up with a jolt from the bed and runs his fingers through his scalp. He clenches a fist of his black hair and yanks once, hard. "*No!*" he screams, his pain stoking the fire.

I swallow as my face and neck fill with this familiar tingling—the predator is loose. I sit still, locked in my chair, knowing that what's begun cannot be tied off. It is fear that now owns me, fills me like an injected drug. And the effects are quick and potent and steeped in shame. I hear Megan's voice outside in Gabriel's room, and I face the door. My father pops to his feet with the cards in his hand and walks toward me.

"I'll do them again, Dad," I say, with my eyes lowered. When I look up at him he winds up with a small skip and throws his hand toward the wall as if hurling a brick. He does not let go of the cards. He does this again and then again, flinging his arm as hard as he can with a deadened pop in his shoulder, a guttural gasp. Trapped in his rage I watch the lunatic dance. He punches his own leg with a closed fist and his knee buckles, nearly toppling him to the floor.

"Stop," I say.

He stares at me, eyes wide.

"I'll do them again."

"Let me ask you something," he says blinking, his jaw jetting forward. "Do you think these are done? Ready for the mailbox!?"

I swallow. I look at the cards he still clenches in his fist and then up at his face, bending over me. "*Do you?*" he hollers from his core.

"No," I say, with a weak and wobbled voice.

"How long did you work on these?"

"How long?" I ask, embarrassed by the shiver in my voice.

"Yes, how long?"

"I don't know."

"You don't know. Okay. The people you are writing these letters to—look me in the eyes."

I look up at him. His face is inches from mine, his skin rattling on his cheeks. He can only hate what he sees before him. I think to put my feet flat on the floor and lean my head slightly back. I stare into the face I can barely see behind his beard and dark lenses.

"These cards, which you *can't . . . can't* give a shit about, are for people who purchased you gifts. *You!* How long do you think it took to *buy, wrap,* and *hand* you these gifts, schmuck? How long?"

"I don't know."

"I don't know, I don't know, I don't know, I don't know," he screams, jogging in a tight circle with his arms flapping. "Like a retarded *chicken.* I don't know, I don't know, I don't know *nothing!* Is that it? *Is* it?" he screams, kneeling in front of me.

"No."

"Do you *hate* this, Jacob!? Do you hate it, do you hate it, do you hate *me?*" he roars so loudly it rings in my ears.

I try to breathe but I can't. I look away but I'm weak and feel the tears, the flooding, rising up from my throat.

"Oh . . . crying," he says, and rams his fist into his eye, grinding it into the socket. "Waaaaa! Waaaaa!"

I let myself go for a moment, though I know my cowardice feeds his rage. I suck for air in quick intakes of breath and gain a semblance of strength from my own mirrored empathy.

"Look at you," he says. "My *son.* The bar mitz*vah.*"

I squeeze my eyes and clench my jaw, drawing from fury I cannot use. When I face my father he's preparing to stab one of the cards, to pin it to my desk with the tip of a pen. He holds it like a dagger and jabs it twice with all his strength. The pen cracks in two and crumbles from his hand. He rifles through my drawer for another. I wipe my nose on my sleeve and try to suppress any sounds that could link me to theatrics. There's a light knock on the door.

"Yes?" my father says in his normal voice.

"Everything okay?" Megan asks.

My father looks down at me. "Everything is fine," he says, and gently closes the drawer.

"Time for bed, Dara," Megan says, just outside the door.

My father hovers above me at my desk, his cranium shivering in bursts. I stay silent, my chin even with his belt. "I just *hate* that you make me this way. I hate it!"

"I know."

"Ya think I'm gonna let you send . . . *slop* to the people I love? Do ya? Pull out a fresh card. Do it now."

I reach for one and place it on the desk in front of me.

"To Lev and Rebecca Saperstein. Write it."

I lift my pen in my hand and watch my fingers tremble. I write the word *Dear* and reach for the gift list.

"*Lev!*" You can't spell *Lev* without looking? *Here!*" he screams, and grabs the pen from my hand. He begins to scribble the name all over my blotter and soon scrapes it into the desk itself, burying the pen tip deep into the wood. LEV. "See it! Are you looking?" he says, and presses his palm to the back of my head. I resist and he pushes harder, bending my face toward the scratched grooves.

"Sssstop!" I whine in a voice higher than my own. "Stop."

And he does. He stops. He lets me sit up. I feel his tangled fingers in my hair as he gently tries to uncoil them. And in seconds he's kneeling at my feet with ever softening eyes. "Jacob," he whispers. "I'm . . . sorry. I'm . . . just . . ."

Asher shoves my door open and we both turn to face him. I can hear his music from down the hall thumping through his speakers, heavy and loud. His fingers and forearms are streaked with white paint and his wide eyes are pinned on the two of us. My father sniffs and slowly climbs to his feet. "Don't you knock?"

Asher moves toward us while looking around the room like a cop.

"I asked you a question," my father says.

"I heard you," he says. He looks down at the embedded word LEV and swipes his fingertips over the wood. "It's enough for tonight."

"Turn around," my father says, flinging his hand at him. "Just leave. The voice of reason. Doesn't even knock. Go on, get outta here."

"Enough. Okay? No more."

My father blinks and folds his arms. "I said get out."

Asher steps toward him with his own churning jaw and looks so geared to pounce that I reach for his arm. "Asher," I say. "Stop . . . wait."

My father broadens his rounded shoulders and actually smirks. "You seem angry," my father says in a softened tone we know well—a voice laced with practiced condescension. "Can you tell me why that is, Asher? Can you tell why you're so very angry?"

"Bedtime, Dara," says Megan, glancing inside my room. "Let's brush those teeth."

Asher looks over his shoulder as my sister runs by. He then turns and reaches to switch my desk light off before walking from the room. As he leaves he swings my door wide open and it bangs against the wall. I want to tell him to stay, to wait, but I'm afraid to make things worse. When he's gone, my father sits on the edge of my bed with his face in his hands. Megan's out of his view but still stands just outside. "You okay?" she says without sound, her face pinched, even frightened. And it's so strange, but as I stare back at her, my instinct is to defend my father, to protect him, to list every kindness and every altruistic breath he's ever taken. I look away from her and begin to lift the crumpled thank-yous off the carpet. My father claps loud, twice, and I flinch and face him.

"Get some sleep now," he says. And I wait. Just wait. For my door to click closed.

## Shattered

Tantrums make the morning feel like the dead of night—always. I shower in steaming water and let the stream beam down on the back of my neck. Megan stands behind me in my mind. She wants to know what happened the night before and she will not let it go. I tell her we disagreed is all, and that I'm fine, everything's fine. She says she doesn't believe me and I feel her fingertips against the ridges of my spine. I turn the shower off and step out of the tub. I grab a towel and cover my head and face. If she asks, she asks. It's all in how you present yourself. If you're fine she'll think you're fine. I smear the steam off the mirror above the sink and press my chin to the glass. "I'm fine. See me? I'm fine."

Meg's in the kitchen, sitting, waiting, tapping her foot. I smile and say, "Hi." She's got no makeup on and wears her silver-framed glasses and a ponytail. She says she's driving me to school before she even says hello and hands me Asher's jacket like she thinks it's mine. I throw it on the table and follow her to the driveway. It doesn't look good. What happened in there? Are you hurt, what'd you do, did he touch you, can I help, what *was* that, who *is* he, where's your mom, does she know, I can help, let me in, blah, blah, blah, blee, blee, blee . . . "Put your seat belt on," she says, for the first time ever, and reaches over me to loosen it.

"I can do it," I tell her. "I'm not an idiot."

She waits a second, and sits back in her chair. "I know you're not," she says. "Sometimes it sticks."

The car is an elderly blue Dodge with a red cap-and-gown tassel holding the glove box closed. There's also a Popsicle stick somehow "clogging" the heating system and a hole the size of a baseball between my feet. I warm my hands under my armpits and lean forward to see the driveway through the floor.

"How'd ya . . . sleep?" she says, as she starts the car.

I nod but keep my eyes from her. I look for something to cram through the hole while we're moving.

"Look a little out of it this morning," she says, and waits for a reaction. "A little sad. Am I wrong?"

I choose to ignore this as she pulls out of the driveway. There's a penny in the front pouch of my book bag and I drop it through the floor. The road swallows it up and I turn to see it tinkling around in the street. Megan rolls her eyes, trying not to grin. "No more." she says. "It's not funny."

"It's not?"

"No."

"Then why are you smiling?"

"This isn't smiling."

"It looks like it."

"It's not. Trust me."

"Wow. Serious today."

"That's right," she says facing me. "I'm not in the mood."

"Guess not."

"Yeah. Guess not."

I lean my head back against the seat and look away from her. Saber Street is strewn with sidewalk trees that stand in line like rail-thin soldiers. My mother calls them "suburban *sick*-amores" and seems to believe they're more fragile than they look. She says she can tell from their dry, pinched-up leaves that they've ingested more exhaust than any tree should. And whenever we drive by she threatens to uproot them and haul them all off to the woodsy slopes of Vernon Valley. I tell her I'll help her. I'll help her unchoke the trees on Saber Street. But, Asher, he can't help but laugh. He knows she's got no time for rescuing trees. And I think she knows it too. Not enough time, not enough strength. She doesn't even own a shovel.

Last night I hear her come in my room. I can feel the cool of the night air on her clothes right through my blanket, and then a kiss to the skin below my eye. She was making her rounds. Before she stands I clutch her lapel in my fist, but it's a dream—so weird—there's really nothing there. And then I hear "Jacob," real soft, "Jacob." And when I open my eyes I see my father standing over me. Protected by the darkness, I squint to fake sleep, my blanket to my chin. He stares down at me but he's blind in this much dark, believes I'm long gone. He calls my name again and then rests on his knees beside me—starving for penance, permission to sleep. He leans his forehead on the mattress and waits before he whispers.

"I cherish you more than you'll ever know." And as always,

the dramatic repeat. "More than you'll ever know." Another long pause and his head lifts. "We'll get them done." One Mississippi, two Mississippi, three Mississippi. "We'll get them done together."

As he slowly climbs to his feet, jostling the mattress as he goes, he leans over me to kiss my cheek. He holds it there for five long seconds, breathing through his nose. "Sleep tight now, baby boy," he says. "I love you . . . I do."

Megan stops the car at the traffic light on Glendale. She takes a deep breath and I can tell she's staring right at me. "Last night," she says, "was hard for me."

Here we go.

"But something tells me . . . it was harder on you."

I keep my head turned from her.

"I had a friend, in high school. Myra Sloan. Her stepfather used to hit her when she—"

I stop her with a laugh. "Is that what you think you heard?"

"I know what I heard."

"He didn't touch me, Megan."

"I heard it."

"No . . . you *didn't*."

She runs her hand through the dust on the dash, shaking her head.

"It's not like that," I say.

"Then what's it like?"

"I don't really want to talk about it."

"But I do. Okay? I was up all night, thinking. Just laying there."

"Thinking about *what*?"

"Let's see . . . about leaving. About staying. About blowin' a whistle, about . . . living with myself if anything ever happened to you, or Gabe, or Dara."

"You don't get it."

"I trust my ears, J."

"You shouldn't."

"I heard what I heard."

I stare out the window as the light turns green. The car doesn't move. "You can go," I say.

"What?"

I point at the green. "Go!"

"Oh." She steps on the gas. We pass Cimeron Field and the frozen duck pond and turn left on Stanyon toward the junior high. Neither of us says a word. My father's usually more careful around Megan. I guess the culmination of issues was just too much for him this time: First, there's this "disability" of mine—a catalyst for all types of failures that remind my father of every crap report card and teacher conference he's ever suffered through. Second, you got these adoring peers of his—people he loves to impress and one-up with the accomplishments of his amazing children. And then you got me—a less than amazing son who actually wowed all these friends on the day of my bar mitzvah but can't seem to thank them for showing the fuck up. I have no idea why my brain is this way. A special ed teacher named Doris says I learn things "spatially" and that I'm actually very smart. But I heard her say the same thing to Ronald Freed, and he wears a helmet with a chin strap wherever he goes.

Megan sighs like a bad actress. "You're not gonna talk to me about this."

I can see my school through the windshield and all the kids out on the front lawn. Megan stops the car in the parking lot driveway and I reach for the door handle.

"Fine," she says. "Swallow it."

I open the squeaky door and keep it open with my foot. "Bye."

"Hey. If I hear it again, I'm gonna say something."

I take my foot off the door and it slams shut. "To who?"

"To him. Or your mother or the cops or anyone who'll—"

"The *cops,* Megan? Are you kidding me?"

She reaches out and takes my elbow in her hand. "It was *vicious,*" she says. "Vicious."

I pull my arm away from her and open the door.

"Wait," she says.

"I'm gonna be late." I shut the door and walk up on the grass.

She gets out of the car, comes toward me. "Just stop for a second," she says.

"I'm late."

"I don't want you to think I'm mad at *you.* Because I'm not."

"I don't really care."

"Don't say that. Why'd you say that?"

I stop and face her.

"I was up all night, J. Just thinking."

"You already told me that."

"I was . . . thinking about your bar mitzvah," she says, swiping nothing off my shoulder. "That dance, the hora, right? Your father, he was . . . flying, I mean, so high with his head back and his arms in the air. In and out of all those friends of his. And I thought, my God, what pride this man has for his boy. Look at him."

"Can I go now?"

She stares at me for a moment and nods her head. "You spoke so beautifully up there," she says. "All that Hebrew. Those songs. Do you know how good you are? Did he tell you?"

I step back from her.

"Say something to me," she pleads.

"Like what? There's nothing to say."

"You have to hate it that he talks to you like that?"

"It was a . . . disagreement."

"Are you kidding? A disagreement?"

"He gets tired at night, Megan."

"That's tired?"

"My father . . . loves me . . . Megan. Okay? I have to go now. I have class."

"Jacob?" she says with a wrinkling chin.

"What?"

She folds and unfold her arms. "You call that love?"

Like a sucker punch, I feel these words in my gut. Tears rise in my eyes with my classmates ten feet away. I try to breathe it away, to erase the sound of it from my heart. I turn once again and face her. "Go home," I say. "Go."

JONNY'S SITTING ON the floor with the back of his head against my locker. As always he's gnawing on the leather laces of his Rawlings, ingesting the cowhide juice of our most beloved game. He doesn't see me yet. I stop in the stairwell and lean my shoulder against the railing. When I run away in my mind I never come back. I catch a bus with my brother to Florida with all my bar mitzvah dough. We move into a motel near Disney World that has a pool with a slide and an ice machine outside every single room. In the mornings we walk barefooted across the soggy AstroTurf lawn and I head for the slide to wake myself up. My mother's always crying when she learns we're gone; some cop gives her coffee and asks to see my room. She doesn't know we live in Orlando now. I think she thinks we're dead.

When Jon looks up and sees me he rolls a brand-new baseball down the hall toward my feet. If I don't stop it it'll head through C wing and end up somewhere in Ms. Kerrigan's science lab. I scoop it up and roll it back to him. Heather Dyer and friends jump over it with a squeal like they think it's a mouse, and Jon looks at me with a laugh, to see if I saw. He's the only person I know besides me who finds it impossible to tire of baseball. When he was seven he stood alone on his driveway and pitched a full nine-inning bout against his garage with a tennis ball. Pop-ups and cleanly fielded grounders were outs, the strike zone a rectangle drawn with chalk. Somewhere around the fifth inning he had to decide whether to take a bathroom break or continue the game. He pissed in his pants and went on to beat the Bosox 8 to 3—squishy britches and all. Seconds after I stopped laughing from this story, I knew exactly why I'd found the perfect best friend for me. We're both human [<Lat. *humanus*] versions of the canine [<Lat. *canis*] retriever: of or pertaining to a genetic necessity to chase after hurled spheres. And what is baseball if not a regimented excuse to retrieve balls all day long. Only the dark can stop us. And when it does, we thumb through nudie mags, watch *This Week in Baseball,* and lie to each other about how many girls we've Frenched. I give the bottom of his sneaker a kick and he pulls the gooey laces out of his mouth.

"Where ya been?" he says, getting to his feet. "I got good news." Jon's a smidge taller than he was in the fourth grade but still stands a foot shorter than me. He wears untied Timberlands and white overalls a lot, and keeps his dark hair long, past his shoulders. I open my locker and throw my book bag in.

"Aren't you curious?" he says.

"Go ahead. What is it?"

He walks in front of me and opens his mouth to speak but stops. "You been crying?" he says.

"Fuck you."

"Sorry. You look like you were."

"Fuck, no."

"Okay, okay."

I grab my gym shorts out of the locker. "So what's the news?"

"The news. The news is Kara Brown. Remember her?"

"Yeah."

"She wants to go out with you," he says. "Fitsy says 'guaranteed hand job.'"

"She . . . touched Fitsy's dick?"

"No, no. He just knows that she'll give you one."

"How does *he* know?"

"I don't know."

"And that's the news?"

"You were expecting something *better*? Fitsy says it's guaranteed."

"I heard you." I hang my coat up and slam my locker. "Come on. We're gonna be late for gym." I walk down the hall and Jon follows me.

"I tell you Kara Brown wants to touch your wang and you're worried about being late?"

"Didn't we know this?"

"Not about the *hand job!*"

"Shhh. Okay, okay."

"She's a fuckin' fox, man. She's an eighth-grade fox."

"I've seen her."

"She let Lyle Hammlin finger her in a movie theater. It's for real—Patrick smelled his fingers."

"What movie?"

"It doesn't matter."

"Patrick smelled his fingers?"

"Yup."

"Lyle probably stuck 'em up his own butt."

Jon thinks this is hilarious. His laugh is high pitched and I can see his uvula fluttering around. We walk toward the gym and he starts jumping around me in a circle. "Oh, Kara, hold it. Hold it tight. Put it in."

"Stop."

"Deeper, Jacob. Deeper."

"Doesn't she go out with Boiko?"

"Fuck Tim Boiko," he says, and swings a punch into the air. "You'll kick his ass."

"I'm not fighting that kid," I say. "He's got facial hair."

"Boiko's a pussy."

"I don't care enough to fight him."

"You'll kill him!" Jon says.

"I don't want to kill him."

"But you *have* to."

I stop in the middle of the crowded hallway and Jon keeps walking. "What?"

He stops and walks back. "That's the other thing. Boiko wants to fight you after school. It's to be expected. She's his girlfriend."

I roll my eyes. "I don't even *know* this girl."

"I say you go nutso," Jon says, placing two fingers in his nose, "and get in his nostrils like this. Then just tear upward, you know? Up, up, up, and just rip like this. Look. Up, up, up."

Jon's got an insane side that makes me love him all the more. His mother, Darcy, blames Jon's father, George, for all his "aggressive energy." His dad left the family for a place called Mendocino after he cheated on Jon's mom with her best friend, Lorna. Jon says they did it doggy-style on his mom's sheets while she was visiting her sister in Miami. I'm not sure how he knows this. George took Lorna with him to California and married her a few years later. Jon was six at the time. His dad visits once in a while and takes us to New York to see R-rated movies. He picks us up at the Hoboken train station in his rented Beetle and we can smell the sweet thickness of his marijuana cigarettes. I love these excursions. His dad is more like a friend than a dad. He lets us sip his beers and curse and once let us spit down an open manhole. I tell myself I'd love every single day if my dad slept with my mom's best friend and moved to a city I'd never heard of. But I know Jon misses his father. I'd miss him too.

After we change, we walk into the largest gymnasium I've ever been in. It's filled with kids in red shorts and Piedmont Junior High tank tops. Everyone's already lining up to use the various apparatus. Three sets of wood rings dangle from the ceiling next to a cocoa-colored pummel horse and a foam vault called a trapezoid. I gaze out at the fat red crash mats and balance beams and all the retractable basketball hoops, folded up high against the fluorescent ceiling. It's just a million miles from the yeshiva blacktop. Jon and I stand with our backs against a long gray mat that protects basketballers from running into the brick wall. We'll wait for Mr. Renna to blow his whistle before we join the ranks. I rub the back of my neck and think about Megan.

"Hey, I got that thank-you note you sent me," Jon says.

"Oh . . . yeah."

"Thanks."

"You don't have to thank me for a thank-you note."

"You got a little messed up though," he says, lightly punching the mat.

I slowly face him. "Why—what do you mean?"

"It's not a big deal. You just thanked me for the wrong gift. You said I gave you a horseshoe set and I gave you a basketball, remember? McGee gave you the horseshoe thing."

I stare at Jon.

"What?" he says.

"I thanked you for the wrong gift?"

"It's no big deal, man. You got a lot of stuff."

"It *is* a big deal. It's a *big* fuckin' deal," I say, rubbing my face in both hands. "I really . . . I really do like the basketball." I feel tears rise up from my throat and into my face. "I'm just . . . *so* fuckin' stupid."

"Hey, man. Relax, okay? You got a lot of stuff," he says, touching my shoulder. "What's wrong with you today? You seem . . . bad."

I wipe my eyes and turn to punch the mat behind me. It makes a *thump* when the flat of my fist hits it.

"Pretend it's Tim Boiko," Jon says, and gives it a kick.

I start jabbing some more, harder and harder. *Thump, thump.*

"You want to mess with me, Tim," Jon says. "You want to mess with my friend because your girlfriend thinks you're a loser. Take that! Hi-yah." *Thump.*

I wind up and throw another punch. It makes a great sound when I connect with a blow. It echoes throughout the gym. I do it again and again. Jon stops hitting the mat to watch me.

"Holy shit, man, you're gonna kill him."

I like that he says this. He's right. I'm crazy, fucking crazy, and don't like being threatened. I'm a goddamn wacko and you've picked the wrong motherfucker to mess with. "You picked the wrong motherfucker to mess with!" I say.

"That's right, he did."

"I'll *kill* you! Get in my face again and I'll fuckin' *punch* your teeth out!" *Thump! Thump! Thump! Thump!*

"Hit him, man. Hit him."

"Are you ready, asshole?"

"He'll never be ready," Jon says.

A flurry of jabs to the face. A gut shot. "Look out now," I say. "Here it comes, Daddy." And for the last punch, I get a small running start and . . . *thump!*

Pain [<Gk. *poine,* penalty]: a wrist that shatters from the blunt impact of a fist against a wall. There's no sound for these seconds. No time.

"Yeah, baby," Jon says. I glance at him, my fist still pinned to the mat. I pull it toward me, against my chest. I try to undo it, to make it all okay. But it's over, cracked, I'm positive, somewhere deep in the purity of the bone. I grab it with my left hand. I squeeze to brace it, the pain climbs and begins to rage. I stumble as I run with wide eyes, confused by direction. My breath held, I see the locker-room door. I kick it open and run into the empty room. "You're fine," I hear myself say. But it's a lie. A lie. The pain expands, pointed and vicious. I suck for air, squeezing the snapped bone. I can't take it. "God, God . . . *don't . . .*" I'm in trouble. It's brutal and rising. I clench my gut and push, push it away, but I caaan't, it's *bad.* The hand, on the end, it's blue and quivers. I try to wiggle the fingers, they're stiff, in shock, I can't take it, I can't breathe, just stop it, stop it, stupid . . . *stupid.* I'll puke, any second, I swallow, stop, stop for a second. Breathe. Fuck, *fuck!* the stinging, *fuck* . . . "Oh Christ." I fall to the floor and slide my back up against a locker. I stare at the twisted wrist I'm squeezing. I'll pass out. I might really pass out, right here, right now. The lights above swirl and I blink and breathe deep but it kills up my arm and into my elllbbbbbbooooowwwww.

"What the fuck happened?" Jon says, taking small steps toward me.

"Get someone," I say, my head rolling on my neck. "I broke it, man. Go."

"Okay. Stay there."

I try to laugh at this but I'll die instead. Die on this floor, this stupid, fuckin' floor. I'm going to throw up, right now, right here, and I *douse* myself in warm milky puke. And then again, all over my chest and legs. "Fuuuuck." The liquid pools and surrounds me, soaks my shorts and naked knees. Breathe, spit, breathe. If I let go of the wrist it'll slip out of the skin. "It's snapped," I whimper to no one in the tiled room. I close my eyes. Just breathe, breathe . . . ride this out, breathe . . . ride it out, breathe. Like a horse, a dying horse, breathe, shoot it, shoot it now, just do it. It's fallen, I see it, a black one, all shiny, the mane, the muscles, that shine, that oiled shine. It's flat in the grass and will die soon, it will, soon it'll end, yes soon it will end. Its long dry tongue, reaches to live, to breathe, breathe, a stunned marble eye. One clean shot, do it. One clean shot. "*Pull* it," I whine, and tears fill my eyes. Breathe now, breathe. Breathe for me . . . beautiful boy. Lie down for me, now. Lie flat and still for me, now. Do not be afraid. *Shhhh.* Stay very still. *Shhhh. Shhhh.*

## Uneven

My father jogs into the nurse's office in a gray three-piece suit, his dark hair tousled. He kneels in front of the folding chair I sit in and rests his hands on my knees. "How bad?" he asks in a gentle tone.

I lick my dry lips, then nod with closed eyes. "Broken."

On the way to the hospital he talks quickly, spending too much time facing me while he drives. He says he and Asher had a long talk after he left my room the night before and that he was "proud" of my brother for standing up to him. "Sometimes I get goin' and there's just, just . . . no talking to me," he says with a chuckle. "But . . . your brother forgave me and . . . I forgave him for not coming to temple on Grandpa's anniversary, and I think we should all just start over on this one. Forgive each other. In fact I told him—"

"Red light, red light," I say pointing at the windshield with my chin. He slows the car.

"I told him that tuition for any of these . . . artsy schools he's thinking about is something I *will* give him . . . if . . . *if* he can come halfway and promises to play more of a role in the family. And I told him, after we apologized, that I don't think it's too much to ask him to . . . come to Shabbat dinner and join us for synagogue once in a while and . . . be a member of this family."

I glance at the speedometer.

"I don't even care what he wears anymore, I swear I don't. As long as it's not in front of people he can wear a burlap bag on his head for all I care. It's a losing battle. I see that now. I lose."

We're moving seventy miles per hour on the **S** curves of Piedmont Avenue. I can hear the tires on his Lincoln Town Car squeal around each bend of the twisting, cement divide. I open my eyes just a slit to see how, exactly, I'd end up dying on this road. The car reeks of pukey gym shorts and pricey new car leather—the combo is just sickening.

"When your brother asked what happened in your room, I told him straight out that . . . occasionally, your learning . . . challenges . . . make me a little crazy and perhaps frustrated with you and that . . . it's *not* always your fault and that . . . patience from me, as your mother has often told me, is something you deserve more of. But, I know you know all of this, and, you know I know you know all of this and . . ."

We're almost there. The sign says two miles. Two miles to the ER at St. Joseph's.

"I need to help you more," he says with a shrug, "and give you more time than I might with others. I get it now, I do. Okay?"

I try to lift my arm. It sits like a lox in an ice pad against the wet numbness of my leg.

"Okay, J?"

"Okay, okay."

"So, that's the first bit of news. Your brother and I are all square. The second thing," he says, "you're just gonna die for. I got this client. Kind of a drip, but a nice enough . . ."

The school nurse said to hold my wrist high against the cold pack and made me a sling which has come undone. The pain is ridiculous. I shift and stare down at it, the darkening skin beneath my thumb.

"So he says to me, 'All you need is a projector, I'll get you any film you want.' 'Any film I want?' I said to him. He said, 'Name it.' So right away I'm thinkin' party, something fun, get us all back on track, and it comes to me—movie night at our house. Invite everyone. No one's done it. Plug the thing in, turn the lights down, and . . . showtime. The guy's got a hundred movies. So I'm about to call you and Asher to ask which movie we should get but then remembered driving cross-country three years ago and Memphis. Remember what we saw in Memphis? It's perfect."

I shake my head.

"*Annie Hall*. Where's your memory? It had just opened and we loved it, remember?"

The lane changes are the most frightening. I lean my head forward to look in the side mirror. It's offset, a reflection of the door handle.

"Annie orders a pastrami on white bread with mayonnaise,

and oh my God, I just roared at that. Just genius. Not a soul in that theater got that joke because we were in goddamn Memphis and who would get it but a Jew, right?"

"Are you . . . watching the road?"

"You're not even listening."

"I heard you."

"Maybe it's not a good time. I thought you'd be excited."

"I'm in pain."

"I know. I know. I was just excited to tell you. I can see you're in pain."

"I just want to be there."

"The guy says next year everyone and his brother will have access to any movie you want. Beta tapes, right in your home."

The tires whine on a curve and my body leans heavy on the door.

"But that's for your TV. This'll be on a big screen, right in our living room, like a huge slide show. It'll be *so* great. You can invite anyone you want, *all* your friends. No one will forget it, I promise you. We'll do popcorn, those hot-dog things, you name it. We'll invite *everyone*. Sound fun, sound good? I'm doin' this for you guys."

I nod.

"I'm gonna invite the whole cast from *Annie Get Your Gun*. An all-*Annie* party. And maybe—bangin' this around this morning—before we start the movie, we'll do the opening number right there in the living room. It's been lookin' real tight in rehearsal. Jocko'll play piano, we'll have mikes set up, it'll be a smash. The only question left is invitations. Should we, shouldn't we. What do you think? I picture Woody Allen glasses or . . . a movie camera or something. Movie night at the Greens. Asher'll throw something together, don't you think? Kid wants to be an ar*tiste* so bad. I'll put him to work."

The car leans on its left tires now. I start to slide.

"So I got the projector for Saturday night, the fifth, and it's a go. The only question left is, Whoooo's got a better daaaaad than you-hoo?"

Oh, he's a jewel. A crisply cut jewel. An onyx, a ruby, a hamantasch-shaped sequin.

"Jacob?"

"No one, no one."

"Bingo! So let me hear your vote. I can get *any* film. I say *Annie Hall*. Funny. Especially for Jews. Poignant. Cerebral."

I see the hospital sign. We're close. We're close.

"J?"

"What?"

"Did you hear me?"

"I agree."

"My God. It's really hurting, isn't it?" he says.

"I broke it."

"Think positively. Could be sprained."

"Doesn't feel sprained."

"Oh, *shoot*," he says. "You have Hebrew school today, don't you?"

I face the window.

"I'll call them from the hospital and tell them what happened. They're sticklers for attendance over there, aren't they?"

Silence. Shit.

"Jacob?"

"Mmm?" I say through closed lips.

"I won't get into it now but . . . are things going better over there? The grades, the homework? How's that Heroes of Israel class coming? Looked good."

I nod. I see the hospital.

"J? Did you hear me?"

I nod again. I see the red sign for the ER. The pain medicine I've been thinking about for the longest hour and a half of my life is in that building. There's relief for me in there.

"We'll talk about all that later," he says, and pulls into a parking spot. "Let's get ya fixed up."

I'm nauseous again. Hospitals make me nauseous. Black suture thread and bloody mop water and cream-colored throw-up bins. "I might be sick," I say.

"You want to vomit?" he asks.

I stop and bend in the parking lot for a minute. "I might breathe through it," I mumble.

"You'll feel better if you get it up."

The words "get it up" do me in. I dry-heave, then hurl twice, back to back, my stomach clenched. I spit and try not to step in it.

"Atta boy."

Kill me.

A HEAVYSET SECURITY guard with folded arms points to a sliding check-in window with his head. My father approaches it alone. I sit in a red plastic chair that's attached to a row of red plastic chairs. I can smell the medicine that will end my pain. It's cold and lemony and will squirt from the tip of a long and daunting needle before filling my veins with love. My father laughs out loud and claps, spinning once before reapproaching the window. "That's *funny*," he says. My luck. She must be attractive. One of those *Playboy* nurses with the cleavage and the lipstick and the surgical gloves that snap. I need a shot, an X-ray, and a cast, and he's winking and spinning. In seconds she'll be invited to our home to watch *Annie Hall* in its entirety. The Green House Cinema. Come one, come all. I look up at the fluorescent ceiling and shut my eyes. Just weeks before we left Rockridge my father invited every Jew he knows to our house. The Chases, the Feigelsons, the Edelmans, the Glucks. After he fed them he packed them all into our tiny den to watch a grainy and never-ending Holocaust documentary that he'd rented through the temple. I fell asleep years before Hitler took over and woke to a house full of drained and teary guests. "Never again," they kept saying as they stood on line to embrace him, "Never again."

"He fell off a—Jacob? What did you fall off?" he says, his elbows on the window sill.

"The uneven bars," I say. Uneven, uneven. I have to get this lie straight.

"He fell off the uneven bars in gym," my father says. "At Piedmont Junior High."

Who breaks their arm punching walls? Maniacs and criminals, that's who. I have to call Jonny and tell him. Uneven bars. Uneven bars. I've never even been on the uneven bars. Maybe boys don't use them. I should have picked a different one. A vault or something.

"Thirteen," I hear my father say. "Bar mitzvahed on November first. A proud, proud day for his papa," he says glancing my way. "A *man* in the eyes of Israel," he says, with a slight bounce on his toes. "Thank you, thank you. He was fantastic."

"Dad?"

He turns to me.

"How long? Ask how long."

"How long does he have to wait? . . . Okay. Thanks so much, Anita. You're a doll."

My father steps away from the window with a clipboard and walks toward me. "Nice woman," he says, still smiling, returning his license to his wallet. "Grew up minutes from what used to be called the Grand Deli on a street that was then known as—"

"Dad?" I muster.

"Yes?"

"Is she gonna help me?"

He licks the fat of his thumb and hones in on a patch of dried vomit on my chin. I turn my face as the thumb comes soaring toward me. "No," I say. "*Get* away from me!"

There's an awkward and silent beat between us. It takes a snapped wrist to talk to my father like that. "Did she say how long?" I try to change the subject.

"*Seconds*. You need to relax."

"I'm trying. It kills."

"It's happening. They know you're here." He sits next to me and carefully drapes his arm along my shoulders. He leans in to kiss my cheek. "You do have some vomit on your chin."

"I don't care. I'm in pain."

"Well . . . Anita said it would be a minute."

"You said seconds."

"A second, a minute."

"It aches."

"I know. I know. I'm trying to take your mind off it."

We sit in silence. My father does the paperwork. I hear the pace of a soap opera on a TV in a nearby room, the room they send you to after you return the clipboard. The electric doors swoosh open and a woman in a long white apron walks through with her hand wrapped in a bloody paper towel. I look away, feeling queasy. A trail of deep red droplets follow her to the window. I pray I'm taken before her.

"Hey, listen," my father says, signing his name. "I don't want you to think about the thank-you notes for a couple of days, okay?"

I close my eyes.

"Just forget about 'em until we get you back on your feet."

I try to flex my fist.

"In a few days, if you're ready, I'll help you get them done. We'll do 'em together. Knock 'em out in a night or two, okay? Bang-bang over with, all right?"

I say nothing. I try to move my arm in the cold pack.

He takes a deep breath that evolves into a yawn. "Noo wwa, wwa, waaaa none, none of my friends will think they're late when they find out what happened to you. And if they're wondering where their thank-you note is, well . . . too bad. You fell off the uneven bars and you might've sprained or even broken your wrist, and you need a few days. That's it. End of story, right?"

I lean forward to see if Anita is still in her booth.

"I'm just sorry you didn't get 'em done earlier, had 'em off your plate weeks ago. But . . . we'll get 'em done. How many you have left?"

The doors spread open again and a man and three little girls walk in. I don't see any gore or agony. I should at least be taken before them. The oldest girl steps in the last lady's blood but doesn't know it. I watch the bloody sneaker prints for a second, then look away.

"Will you try Mom again?" I say.

"Oh my gosh," he says, popping up. "Phone, phone," he says, neck swiveling. "I'll be back."

The second he disappears the doors swoosh open again. It's my mother and Dr. Nathaniel Brody. Her eyes dart around the room, frantic. When she sees me, her hand reaches behind her to grip Dr. Nate's fingers. She runs over to me.

"Oh, sweetie," she says, and I hold back tears. She presses her cool cheek against mine and my nausea is somewhat quelled. "Where's your father? Are you checked in?"

"He's calling you."

Dr. Nate sits next to me and flashes some tender eyes. He looks down at my arm. "Can you bring it up to your chest?" he asks, and then helps me raise it.

"I think it's broken," I tell him.

"Yeah . . . maybe. But you're okay." He smiles at my mom. "Even if it is. It's just his wrist, Claire," he says, and reaches to rub her back.

"We didn't know how we'd find you up here," she says, her open palm on her chest. "We couldn't get *any* details."

"But he's fine. He's fine."

"Nathaniel drove a hundred miles per hour." She looks at him and chuckles. "Or should I say flew?"

"My tires never left the ground."

Dr. Nate's a lot shorter than me and is bald on top. He also has a Wilford Brimley mustache and wears the required professor patches on the elbows of his corduroy blazers. After he began spending every waking hour with my mother, Dr. Nate's wife and three-year-old daughter, Amy, began attending all my father's parties. We see them a lot. He's my mom's mentor, research partner, colleague, and friend—a professor with tenure at Rutgers University. My mother says their grant allows them to write articles and textbook chapters on the intricate decisions of birth mothers and surrogate mothers and that they're basically preparing themselves to be experts in the psychology of adoption. Dr. Nate is kind and soft-spoken, intelligent and confident—a practicing psychologist with an innate gift for listening. But it isn't until this moment, with each of them by my side, that I realize what else he is to my mother.

"Jacob?" says a heavy nurse in *Fraggle Rock* scrubs.

"Yes, that's me."

"Want some relief, babe?"

AFTER A SHOT of something in my butt, I feel delight-
ful and free. My mother, father, and Dr. Nate all stand around
me in my curtained sectional, waiting for the X-rays to come
back. My dad pitches them both on the *Annie Hall/Annie Get
Your Gun* extravaganza and encourages them to invite the entire research team from Rutgers. Dr. Nate says he likes the
idea but that he'll be in Atlanta at a conference on the fifth.
My mother wrings her hands and says she wishes he'd checked
with her first. She'd hoped to be at that same conference. My
father nods and stares at them both. One Mississippi, two
Mississippi, three Mississippi. He rolls a metal stool over to
the far wall and sits with his head turned, as if punishing them
with his distance. I tell myself he won't lose his temper as I
watch his jaw churn forward. Not here. Not now.

The doctor walks in and sticks up the X-ray for viewing. He
wears a goatee and wrestling shoes and tells me to call him
Lou.

"He's got a Colles' fracture," he says to the room. "It's an un-
usual break for the way he fell. It's in the radius bone, near its
end. See that? There's a natural weak spot in the bone where
it widens *right* here, and because of the flare in the shape of
it the broken piece is usually wider than the piece right next
to it. See what I mean? So if the pieces don't lock back together like a jigsaw puzzle, the bone can shorten like one of
those collapsible drinking cups."

"Could that happen?" my mother says, stepping closer to
the picture.

"I don't think so. The way it's set will most definitely prevent
that. . . . Soooo . . . I'm gonna need to ask you to leave for a
moment or two. I'll give Jacob's hand a little tug which could
be *slightly* painful, but it'll then be lined up for proper healing.
I'll set it, put him in a cast, and you can all go home."

"I'd like to stay with him," my mother says.

"I'd prefer you didn't," Lou says.

"But I'm asking you to let me."

"I'd still prefer you wait outside."

"Is there someone who's in charge here?" she says. "A head doctor I could speak to?"

"*Claire!*" my father says, standing from his corner.

Lou flinches and cranes his head toward my dad. "Whew, scared me. I didn't see you back there."

"I'm his father."

Lou waves at him and pats his heart. "Hi, Dad."

"The doctor asked you very nicely, Claire. Why don't you just let the man do his job?"

"I'd merely like to stay in the room with my son. I'm asking nicely as well, and I *certainly* don't need any assistance from you, Abram."

He's frozen by this retort. He walks toward my mother and she steps away, closer to me.

"Come on you two," Nathaniel says with a grin. "This is no time for an argument."

My father blinks with exaggeration and folds his arms. He smiles at Dr. Nate. "You thought we were arguing? Is that your professional opinion, Dr. Brody?"

Nate looks at my dad with a tilted smirk. "All right, Abram."

"Maybe you'd like to . . . be our therapist, Doctor. Help us *bang* out any snags we might come across in our relationship. Can ya help us out?"

"Come on now," he says. "Get past it."

"Come on where? Nathaniel. Where to?"

Dr. Nate shakes his head and lifts his coat off the chair. "I'll be outside, Claire."

My father turns to me and points at Nathaniel. "Who the hell is this guy?"

Lou looks up at my father when the silence gets awkward. He then faces me. The *Fraggle Rock* nurse enters the room. "Hi there," Lou says to her. "I need the plaster cart and five ccs of Xylo." She nods and leaves.

Dr. Nate follows her to the curtain. "See you in a couple of minutes," he says to me at the door, and avoids my father's stare. My mother doesn't budge. When Nate is gone my father reaches for her elbow. She yanks her arm from him with force and I see it recoil high above her head, her eyes enraged.

"What're you *doing?*" my father screams in a whisper.

She steps toward me on the table and takes my face in her hands. "If you want me to stay I will," she says. "Just say it. They can't make me leave."

"I'll come get you in two minutes," Lou says.

She kisses my cheek and my right eye mushes against her face.

My father waits by the curtain for my mother, his fingers clasped behind his head. With his eyes locked on her, he says something into her ear as she tries to pass by. She leans away from him.

"Don't be a *child!*" he barks, and the doctor faces them. "It's *grown*-up time, Claire."

"You . . . uh . . . have any questions for me, Jacob?" Lou says.

I wait for my parents to disappear behind the curtain. "No . . ."

The nurse wheels the cart in and parks it at my feet. I watch her prepare the needle as the doctor snaps on gloves. "Take a deep breath for me," he says, and inhales deeply through his nostrils. "I need you loose right now, all right? Don't think about any of that stuff," he says, waving at the curtain. "Hospitals make people nuts."

"Is that what it is?"

"Sure, sure. One more deep breath. Good, fill those lungs. Fill 'em up and blow it out slowly through your nose."

I exhale through my nostrils and look down at my hand.

"Perfect. Now, how do you feel?" he asks.

Embarrassed.

"Embarrassed."

Lou smiles. The nurse hands him the syringe and he walks it toward me. "You shouldn't. They're just worried about you. Just as you'd worry about them. Ya ready for me?"

I nod.

"Okay, friend. Easy part. Just . . . a . . . prick."

## Lucky

Lulled and foggy from needle number three, they tell me it's time to go home. My parents in the front seat, me in the back, I watch the speedometer flutter near twenty and listen to the drone of my father's haughty words. The sermon reflects on what he calls the "distance" my mother's created with her newfound life—a distance first hatched, he suggests, the morning she met her "little" mentor. Enunciating as if speaking to a room full of toddlers, the critique raises the question of how someone so attuned to familial dysfunction can justify "vanishing" from her very own home.

"Vanishing?" my mother asks. "Twice a week I'm home after nine. The rest of the time I—"

"Does *Nathaniel* get home before nine, ten at night?"

"I'm not having this conversation now."

"Consistency," he says. "Tell me if I'm wrong, Doctor. Being there. Being home when they're home. *This* is motherhood."

"You, Abram? You want consistency for your children?" She lets out an incredulous chuckle. "Is that what you said? Consistency?"

He stares at her and tries to control his jaw. "Are you cute now? A little act? He tells you you're witty, doesn't he? He tells you you're cute? Before he makes you stay after class and—"

"Don't!"

There's a blip of silence before she turns to face me. Our eyes meet briefly and she looks away, out her window—wanting to stop the flood. "Jacob," she says, as if reminding him I'm there.

"Yes?"

"How does it feel right now, honey?" I look down at my cast and then up at her. She rests her head against the back of the seat and her curly brown hair is flattened. How does it feel? How does it feel to be here, is what she means. Stuck back here, in earshot of this ugly privacy. How does that feel? How does that feel, Jacob? To be so lucky.

My father flips the radio on and turns it right off. He shakes his head a few times and leans into her ear. "Do you know you have a *six*-year-old boy?"

"Stop it."

"Just answer me."

"We both do."

"But I *work*," he says. "I make a living, remember? Remember?"

"And I raised babies."

"You're not done yet."

"I never said I was."

"I'd take over for ya, Claire, but what would we eat? Where would we live? *I* never signed up to be a housewife. *Did* I? It wasn't my role."

"I did it for years and I still do it."

"When? How? How could you still do it?"

"Every second I'm home."

"It's not the way we discussed it."

"Discussed it . . . when?"

"In Rockridge. I know where we were *sitting*, what we were *eating*. Asher was a baby. Early November of 1964."

"Nineteen sixty-four? We had a conversation in 1964?"

"So that makes it less valid? Because you say *sixty-four* as if it was . . . the turn of the century?"

She looks down at her hands, her head shaking. "I've never stopped you from growing," she says. "Never."

He pokes himself in the chest. "I kept my part of the deal. You *didn't*. Tuna casserole in the kitchen in Rockridge and you said you wanted four kids, and it was *you* Claire, *you*, who said you'd—"

"So I grew."

"You're their mother!"

"And I'm *still* their mother."

"Are you? Are you?"

I see her head dip forward, down into tears. I see a hop in her shoulders. "How dare you ask me that," she says. "My son can hear you."

My father blinks and sits taller in his seat. He looks at me through the rearview and then back at the road ahead. The speedometer finally climbs as we curl through the S curves and no one says a word until we reach Westlock Drive. I stare down at the still hardening plaster that warms my swollen hand, and gently flutter my fingers, chalky and stiff.

"How does it . . . feel?" my father says, trying to see me again in the rearview.

I ignore him as long as I can. Until he finds me in the mirror.

"Feels numb."

He nods and pushes in the eight-track. Itzhak Perlman at Carnegie Hall. "Well," he says, exhaling a long sigh. "That has to be better than pain."

As we pull in the driveway and park, my father says that he and my mother will be staying in the car for a few more minutes. He asks if I'd give them some time alone. My mother cranes her neck to see me and pushes out a smothered grin I know well. "I'll be there in a second," she says softly. "I'll be there real soon."

Asher's in the hallway when I get upstairs. He's wearing torn jeans and a Squeaky Fromm T-shirt, and his long hair sprouts like a fountain from the center of his head. He wants to know why I'm home, who brought me here, and what the fuck happened to my hand. I ignore the asshole tone and try to walk past him. He stops me with his chest. "Did you hear me?" he says.

"Move."

"What the hell happened?"

"Get out of my way!" I say, without facing him, and a softer and surprisingly gentler person lifts my chin with his thumb. "You all right?"

I slowly nod.

"Good. Now what the fuck happened to your hand?"

"I fell, okay? Get off me now?" I walk past him into my room and slam the door. In seconds he's there again, sighing with impatience, his arms now folded. Squeaky Fromm is winking at me, a close-up of her pink and freckled face. I stare at her instead of him and try to suppress a strange and sudden need to cry. Asher cringes with more empathy and moves to touch me but stops. "What the hell happened, man?"

"I was playing around and I . . . punched it."

"What? I can't even hear you."

"I punched a waaaall," I yell. "*Happy* now? You got what ya want, now go, leave me alone." I lay facedown on my bed and feel the tears roll off my lips and into the fabric of my pillow. I hear Asher coming closer, and soon he's sitting there, his body next to mine.

"Shhh, it's okay," he says. "It's okay, man."

I shake my head, and turn to face the other wall. "Bullshit. You're wrong. It's not. She's not—"

"Who? Who's she?"

"Mom."

"She's not what?"

I take a deep breath and let my eyelids gently close. "Staying. Here. With him."

Asher waits a few seconds before he slowly stands. He walks to the window and looks down at the car in the driveway. I watch him from the bed as he leans and rests his forehead against the glass, and in the silence that follows I listen for the car doors to open. She's telling him now. That's what's taking so long. When should we tell the kids, Abram? How shall we split them? I'll take Dara and Gabe, she says, jotting it down on her palm. You take the boys. *Fuck you!* he screams, and I hear it rattle in my thoughts. When I open my eyes my brother is back. He reaches to touch my swollen fingers like someone new to affection. His thumb just rests on mine at first, barely there, as if uncertain to give too much. And when he lifts my whole hand into his and holds it, I am safe somehow in the foreign tenderness of his touch. I try not to move, to not scare him away, and look down at my cast when his eyes meet mine. "If this ends," he whispers, "I'll be here for you. I won't leave you."

We hear a siren in the distance and we both face the window. We listen to it fade.

"I'm gonna get into an art school in Rhode Island, J. My guidance counselor says it's the best. They call it RISD. He says if I try hard I could get a scholarship. Do you know what that means?"

I say nothing.

"It means I'm not going to need him anymore. I'm not going to need him ever again. All I need is the grades and the diploma, and we could leave here. Ya hear me? No more of this." He looks down at our hands and then back up to me. "But we got to play ball for now, ya know? Wait it out. Please him. 'Cause I need some time," he says. "I need more time."

I glance up at him.

He kneels to touch my fingers to his cheek, and holds them there for a long second. "I gotta go," he says. And quickly stands to leave.

I blink once and my eyelids burn and stay glued to my face, closed. Rhode Island. Rhode . . . Island. Just me and my brother. I'm fading and can taste the liquid drugs in my veins, pouring into my wrist and palm, the very tips of my nerves. How shall we split them, she says, and I drift away into this blissful and airy space, somewhere between the truth and sleep.

I've been away for years when I wake again. The sun has gone down, just blackness out my windows. I hear footsteps outside my door and see a light from the hallway. Someone knocks lightly and enters my room. When I hold my head up I hear, "No, no, lay back down." It's Megan. She walks over to my bed and sits on the edge. "I just got back from school," she says softly. "You okay?"

I take a deep breath and let my eyelids close. "I broke my wrist."

"I know, poor baby. What happened?"

"I punchdawall," I whisper.

"You what?"

I open my eyes. "Uneven. Uneven."

I feel Megan's hand lifting the back of my T-shirt. She scratches in long, feather-light strokes, up and down my spine. "Oh."

"Relax," she says and pulls the shirt higher. "Just let me touch you."

An erection seems untimely and impolite. My body has no tact, no choice. Just this pumping flow of gasoline from some unseen vat.

"We'll talk tomorrow," she says, and pulls my shirt down. When she stands from the bed I can see her body lean over me. I feel her long black hair against my cheek and then her breasts against my chest. She puts her mouth against mine and kisses my lips. One Mississippi, two Mississippi. I lift my left hand to touch her face but she stops before I reach her. As she stands in the dark my palm brushes her thigh.

"Good night," she says, walking away from the bed.

"Good night."

I stare at the ceiling, awake. I move my left hand down my stomach and hold myself in the grip of this naughty fog. It is not a touch I know. This lefty with no name. But she is real, she is, I feel her. And tonight, I'll call her . . . love.

*Just let me touch you. Just let me touch you.*

Dear Sid and Adina Weintraub,

Sorry this is late. Thank you for coming to my Bar Mitzvah and for your generus gifts. No one has ever given me a sweater and snow hat and mittens with the Israeli flag embroidered into them. I love the socks too. I will think of both of you when I wear them places like Hebrew school and other Jewish places too. I hope to see both of you somewhere in the future but it's likely I'll be moving to Rhode Island with my brother some day and will never think of or see you again.

Sincerely,

Jacob

Dear Effie and Mel Greenstein,

I'm so sorry this card is late. It's been two and a half weeks since the incident regarding the uneven bars. I hope you understand that my writing hand was injured in the aforementioned uneven bar incident and that this fact caused the lateness regarding this tardy note. I really like the generous gift you gave me for my Bar Mitzvah. I had no idea that they made bookends out of Jerusalem stone. With the help of my brother and my friend Jon we were able to hoist them up on my bookshelf yesterday. They looked really great up there before my shelving collapsed into a cloud of snapped particleboard. No one was hurt. I think I'm going to keep them on the floor.

Thank you very much again. You both *rock*, Effie and Mel. Get it?

Sincerely,

Jacob

Dear Jack and Bella Weingarden,

I'm so sorry this card is late. My father told me that he called you last week to apologize for my tardy thank-you notes. He is sitting here with me as I write. He wants me to apologize once again and to remind you that parking will be tight the night of the *Annie Hall* party. He says to tell you that it's okay to park on the lawn to the left of the driveway, but to be careful not to hit the Sinkovitz's porch or mailbox. He also says to arrive on time because just before the movie starts, the cast of the Leiland Community Theater's production of *Annie Get Your Gun* will be performing in our living room. If you didn't already know, my dad is in this chorus.

Thank you for the generous Israel Bonds and thank you, Jack, for resharing that detailed story about my bris during dessert.

Sincerely,

Jacob

Dear Morris and Dora Bitterman,

Sorry this card is late. My father told me that he called you last week to apologize for my tardy thank-you notes. He is not sitting here right now as I write this and I am so very happy about it. I might be a retard but when he's standing over me, watching every stroke of my pen, I become a much more substantial retard. I love that I can write anything I want right now and he's not here to see it. For example: Ass. Fuck. Fist. Shit.

Boink. Dick. Fiddle-fart. Titties. Etc. Rhode Island, Rhode Island, Rhode Island, I'll soon leave here and live on an island. I can write that Megan takes her bras off in front of me now. I don't know if you know her or not. She lives in our attic and eats dinner with me. We've been doing a lot of back scratching up in her room and I'm getting used to seeing the raised and pinkish part on each of her breasts. My friend Jon says that this area is called the ariolla. The other day she sat up with her bra off and it didn't seem to bother her that I was sitting there, two inches away, pretending not to care that her nudity was so close to me. I try not to stare at her chest when she sits up to light her cigarettes. But as it turns out I'm a great deal interested in nakedness and the beauty of girls and that raised and pinkish part of the female ariolla. Lately, after I go down to my room and my boner (slang for "erect penis") deflates, I've been seeing something wet in my underwear that I don't think is pee. I think it's what they call sperm. In the sixth grade a classmate named David Barnett told me we only have a million of them to spend so we should be careful with every drop. I've got to tell you, Morris and Dora, I'm a little concerned. I have no way of knowing how many sperms I have left in my testicles.

Thank you so much for the dartboard and for the darts. Asher likes to hang pictures of people he despises on it. He then hurls the darts from very close range with a running start. He completely ruined my Hall and Oates album cover. The record just sits in its paper sleeve now. Thanks again. See you at the *Annie* party.

Sincerely,

Jacob

Dear Abe and Judith Frazenberg,

I told Megan about Rhode Island the other night and how

nice it would be if she'd visit. She says it's not really an island but to call when I get there. We were spooning at the time. This means that I lay behind her with my body against hers and we curl our knees up and watch sitcoms. For the first few times we did it I wore my jeans under her sheets but when she changed into sweatpants I decided to do the same. Each time since then I've felt a little worried that she'd feel my erect skin-flute (slang for "penis") against her body. The way I lay behind her leaves nowhere for it to go except pressed up against the crack of her butt. I don't really know the words to describe how good this feels. I've never felt anything like it before. The more we do this together, the more I realize that she probably does feel me against her. But she doesn't say anything or seem to mind. She just watches TV and lets her whole body jiggle when she laughs at the jokes. It feels good when she laughs. At times our feet touch or her hair gets in my mouth or I feel her fingernails against my forearm and I pretend that's she's my girlfriend. But I don't think she likes me like that. I just think she sees me as someone who's alone a lot. And she is too. Ever since she heard my father in my room she's been telling me I'm handsome and smart and that the girls will always like me because I know how to listen. She also says she loves my blond hair and that I'm funnier than my dad will ever be. I think she only says these things because she thinks I need to hear them. But she's wrong. I don't like sympathy. I want her to like me for me and not because she thinks no one else does. I want her to wake up in the morning like I do and think of her face and her mouth and the way her arm sometimes drapes over me during sitcoms. I'd also like to press my penis against her without any clothes on.

Thank you so much for the Johnny Bench Pitch-Back. Asher threw a bowling ball at it yesterday and it crumbled into a heap of orange aluminum and tangled netting. He says he can fix it. My father told me to ask if you have any extra folding chairs you could bring to the *Annie Hall/Annie Get Your Gun* party on the fifth. If not, do you have any large floor pillows? See you then.

Sincerely,

Jacob


Dear Aunt Gert,

Last night with Megan was different. We got into the spoon thing again during *M\*A\*S\*H* but this time I started to move my hips in a different way than I have before. I wasn't sure if she felt me doing this but soon I was sort of grinding without thinking and began to feel a dizzying and sexual flutter in my testicles and ribs. It was like a risky and swirling dream, Aunt Gert. A rush that rose from my stomach to my shoulders and on through the nerves in my face. I noticed that if I raised my pelvis in tiny increments, higher and higher up her back I began to lose control of the nerves in my eye sockets. And just as Megan let out a laugh at the TV my eyes squeezed closed as if light was pouring in on them, and I felt a great and flowing squirt from the tip of my Johnson (slang for "penis"). My whole body stiffened and shivered and my toes and fingers clenched up tight with spasm. And when I opened my eyes I saw something I'd never seen in my life. Sperm, Aunt Gert. About a liter I'd guess. White and sticky and all over the back of Megan's gray sweatpants. It must have come out of my penis when my eyes were shut. She sat up at just that moment. I didn't move, still unsure of what I'd done, so shocked at how much came shooting out of me. I watched her reach her hand around and slowly put her fingertips in it. When she turned to look at her hand, her fingers were webbed. She didn't look at me at first when she got off of the bed. But when she stood up she gave me sort of a half smile and said, "Whoops. I think I'll take a shower." I went down to my room after she went into the bathroom. I curled up into my own spoon and wished to God it hadn't happened. I wish to God I was already in Rhode Island. Humiliation, Aunt Gert. I had no idea. How am I going to look at her?

Thank you so much for the stationery with my name in bubble letters, and for the book *Jews Say the Funniest Things*. My father suggests you take a cab to the party tomorrow. He's very tense right now about the parking issue, the dance number, the projector, the food supply, the amount of chairs, the number of people coming, what we're all wearing, cleaning the house, my mother's "attitude," Gabriel's speech, and whether people will enjoy themselves enough to call and thank him the day after. It's gonna be great. See you tomorrow.

Love,

J

## Show Business

My father's been wearing his makeup and costume for
two and a half hours. His oversized overalls are a worn-down
denim and have a polka-dot patch sewn into the seat. There's
also a blue and white bandanna around his neck and a piece
of fake straw behind his right ear. As some very early guests begin to arrive he asks me to gather the family into the kitchen.
I can't find Gabe or Asher and I'm way too embarrassed to
knock on Megan's door. I decide to just get Dara to do it but
then I can't find her either. My mom says she's in the backyard
cleaning off the lawn furniture for my dad. When I look out
the kitchen window I see her on Asher's shoulders, laughing
her ass off as he races around the patio. She bear-hugs his
head for dear life as he jumps up on the lawn furniture and

starts pogo jumping with his arms out like a plummeting air-
plane. I can hear her scream through the window as Asher
tumbles onto the lawn and begins tickling her armpits like a
madman. My sister's going to pee any second—I've seen this
before. "Jacob!" my father says behind me. "Where is everyone? It's *five* twenty."

"Out there," I say, and knock on the glass. They both look
up at me and I wave them inside. My father lifts his glasses to
his forehead and begins to read from the back of one of the invitations. "Ushers, chairs, popcorn, and lights," he says, and
lowers the paper. "There's tons to do. Megan. Where's Megan?"

**Rule Number 7 of the Green House Rules**

*Any member of the family that proceeds to ejaculate on
Megan should feel a torturous and unrelenting sense of
mortal shame, coupled with a near psychotic desire to disappear from this God's earth.*

　　*a. But I wasn't trying to. (It doesn't matter.)*
　　*b. I couldn't hold it. (No shit.)*
　　*c. I felt it rising and . . . (Yuck, who cares?)*

"Jacob?"
"Yes."
"Did you knock on her door or not?"

Asher walks in the room in torn red pants and bare feet.
Dara's right behind him with lawn grass on her poodle sweater.
"Murray Blatt needs some help," says Asher, tying his hair up
off his neck. "He says the toilet in the den won't flush."

"Again?" my mother says.

"Why are people here already? The invitation said six." My
dad takes a deep breath and exhales in spurts through his
nose. "What did he put in the toilet?"

Asher looks at me with a smile and shrugs his shoulders. "A doody? I don't know, Dad . . . uh . . . the seat's down."

Dara and I *have* to laugh. The word "doody" is too much for us. My father's eyes leap to Asher knees. "What the hell is this? Change now. You're *not* wearing those. Go. Go."

Asher leans over to look at them and swipes at the holes. "I've been cleaning up all day. They're old."

"They're rude. Get out of my sight."

Asher looks at me and then back at my dad. "Since noon I've been . . . runnin' around for this bash of yours and you—"

"This bash is for *you*. It represents *you*. People are arriving and you're in clown pants. Torn clown pants."

"Okay, I heard you. I heard you the first time. You can relax now."

"And you can kill the condescension while you're at it. Got it?"

Asher shakes his head. "Got it . . . *Dad*."

"Look at these pants he's got on, Claire. In tatters. Are you homeless? Seventy-five people coming and—"

"He'll change them, Abram. He's been cleaning and moving furniture all day."

"So has Gabriel. So has Dara. I don't see *their* knees."

My brother walks past my father toward the fridge. "It's happening, right? The fun? This is it?"

"I'd like *all* of you to dress nicely tonight. It should go without saying. Nothing crinkled or . . . *torn*, for Christ sake."

Asher pops a grape in his mouth and faces my dad. "What's on your face?" he says, squinting.

"Freckles," says Dara. "I helped him draw 'em on."

"Why freckles?"

"Freckles for the show," my mother says. "He plays a country bumpkin."

"There as big as Raisinettes. Are they moles?"

"They're freckles," says Dara.

"Freckles are tiny."

"Enough!" my father says, waving the list above his head. "Just stop. Listen to me. People are arriving. People are here already. It's buckle-down time. *Focus* now, eyes here. Please. I'm going to list your tasks. Asher will be on lights and the projector, which means—"

"I know what it means, Dad."

"Humor me will ya, *please*? Just clam it for ten seconds. Don't tell me what you know . . . all right? Why would I need that?" He reaches in his pocket and pulls out a black Magic Marker. "Claire. For Gabe. I almost forgot. It's nontoxic." He flips it to her. "Now, lights and projector."

"What is this stuff?" My mother pulls the cap off and smells the tip. "I'm not putting this on his face, Abram."

"It's fine. I asked the guy at the store."

"It smells too chemical-ly."

"I just told you. I talked to the man who sold it to me. It *can't* harm skin. Now can I continue? Do not underestimate our time constraint. Listen to me. Lights and movie projector involves the lights for the dance number *and* the film, so . . . due to the fact that Asher'll be working the projector as well, I need Megan . . . where the hell's Megan?"

    d. *and then I guess I gyrated a little and—*

    e. *What do you mean you gyrated?*

    f. *Maybe that's the wrong word.*

    g. *Did you thrust into her?*

    h. *Not into her.*

    i. *Against her? Did you press your boner against her over and over?*

 *j. Yeah.*
 *k. Well, there ya go.*
 *l. Right. I feel so stupid.*
 *m. Ya should.*
 *n. Pressed it against her too much, huh?*

"She's in her room," Dara says.

"Go get her, please."

Dara runs out the door.

"I told her five thirty, did I not say five thirty?" He checks his watch but he's not wearing it. "*She*, Megan, will turn the lights down when the film starts. Asher, you just handle the lights for the performance. Now, quickly, do you have the colored filters I gave you?"

"I have them," Asher says. "For two days now."

"Okay," he says, reading the list. "Jacob, you will usher people in and make sure they have a place to sit. Now . . . we're limited, so, we'll be using the lawn furniture. Have you cleaned it off yet?"

"Me?" I say.

"No, the *wall*. Yes, you. I told you to do it yesterday."

"You told Dara to do it."

"Did she do it?"

"I don't know."

"Find out. Next. Claire," he says, lifting the list. "You're on coffee, popcorn, and food in general. Fine. That's . . . all great and needed. But I want to emphasize how much I need you . . . out there, with me, to show your face and to mingle and greet and . . . play hostess like you're so very capable of doing. Right? They're your friends too so . . . I'll thank you for helping me with your . . . with your presence."

She seems to freeze at the sink, her back to us. She slowly lifts her head from the chore.

"Tell me you'll be out there."

"Of course I'll be out there," she says without turning. "Where else would I be?"

He lifts the list but lowers it again. "They're here to see you. To share this time with you so—"

"They're *here*, Abram because you invited them."

Megan and Dara walk in the room. "Sorry. I didn't realize how late it got," Megan says.

She's wearing *the* sweatpants and a Moraga College T-shirt with a cougar on the front. When she looks at me I drop my eyes to a patch of bubbled linoleum under the stove.

"How dressed up are we getting?" she says.

Hi, Meg. Sorry. I'd take it back. It snuck up on me when I was doing that thrusting thing. It wasn't on purpose. I've only seen the stuff once before and it didn't come out of me. It was on the chin of a Chinese girl in one of Asher's magazines. She was winking at the guy who did it and I wondered if it smelled like glue.

"A nurse with a punctuality problem," my father says.

"I said I was sorry."

"I know, I heard."

Megan stops and faces him. "Good," she says. "Then I won't say it again."

Silence. He tracks her as she walks farther in the room. She leans against the stove with her elbows. "So . . . are we all wearin' *Dukes of Hazzard?*"

Asher laughs. "Just a good ol' boy."

"What's that mean?" my father says. "*Dukes of Hazzard?*"

"She's kiddin' you," Asher says. "It's a TV show."

"Huck Finn with a beard," she says. "Howdy, Rabbi Finn."

"What's that? That's not funny," says my dad. "Rabbi Finn? Is that funny?"

"Oh, come on," she says. "Look how tense you are. It's a party. Have some fun."

"What does that mean?" he says, looking at Asher. "Rabbi Finn, what is that? Is it anti-Semitism? I'm lost."

"*No*, Dad," he says. "Joking, she's joking."

"She's kidding you," my mother says, shutting off the sink. "My God. Meg's right. This is supposed to be about fun. Entertainment, right?"

"Making fun of someone is *fun?*"

"I'm not making fun of you," Megan says, her face flushed, a little stunned. "You're wearing overalls and there's eyeliner on your face. It's a *little* funny. Anti-Semitism? Really?"

"Okay," he says, his jaw churning. "Terrific." He plops down in one of the kitchen chairs and slams his list on the table. "You run it. Take control. Thank God you're here. She's *here* everyone! Watch. Watch how much gets done."

"I heard you," Megan says. "Go ahead."

"So I can continue? You're done?"

"Yes."

"You can do that? Save the routine? For when I'm asleep or *dead.*"

"Abram," my mother says. "Please."

Gabe walks in the room wearing the tiniest tuxedo I've ever seen. "Mommy?"

"Hi, baby."

"I don't like this costume," he says, tugging at the bow tie.

"You look fantastic," my mom says. "So handsome."

My father lifts the Magic Marker from the table and hands it to Asher. "Will you please draw some Woody Allen glasses on

Gabriel? Your mother's afraid it'll sizzle his skin off. It's a *marker*. Tell her."

Asher begins to read the warning on the side.

"Do *not* draw on his face with that thing," my mom says. "The tux is cute enough."

"I spec*ifically* asked the man at the store and he said it wouldn't harm him."

"You think yelling at me is gonna change my mind, Abe?"

"Who's yelling? I'm telling you."

The front door slams closed. We all hear a woman sing, "Helll*ooo, Greeeeeeeens*. It's Wendy and *Laaaar*rrrr*yyyy*."

"Hi, Wend," my father yells out the kitchen door. "We'll be out in a jiffy, just give us a sec." He shuts the door. "You know something?" he says, nodding and facing my mother. "You'd never believe this, but I'm doing this—all of this—because I *love* you. Do you hear that? Do you *buy* that?"

"Do I *buy* it, Abe?"

"*Allow* me to love you. All of you. Allow me to love you and to do this my way and you'll see what it can be. This is for you. For *your* pleasure."

"Abram."

"Say nothing! Can you do that, Claire? Can you just stop? Why is there resistance through every inch of this? Why? It's like . . . *trudging* through a swamp with bickerers on my back. None of you know what it takes to pull off a flawless show. It's *not* fluff. Freckles and makeup and time and discipline and attention and *passion*. *Laugh* if you want, go ahead. You're so funny, all of you, you *really* are."

Megan starts rubbing her forehead.

"People who care about us are pulling out of their driveways, right now, to come and be in our home. To be with you. And look at you."

We all just stand there and wait for him to lift his list. One Mississippi, two Mississippi, three Mississippi. "Now, Megan."

"Yes?"

"You will shut the lights off in the living room when I point at you . . . just seconds after Gabe does the intro to the film. So again, the order. One, the cast performance of "There's No Business Like Show Business." Two, I'll do a very quick introduction of the family. Three—"

"Time out," Asher says. "I said earlier, days ago, that I don't want that . . . this time. To be introduced."

Everyone looks over at him.

" I just—"

"Why are you inter*rupting* me? Why? I always introduce the family."

"That's what I'm talking about. You don't think Shel Friedman knows that I skateboard and Dara swims and J reads good Hebrew? You said yourself you had a time constraint. Everyone coming to this thing knows us. Am I wrong, Ma?"

"I . . . see what you mean," she says. "To save time, Abram."

My father slowly puts the list in the chest pocket of his overalls and walks to the sink. He folds his arms and looks out the window with a tilt of his head, as if searching for clouds. "Three," he says calmly. "Gabriel introduces the film. Four, viewing. Five, dessert and coffee. Six, discussion of film. Gabriel?"

"Yeah?"

"Are you ready to try it for Daddy?"

"Noooo," he says, pulling on his bow tie.

My father turns around. "Don't do that, Gabriel. Don't *pull* on that. Daddy tied that for you and I don't want it loosened. I want to hear your introduction, the one we practiced yesterday. Are you ready to show Daddy?"

"I don't want to."

My father drops to his knees and takes him by the shoulders. "You're going to give the introduction to *Annie Hall*. We practiced for two hours yesterday and tonight you're going to make everyone very, very happy when you go out there and say what I told you to say. It's very cute. *You're* very cute."

"I don't like this costume, Daddyyyy."

"The costume is fine. Everything is fine. The people coming today love you . . . and they're going to love you *more* in about an hour. So, tell me you're ready to show me that you know your lines. You're a big boy today and I don't want to hear that you don't want to."

"But I don't want to," he says, and his bottom lip protrudes.

My father stands from his crouch with his eyes closed. "*Damn* it!"

"Abram," my mother says, walking toward Gabe. "Don't. Don't make yourself nuts over this. Just do the introduction yourself."

"He knew every inch of it, Claire. He's doing it tonight, right out there. He is. *Some*one draw those glasses on his face and do not discourage him. I *mean* it," he says, his finger raised. "Gabriel, in five minutes I want to hear that intro. You did *wonderfully* last night and I want it again. So you be ready for Daddy."

Asher shakes his head and starts to leave the room. "Where are you going?" my father says.

"To change my clown pants, remember?"

"Is that sarcasm? Is it? 'Cause you can *keep* it if it is."

Asher stops at the door and turns to my father. "Why do you even . . . have . . . these parties?"

"And this is my son, Asher," my dad says. "He's into sarcasm and disgusting pants and doesn't like to be introduced."

"Do you need me anymore?" Megan says, glowering, her elbows on the stove.

"Do you know your role?" my father asks her.

"You point at me and I turn the lights off. I got it."

"More sarcasm," he says to my mother. "Go. Go away. Go do whatever you do up there. Have fun."

Megan points her tongue at the back of my dad's head as she and Asher leave the room. My father lifts the list to his face. "Lawn furniture. Did you clean it off, Dara, like I asked you to?"

"Yeah."

"With what?"

"A towel."

"Good girl. Now drag it all to the back steps and Asher'll help you bring it in."

"But it's heavy."

"Anybody home?" someone says from the front hall. "Abram? Claire?"

My father runs to the door and opens it. "Out in a *sec!*" he barks, and slams it.

"Abram," my mother whispers. "What are you doing?"

"Just . . . quiet," he says. "Can I have quiet? Dara, go see who that is and bring their coats upstairs. If they're in the show, point them to the wardrobe rack in my room. Go, go, go."

She runs out. He looks down at his list.

"Is the coffee made?" he says. "Is there tea? Is there ice?"

"Yes," my mother says, opening the fridge. "I have it handled."

"Jacob, go drag the lawn furniture to the back steps and I'll help you from there."

"Even the—?"

"All of it. Make sure it's clean. Bring a towel."

Asher pokes his head in the room. "Someone's parkin' their Benz on the Sinkovitz's lawn."

"Stop them!" my father says. "Tell them to park in the driveway. What's *wrong* with people? Ten bucks it's Saul Dardik. Putz!"

"I'll try," Asher says, and walks back out.

"I'll talk to Saul," my mother says, and she leaves right behind him.

My father turns to me and glares. He is tortured with rosy cheeks of red. Gabe lets out a long yawn and tugs at his bow tie. My father's still staring at me. I crack my mouth into a smile.

"Lawn furniture, lawn furniture, lawn furniture." I start to walk toward the door. "Lawn furniture, lawn furniture. *Wait!* Take that marker and draw glasses on Gabriel. Do it quickly, please."

"I can't draw glasses, Dad."

"Woody Allen glasses."

"What?"

"Black glasses. Clark *goddamn* Kent."

"My cast," I say lifting it. "I can't even hold a pen."

"Gabriel, come over here," he says, and pulls the cap off the marker.

Gabe steps closer to him and my father kneels on the kitchen floor. "I'm going to start the introduction that we practiced yesterday and when I stop I want you to take over, okay?"

Gabe lowers his chin.

"In . . . the sum-mer of 1977, remember? My . . . my. Come on. My daddy and two brothers drove to California. Remember now? One night in Memphis they stopped to see a movie called *Annie Hall*. Okay, now you."

Gabe looks up at me for a second and then back at my dad. His eyelids are half closed.

My father says, "When the . . . when the . . . cha-rac-ter of An-nie . . . ordered a pastrami on . . ." He waits with his head tilted, his eyes wide with mascara.

"White . . . bread," Gabriel whimpers.

"Right. Good."

"My . . . daddy . . . laughed harder than he ever . . . ever laughed."

"Good! Good, boy! Little faster. A lot louder. Now you're almost there. "It's . . . safe . . . to . . ."

". . . say . . . that my daddy and my brothers . . ."

". . . wwwwerrrrre . . ."

"Were the only Jews for . . ."

"For what?" my father says, his hands spreading apart. "For . . ."

". . . miles," says Gabe.

"Good *boy! Great* boy! Okay," he says, with a sigh and smiles hard. "Fabulous. I knew it was in there. Now, come closer so I can draw these glasses on you. This is the *cutest* idea. Now from the top. In the summer . . ."

I watch my father press the wet tip of the pen into Gabriel's cheeks. "Turn this way now. No, this way. Good, stay still. Okay, ready? In the summer . . ."

Asher and my mother walk back in the room. "It's Bernie Shapiro, Dad. He says you told him to park on the lawn."

"What the hell are you *doing*?" my mother says. Gabriel has a black circle around his right eye. He starts to touch it and it smears to his nostrils. "I *told* you not to draw on his face." She grabs the marker from his hand. My father jumps to his feet and runs at her. "Give me that marker this second, Claire."

She grips it with both her hands. "You . . . *heard* me, Abram.

Why would you ignore me? If I did that to you, you'd . . . go insane."

"Hand it to me."

She brings the marker behind her back. He lunges for it but misses.

"What are you doing?" she says.

"I told you *forty* times that pen is safe. Give me the pen. Give me the pen."

"I'm not giving it to you. Step away, Abram!"

"A *child*," he says, grabbing her wrist.

"Stop, Daddy," Dara says.

"Let go of me," my mother says, with tears in her voice.

"Daddy, get off."

"Asher," I say, walking toward them.

"Whoa," Asher says. "Dad!" He tries to step between them and takes my father's elbow in his hand. "Whoa, whoa, take it easy, take it easy."

My father lets go of her and she slides to the floor with the pen in her grip. "What the hell is that?" he says to Asher. "Keep your hands off of me, *hero*. Mister clown pants."

"Just . . . calm down. You have a party going on out there."

"The voice of reason," he says, and throws his arms to the ceiling. "Come to save his mama. Yay the clown. *Yay* the clown!" he barks.

"Don't do this now," Asher says softly.

"You think I'd hurt my wife?" he says, stepping into his face.

"No . . ."

"Abram," my mother says. "Take the pen."

"The savior? Gonna save us all?" My father hooks his finger into Asher's belt loop and yanks down. Asher spins away, stepping back.

"You're gonna tear my pants?" he says. He smiles at me. "Ya

know you got friends out there, Dad? Outside that door? A lot
of them. Tell me you know that."

"Come over here," my father says and points at the floor.
"*Right* now!"

Asher just stands there blinking with amazement. "That's
what you want. You *really* . . . do." He lowers his chin to his
chest and laughs out loud. "Wants to rip my pants."

"Abram," my mother says. "Let's start over!"

"Why? To humiliate me? Twelve cars in the driveway and he
wants a . . . *rrriiippp* down memory lane. Here. Wacko. Take
it." He skips toward my father. "I'll stick my leg out for ya. Go
on, *tear* 'em, ya lunatic. Spend it, right here, in front of your
family. *Spend* it!" he yells, and his smirk fades to rage.

My father gets a finger inside and yanks down with all his
strength. The pants don't tear. He drops to his knees and goes
again with both hands. Nothing. Dara starts to cry and my
mother surrounds her in her arms. Asher looks down at the
top of my father's head. He begins to find a smile. "Look at
you," he says. Another jolt of the arm, a tiny tear. Another and
another quickly, his glasses flopping to the floor. Gabriel moves
to my mother, his eyes pinned on his dad.

Someone knocks on the kitchen door.

"Abram, stop now," my mom says. "They'll hear you."

He jolts again and Asher wobbles, nearly stumbling, with a
lazy laugh.

"Anybody home? Claire?" I step toward the door and my
mother does too.

"Time's up," Asher says, and bows over his own knee. In a
blink the fabric is torn clear off his right leg and fills his fists
with floppy red flags. He throws them at my father and they
drape over his slumped shoulders. My mother opens the door

and sticks her head out. I wait for the tantrum, we all do, the metal in his molars. But he doesn't move. His overall straps have come undone and the dust of his makeup now peppers his beard. He breathes hard on his knees and just stares at the floor.

"What is it with you?" Asher nearly whispers. "Your children are watching."

Out of the corner of his eye, my father sees me. He is lost in this moment, startled from the dream. He looks cold and somehow childish, exposed to even himself. No one goes near him. My mother shuts the door and leans her back against it. "I'm not going to live like this anymore," she says. "I'm just not."

I reach under the table for his glasses and hold them out to him. "Dad. Here. Take these."

His chest and shoulders begin to cave as he lowers his forehead to the floor. I see his mouth widen and lock as a very high and soft sorrow whines from his throat. My mother kneels toward Gabe and Dara and buries her face in their clothes. We listen to him together. We listen to him fall.

Another knock. "Anybody home?" says a voice from the hallway. "Abram? Claire? I got kugel here. It's heavy."

My mother stands from the floor and wipes her eyes. She walks to the door and slips out of the room. My dad lifts his head and breathes deep; he stares at his hands. Asher bends to lift the strips of red denim off his back. He tosses them in the garbage and faces me. "Go get the lawn furniture, okay? I'll help you bring it in." Two men laugh out loud in the dining room and one of them claps his hands.

"Dara?" Asher says. "Dara?"

"Yeah . . . ?"

"He's . . . gonna need more makeup. You helped him before, right?"

She glances carefully at her father's hunched back.

Asher points at his own face. "Freckles," he says. "He's gonna need new freckles."

## Curtain

Temple congregant Gabby Minkowitz went to high school with my dad. She stands in the sea of guests and waves vigorously at the cast members before chasing a piece of popcorn down her wrist with her tongue. I sit right behind her on the living-room floor. Two of the actors wink at her in unison and wear white cowboy hats and droopy plastic holsters, while the third wears overalls like my dad. The cowgirls are in long denim skirts and boots with pinkish white frills, and Jonny, who sits next to me, says one of them is a lunch lady at our school. I think he may be right. The ten-foot movie screen is set up to the right of the cast and ripples in silver waves from all the commotion. When I look behind me I see my mother, kneeling and mingling amid the Altmans and the Schaffers and the Kriegers and the Harsteins and the Ryzmans, the Bulawkos, the Meirs, the Krasnobrods, the Weisses, the Barneses, the Wendels, the Reselbachs, the Grossos, the Lantos, the Mautners, the Kozlowskis, the Levys, the Schwarzbats, the Offens, the Gabanys, the Tennenbaums. And then there's the accounting firm crowd that all sit on lawn chairs by the far windows: the Nelsons, the Browses, the Perlsteins . . .

"J," Jonny says, leaning close to my ear. "Where's Asher?"

As I look back at the projector the crowd roars with applause as my father runs in the room shooting the only cap gun that has ever been allowed in this house. He dips his hat to his guests as he hops over their legs and finally makes his way to the "stage." An obese guy the cast calls Jocko is wearing an Indian headdress and sits behind our piano. He hands my father a microphone in exchange for a friendly mock punch to the jaw.

"Howdy, loved ones!" my dad yells into the mike, and Jocko starts a two-key intro for the big welcome. My father taps the mike against his palm to the beat and gets the audience to do the same.

"*Whoooooo's* got the stuff that made the Wild West *wiiiiiild?*"

"You do, Abram!" yells Judy Sempel from behind me and the crowd laughs.

My father shuts his eyes and smiles as Jocko keeps the beat. "My vaudeville partner of twenty years, Mrs. Judy Sempel, ladies and gentlemen!"

Laughter through the rhythmic clapping. Judy stands and curtsies.

My father steps three rows deep into the crowd and stands above me. "I said, *whoooooo's* got the stuff that made the Wild West *wiiiiiiild? Whoooo* pleases *eeeeevery* wo-man, man, and child?" His hand ruffles my hair and Jonny cackles with his mouth wide. "I'll tell ya! I said I'll tell ya, *buckaroos!* The cast of the Leiland Community Theater's *Annie Get Your Gun!* That's whooooooo!"

All nine of the cast members pull out cap guns and start firing them at the ceiling. Jocko sweeps his hand down the row of piano keys and kicks into the intro to the main event. The cast lock elbows and begin to do-si-do their way around the small square of space as the crowd continues to clap. After a solid minute of this, Jocko snaps three times and they all shoot their guns and line up to face the audience. "Two, three, four . . . 'There's no bus'ness like show bus'ness, / Like no bus'ness I know. / Ev'rything about it is appealing, / Ev'rything the traffic will allow; / Nowhere could you get that happy feeling / When you are stealing that extra bow.'" They all bow. "'There's no people like show people; / They smile when they are low. / Yesterday they told you you would not go far, / That night you open and there you are, / Next day on your dressing room they've hung a star— / Let's go on with the show.'"

The applause goes on for a while. Gabby is standing and clapping and rocking her giant Jewess hips near Jonny's face. My father wipes his forehead with his bandanna and lifts the mike off the piano. A standing ovation begins and Jonny and I look around the room before slowly joining the masses.

"Ladies and gentlemen, the chorus of *Annie Get Your Gun!*" he says over the applause. "May fifth through the fifteenth at Wilford High School in Radison. Take I-80 north and exit at Tankhill Road. If you see the Howard Johnson's tower you've gone too far. Thank you. Thank you, aren't they superb? Thank you. You're wonderful, thanks." The applause rages on and my father hugs each of them and faces the crowd. "Ladies and gentlemen, Bruce Finkel, Diane Mead, Henry Tasko . . ."

The applause climbs.

"Margerie Danes, Brian Levy, Fran Angel, Pauline Crane, Kim Woo, and Gail Trotsky. The chorus—and heartstrings—of this *beloved* American classic."

Applause.

"They are wonderful, wonderful people to work with and to know. The show is just dynamite because of them. Truly, I mean that," he says, and bows to them with his palms pressed together.

Applause.

"Thank you so much. Thank you," he says, lowering everyone with his hands. "Shhhhh. Thank you. Thank you so much. We did an abbreviated version because of time but it's a taste and we'd love to see you out there. Thank you so much for your energy. We really feel you."

"We love you, Abe!"

Laughter and some light applause.

My father shades his eyes and looks out on the room. "Who said that? Irv? Is that you, Irv Dreisen? I'll get the twenty I promised you right after the show."

Laughter. Irv blows a kiss.

"Shhhhh. All right now, thank you. Settle down now, thanks." The sound slowly dies out.

"Now before we hit the lights and break into the wonderful world of Woody, I'd—"

More applause.

"I'd like to introduce my family to you. It'll just take a second."

Jonny pats my back and says, "Show time," into my ear.

"My oldest—Asher says to me, 'They all know us, Dad. Come on, give me a break.' Well . . . to that I say . . . one day you'll know how proud it makes me to be your father. Ladies and gentlemen, I love him like a son—" My father bops himself on the forehead. "Wait a minute, he *is* my son. Asher Green."

Jesus Christ, he does it. The one thing he asked him not to do. I look down into my lap as everyone in the room claps for Abram's firstborn son.

"Anyone seen him?" he says into the mike, and I look up. My father's blinking nervously and searching the room. "Asher?" he says with a chuckle, and I stand to search the room for myself. The Friedmans, the Kramers, the Brewsters, the Milks. He's not in the room. I stand quickly and step over Jonny. "Excuse me, I have to get by," I say, and start to shuffle through the bodies and legs. He's up in his room, I'm sure, or definitely in the kitchen or something, hiding out until the intros are done. "Jacob," my father says into the mike. "I'll go find him," I say, not facing him.

"Wait, wait, wait, come back here—we'll just move on. My blond boy, Jacob. Come on up here for a second."

Nearly out of the room and straddling Lilly Jacobs, every face around me lights up with celebration. I'm a son they can see. And I've just been announced. I carefully step back over Gabby and the Gilmans, Milt and Sari, and walk straight for my dad, into the spotlight. He puts his arm around me and kisses my ear. He gazes out at his audience. "Can read and sing Hebrew better than Theodore Bikel, Moshe Dyan, and Golda Meir all wrapped up into one."

Some laughter.

"It was stunning when he read from the Torah, wasn't it?" Some applause.

"Well, he'll be doing it again. Soon I hope. What else could a father ask for?"

I smile out at the audience and have no idea what he's talking about.

"And this semester . . ."

Good Lord.

". . . he's gonna get a B in math for the first time in his life. He promised me." As the applause starts I glance up at him. He reads my eyes and tries to dilute his words.

"Overcoming . . . obstacles is . . . to me . . . one of the hardest things in life, and my son can overcome anything you put in his way. He's a hurdler. And I *love* him. Friends, this is Jacob, let's hear it." He leans in to kiss my head but I dodge it. I walk back to my spot with a tingly burning on my cheeks and neck, trying to avoid eye contact with all seventy-five people. *My son, the retard!*

"Dara and Gabriel? Where are they? Quickly, both of you."

Applause as they make their way to the front of the room. I get eye contact with my mother and mouth, "Where's Asher?" She shakes her head and shrugs.

"Down in front," yells Rod Strauss. I drop to my knees but still search for my brother. I can see the staircase if I move forward. I ask Gabby for some room.

"Dara . . . the beautiful," my father says, and pecks at her head with his lips. "Looks just like her mom, doesn't she? Still the fish of the family. Took fourth in her age group on Sunday, but don't you worry," he says, bumping her hip with his, "her coach says she'll be just fine. *Dara,* my only daughter!"

Applause as she steps back into the crowd.

"And my Gabriel. Looks sharp today, yes? He's off to his prom after this."

As they laugh my father licks his finger and swipes at the faded dots of marker on his cheek. Gabe ducks and cringes.

"No limits here. Bright, funny, just look at that face, folks, that *punim.*"

Light applause.

"Gabe works with the lighting crew for the show and . . . the whole cast," he says turning to them. "You just eat him up, don't you?"

They all nod with too much energy, the way chorus people do.

"Seven years old and knows more show tunes than all of us combined. The not so baby of the family. *Gabriel!*"

Applause as Gabe steps forward and bows. I see someone on the stairs and I stand to get a better look. Saul Dardik.

"And now, my wife. Come on up, baby."

Through whistles and applause, she slowly makes her way to the front.

"Before anything else—before lights, before cameras—I'd like you to see the greatest gift that God has ever given me."

When she arrives he puts his arm around her waist and pulls her close to him. "How beautiful is this woman?"

Whistles and more applause, a light chant of her name.

"'Along the garden ways just now / I heard the flowers speak; / The white rose told me of your brow, / The red rose of your cheek . . . / The lily of your bended head, / The bindweed of your hair: / Each looked its loveliest and said / You'—Claire Green—'were more fair.'"

Some applause.

"I just love this poem. I call it my 'Poem de Claire' because . . . it . . . helps me . . . encompass, in so few words, the . . . *love* . . . I have for my wife. The true love. I think she looks a little like Annie Hall, don't you?"

Many in the room agree. Gabby turns to me, nodding.

"Would you like to say anything to our guests, love?"

He holds the mike out for her. At first she shakes her head and just smiles out at the room.

"Come on, just a hello. They love you. Brief."

Another body comes down the stairs. It's Nora Butensky and her daughter, Sil.

My mom reluctantly takes the microphone and glances out at us. "Thank you. Thank you all for coming to our home today."

"Where's *your* cap gun, Claire?"

Laughter.

She pats her pockets and smiles. "Musta left it in my other holster."

More laughter.

"That's *funny*," my father says with surprise, nodding at the audience. "Not bad."

She dips her head for a moment and when she lifts it, she's looking straight at me. One Mississippi. Two Mississippi. Three Mississippi. Speak. Say anything. Please. She swallows and bites her bottom lip.

Just. Say. Anything.

"Weren't they great?" she says with her arm toward the cast, and the clapping briefly erases the lengthy pause. As it slowly dies down she grips the mike with both hands and stares down at it to speak. "Know that . . . there's plenty of food and of course popcorn on the dining-room table. Just . . . help yourself. If that runs out just let me know. Don't panic. And there's coffee, both caff and decaf, and soft drinks and juice in the kitchen, and plenty of ice in the freezer so . . . let me know if you have any questions with that." And lastly, since I have you all here in one place, I have something to share with you. Along the garden ways just now . . . I too heard the flowers speak. They told me that our family garden has all but turned to sand. I want you to know I've watered and nurtured this square of earth for nearly twenty years, and waited on my knees each spring for these gentle bulbs to rise, reborn. But *want* does not bring such breath to life. Only love does. The plain, old-fashioned kind. In our family garden my husband is of the genus *Narcissus,* which includes daffodils and jonquils and a host of other ornamental flowers. There is, in such a genus of man, a pervasive and well-known pattern of grandiosity and egocentrism that feeds off this very kind of evening, this type of glitzy generosity. People of this ilk are very exciting to be around. I have never met anyone with as many friends as my husband. He made two last night in line at Carvel. I'm not kidding. Where are you two? Hi. Hi, again. Welcome. My husband is a good man, isn't he? He is. But in keeping with his genus, he is also absurdly preoccupied with his own importance, and in staying loyal to this, he can be boastful and unkind and condescending and has an insatiable hunger to be seen as infallible. Underlying all of the constant campaigning needed to uphold this position is a profound vulnerability that lies at the very core of his psyche. Such is the narcissist who must mask his fears of inadequacy by ensuring that he is perceived to be a unique and brilliant stone. In his offspring he finds the grave limits he cannot admit in himself. And he will stop at nothing to make certain that his child continually tries to correct these flaws. In actuality, the child may be exceedingly intelligent, but has so fully developed feelings of ineptitude that he is incapable of believing in his own possibilities. The child's innate sense of self is in great jeopardy when this level of false labeling is accepted. In the end the narcissist must compensate for this core vulnerability he carries and as a result an overestimation of his own importance arises. So it feeds itself, cyclically. And, when in the course of life they realize that their views are not shared or their expectations are not met, the most common reaction is to become enraged.

The rage covers the fear associated with the vulnerable self, but it is nearly impossible for others to see this, and as a result, the very recognition they so crave is most often out of reach. It's been eighteen years that I've lived in service to this mindset. And it's been devastating for me to realize that my efforts to rise to these standards and demands and preposterous requests for perfection have ultimately done nothing but disappoint my husband. Put a person like this with four developing children and you're gonna need more than love poems and ice sculpture to stay afloat. Trust me. So. So, we're done here. The family you've known is over. And I'll be building a new garden with a man some of you know and I imagine this will be infuriating to learn. But I am very much in love with him. So much so that tomorrow I will alter my children's lives forever when I tell them the truth. My husband has known for quite a long time that this day would arrive. He'll need your love and your friendship. And he very much deserves it. "Also, the downstairs toilet, the one in the den, keeps clogging with a kind of tinkling sound if you don't jiggle the handle after you flush it. We apologize. Old house. Be as comfortable as you can, those of you on the floor. Halfway through we'll do a quick—"

"*Very* quick," says my father.

"A very quick intermission so you can all stretch your legs. Thanks so much again for coming. Enjoy."

Applause. My father kisses her and wraps his arms around her. He lifts and spins her before letting her down. She stumbles over a speaker wire as she's lowered but quickly gets her balance. "And now," my father says, "to introduce our feature film . . . Ladies and gentlemen, you know him, you love him: Gabriel Woody Allen *Greeeeeen!*"

# Over

When a man takes a woman and marries her . . . if she find no
favor in his eyes . . . then he shall write her a bill of divorce-
ment and send her out of his house. Deuteronomy 24:1

**Rule Number 8 of the Green House Rules**
**(Jacob's Copy):**

*You will now be part of a joint-custody agreement. The
agreement states that you will be "shared," or parented,
equally by both your mother and your father (although
never again in the same home). Within the week you will
have a second house in nearby Hayward, New Jersey. It is
here you will notice that your mother is sharing a bed with*

*a man you've known as Dr. Nate. As this particular rental house has one bathroom, you will see this virtual stranger in the early mornings and often find yourself attempting to urinate next to him while he hums and shaves. He will be wearing black "banana hammock" bikini briefs and have a great deal of hair on his back and shoulders. In time his presence will become less strange and the very notion of his bearlike nudity, pressed up against your mother, will begin to dissipate. Every other Sunday until you graduate from high school, you and your two younger siblings will move back to your father's house and spend a week under his parental guidance. Your older brother will have a choice. He can travel back and forth with you or he can pick one house and settle there until his graduation. Dr. Nathaniel Brody's three-year-old daughter, Amy, will be on your schedule and she too will pack a suitcase each weekend and alternate between Hayward and her mother's home in Evansville. Megan has been given a choice to remain at your father's house but needed less than two seconds to decline. It is undetermined where she will move. You will have two rooms and two toothbrushes and two beds and two phone numbers and you won't need to change schools or meet new friends. Your immediate challenges, given your age and level of maturity, are the following:*

*a.  With puberty upon you, you may find this early "honeymoon" period between your mother and Nathaniel to be a tad more nauseating than most. Entangled legs, the stroking of earlobes, a glimpse of the sides of their tongues during overly affectionate greetings—all possible triggers. And as you are too young to voice this gripe with effective language, the resulting emotional outcomes range from irritability to anger to varying degrees of depression. Knowing your history and the way your father handles fury, you are also in a high bracket to smash something with your own closed fist.*

b. *Also due to early sexual awareness, the sight of Dr. Nathaniel's naked body will be more disturbing in that it's a body with whom your mother has obviously commingled. When, for example, his penis is brandished during your time together in the aforementioned bathroom and, let's say, draining like a fire hose into the toilet next to you, an early teen might have trouble erasing the sounds and smells of such image, and how it pertains to his mother and her use of said penis.*

c. *You may encounter at this age a grave sense of abandonment from this circumstance. Your dreams will often be scenarios in which you are left alone, trapped in small places, falling from great heights or submerged in sand, water, or some type of clingy mud. Depending on your emotional drive, you will either survive and fight your way out of these corners or just wait to die. You're currently in a high bracket for the latter but dying in a dream state just means waking up all sweaty and frightened and uncertain where you are.*

## Rule Number 9 of the Green House Rules

*Keep loved ones and people you trust close to you. Remind yourself that you're truly and actually and technically not alone. And remember that most kids lose their fathers entirely when their mothers fall madly in love with their college professors and move with them to neighboring zip*

*codes. You're lucky. You still have your father in these vul-*
*nerable and blooming years of early adulthood. And you*
*know what's even better? Your father still has you.*

"Mmmmthinkmmmmmgonnathrowup," says Gabriel, as he
stands and gags twice like a cat. My mother leaps to her feet
and puts her palm on his chest. "It's okay, baby," she says, pulling
him into her arms. She kisses the top of his ear as he begins to
cry in silence. "I'm *not* leaving you."

I look at Asher on my parents' bedroom floor, propped up by
his elbows, his shoe tips pointed at ten and two. He peeks at
me from the corner of his eye and lets his head flop backward
between his shoulder blades. "Kabooooom," he says softly, and
my father looks his way. There's a blur in the air as the truth
settles in my skin, a slowing of time. I am awake, I think, as I
touch my own face and eyelids, reaching for tears I can't even
feel.

"I'm not leaving any of you," she says with a wobbly voice.

"Are you leaving Daddy?" Dara asks.

My mother pulls Gabe even closer and faces my sister. "Yes,
I am."

"I . . . worked very hard," my father says, "to make this all go
away."

"I'm confused," Asher says, a sarcastic tone. "Who lives
*here* . . . and . . . where do I sleep on Tuesday?"

"Here," my mother says. "We'll all sleep here for now. I'm
not going anywhere for a few days."

"Why not?" he says harshly, sitting up straight. "Why draw
it out?"

"Can't you see your brother's upset?" my father says. "Can't
you—?"

"We're all upset," says my mother. "I'm staying for a while,

Ash, so we can all adjust. So we can ease into . . . what has happened here."

Gabriel suddenly looks up at her. His face is drained of all life, a ridiculous pale of confusion and fear. He burps and bends as his cheeks fill with air. My mother shuttles him to the bathroom and I run to open the door for them. The toilet seat clinks the tank and I hear the thump of Gabe's knees as they hit the floor. We're all frozen as we wait, listening to the mourning of this shocked little boy. Burp. Gag. Puke. *Puuuke!*

"Good."

Flushhhhhh.

"Good, sweetie. Any more?"

"I don't knooooow."

"Wait a few seconds," she says out of breath. "Just wait."

A somber whine pours from Dara's mouth and she stands and walks to my father. He embraces her off her feet and wears her weeping body like a sash.

"Agaaain," says Gabe before a burp. Burp. Puke. Puke. *Puuuke.*

"Okaaaay," says my mother. "That's the one we needed."

"I just want this to go away," says my father. "I just want it all to . . ."

Flushhhhhhhhhhhhhhh.

It's two hours later when my mother ushers Gabe and Dara to bed. Asher stands slowly for the first time all night and walks without a word from the bedroom. My father watches him go, and waits for the door to close before covering his face with my mother's pillow. I sit alone with him now amid the smells of their sheets and clothes and skin and wish, with a pain I can touch, that I could love him enough tonight. "I need to leave this marriage" is how she began, her hands out and cupped like a Christmas caroler. There was a long beat of silence before Gabriel stood, and somewhere in that quiet, deep inside my mind, I actually felt free. My father pulls the pillow away and stands. He claps his hands twice and rubs his palms together. "I think I'll do a little dance," he says with a teary smile, and starts to tap dance on the carpet with his bare feet. I move back to give him more space as his arms whirl around and his feet go through the motions. When he stops after a minute his breathing is heavy and the sound of this fills the room. He sits on the edge of his bed again and looks over at me.

"How's my boy?" he says, and a grim smirk lifts the corners of his lips.

"Okay" is what comes out.

He pats the mattress next to him. I stand, pretending not to see, and sit in my mom's wicker chair near the TV.

"I . . . tried, over these last few months, J. I tried to imagine all your faces . . . when you heard . . . what you heard." He fluffs her pillow and keeps it on his lap. "I tried to hear your mother's voice and . . . tried to guess where she'd be sitting when she told you." He tosses the pillow to his side and walks across the room to open my mother's closet. With his back to me he runs his fingers down the sleeve of a striped blouse. "I saw you," he says. "I saw you the clearest."

He gently shuts the door and leans on it with the weight of his shoulder. "You held me," he says as the tears roll from under his dark frames. "In my thoughts. That's the first thing you did. You stood up, walked over to me, threw your arms over my shoulders, and . . . told me we'd get through this."

I hear Gabe's voice in the hall. I look toward the half-open door and my father walks to shut it closed.

"Do you love me?" he asks, with his hand still on the knob.

"Yes."

He faces me and says nothing. I shift in my seat, unsure if he heard me.

"But do you love me as much as I love you?"

I look down at my hands. "I think so."

"You think so? Is that what you said?"

"I mean, I do."

"Because lately I've been feeling a distance between us. Okay? I come home from work and . . . you're here and I know you hear me but . . . you don't come to see me. You don't come and ask me about my day."

I sit taller in the chair and it squeaks beneath me. I keep my eyes from my father.

"And as you can see," he says, pausing to swipe his cheeks, "I need that now. I need you to tell me it's gonna be okay." We stare at each other for a few seconds and I'm not sure if he wants me to say it right now.

"It's gonna be okay," I say.

"Then tell me that. Tell me that again and again. Will you?"

"Yeah."

"Promise?"

"Yes."

"Because . . . right this second, I'm trying to figure who I have and who I don't have, ya know? So do I, Jacob? Do I have you?"

I nod when he looks up at me. "Yes."

"Then tell me right now," he says, moving toward me.

"Tell you . . . ?"

"Tell me."

"That . . . it's going to be okay?"

"No," he whispers. "That you love me."

He steps right up to my feet and I look up at him. "I love you," I say.

He nods, and runs his finger along the wood of the bed frame. "It would be nice . . . if I could have a hug now," he says. "It would be nice if I didn't have to ask you to give me a hug when I need one."

I stand and place my arms over his shoulders. He begins to cry and pull me against his chest and I can feel the coarse hairs of his beard pressing into my neck. He begins to whimper, to sob, his body shakes.

"It's all right," I hear myself say.

He shakes his head. His tears streak my face, my mouth and I tighten my lips to avoid the taste.

"I only have you," he says.

His arms begin to squeeze my frame, tighter, closer to him and the weeping is now joined by a rhythmic hum. He starts to sway in this dramatic dance of grief that pinches the skin of my arms and presses my eyelids against the buttons of his shirt. He moves us closer to his bed with small steps and begins to lean onto it with my body beneath his. We then topple together like a cut down tree and bounce on the mattress. His weight is crushing my chest and I can feel the cold of his tears in the collar of my T-shirt. I try to push him off but I can't.

"We don't de*serve* this, Jacob," he sings, mouth wide, an angel hair of saliva connecting his lips. "My family."

"Dad."

"My whole *life*."

I try to move my legs but they're entangled in his. I can feel his breath on my neck and chin.

"Don't leave me. Never leave me. We need to be closer. Like you and Jonny."

"Okay . . ."

"Your brother is so angry. Did you hear him? He's . . . a *blamer*, he is; he'll blame me till the day I die, he will. I *need* your love. How do I get that? Tell me!"

"Dad."

"What?"

"I can't breathe."

"What did you say?"

"I just can't . . ."

"Can't what?"

"You're hurting me."

He shifts with a jerk and stares down at me. "I'm hurting you?"

"I just can't breathe with you on me like that."

"I'm *loving* you," he says, lifting his torso from mine. "I'm holding you and letting you know that *I'm* hurting and I need you right now. You can't give me that? *So* dramatic. 'I can't breathe, get off me, get off me.' You really can't *breathe*?"

"I can now."

"I ask *nothing* of you. My life is turned inside out. I need you and all you can do is —"

"I just couldn't breathe."

"Or maybe it's more than that, huh? Maybe you want to get away from me. Is that it?"

"It's not that."

"You got somewhere you need to be, right?"

"No."

"*Any*where but with me. Alone is better than with me. Say it."

"I didn't say that."

"Can't hug your father for . . . two goddamn seconds?"

"I can."

"Well, then *hold* me. Open your arms and hold me like I'm someone you love."

From underneath him I place an arm over each of his shoulders. I turn my face to the wall and feel him staring down at me.

"That's it? That's how you hold me?"

I pull him closer with my arms and his chest presses into mine. He begins to cry, and as I hold my breath he suddenly rolls off of me with his legs still entwined.

"*Get* out of here!"

I look up at him. "I'm holding you."

"I said *go!*" he screams, an inch from my ear and punches the pillow by his side. I wait a few seconds and push his dead weight with both my hands. I slide out from under his legs. When I get to my feet I walk quickly across the room and close the door behind me. I stand for a moment, blind in the darkness of the hallway and soon see my mother on her way up the stairs. I turn and walk quickly toward my room.

"Can we talk?" she says.

"I need to go to bed."

"Will you let me tuck you in?" she says, and walks over to hug me.

I keep my arms at my side as she pulls me into her chest.

"It's . . . been an awful night. Hasn't it?" She rests her cheek against mine. "You're so stiff."

I clench my jaw and shake my head. "I'm tired, Mom."

"It's gonna take some time to understand all of this," she says. "Ya know?"

"I understand," I say.

"Do you?" she says, holding me tighter. "Do you understand?"

I shift my feet and clasp my hands behind my back. "You're leaving him," I say. "You're leaving him behind." I close my eyes and for a second I see them, my mother and my father, a photograph I've known forever.

She pulls away from the embrace and takes my face in her hands. "Yes," she says. "Yes, I am."

I reach for both her wrists and toss her hands back to her. "With me. You're leaving him behind with me."

—⚹—

June 3, 1981

Dear Megan,

I will send this letter to your mother's house in Pencilvania and I hope you will get it. You left a sweater here. It is the red and too big one that is hard to push up the sleeves. You left two plants. The one you call Bonzeye Sammy and the one that I said looked like an old man's elbow with leaves on it. I gave them water but I don't know how much to give them. You left five cassette tapes, the belt to your bathrobe, and some socks in the laundry room too. Not the socks with the cat whiskers that I teased you about. Ha Ha. These are normal and white but have little balls on the back. If you call me and give me your number we can talk about when you will come here. I am not mad that you did not say good-bye. I have to go. It is late here. Are you in New Jersey?

Sincerely,

J

June 21, 1981

Dear Megan,

I put your things in a box in my room. If you want to come and get them it is okay. I hope you will call so you can get your things. I live at my mother's house in Hayward when I don't live at my dad's house. If you call my dad's house and I am at my mom's house then you should call my mom's house so I can meet you at my dad's house. If I'm not at either house, I may be in Rhode Island in my own apartment with Asher. You should call soon or I may be in my own apartment by then. In Rhode Island. How are you? Did you get my last letter?

Sincerely,

J

July 2, 1981

Dear Megan,

I had a dream you were in a coma. I hope you are not. In my dream you were in the hospital and my mom and Nate were tongue-kissing next to your electric bed. Nate was wearing your whiskers sox and my mom said, oh, oh, baby to him, and then my teeth turned crumbly but Asher caught them. In real life my mom and Nate kiss all the time and my room is very close to their room. I sometimes hum so I won't hear anything revolting. Nate has huge calves and sometimes bad breath but he is nice to me. He was on TV last week on the news for being a psychologist in a court thing. It was weird to see him on the screen and be in the room with him too. My mom says his career is "taking off" and that's why he has to travel a lot for his work. I hate this because she needs to go with him every time. This means I have to go to my dad's house and he makes us go to Beth Tikvah because he wants to be president of the synagogue. The president sits on the *beema* with the rabbi and cantor during services. He gets to make a speech to the people afterwards too. He says I can help him if I volunteer to be a leader for the kid services they call Tot Shabbat. I wish I never learned Hebrew because you have to read it good to do the Tot Shabbat. I told him I don't want to volunteer and he said I had to. I don't think he understands the word *volunteer*.

I have to go now. Asher is coming here to get his mail. I'm going to tell him that I found a map of Rhode Island at my school. I made a Xerox of it and I keep it in my closet. You are right and I feel stupid. It's not an island. But there really is a lot of water near it. I put a red dot where I think me and Asher should live in our apartment. It's very close to this bay and near some real islands too. If he's in a bad mood I'm not going to show it to him because I don't want him to change his mind. My father puts Asher in a bad mood every time he sees him. It's because Asher wants to live at my mom's even when she's on trips with Dr. Nate. My father really hates this. He calls over there all the time and wants to know what he's doing or if he's drinking or if he went to Hebrew school or not. Asher? Hebrew school? My father still thinks he actually goes to that fuckin' place? How does Asher get away with it? Why doesn't the rabbi just call my dad? Is he paid off or something? I'd be expelled in seconds. Wouldn't I, Megan? Wouldn't I be expelled in seconds?

If you don't want to write me back just call and tell me you don't. I am wasting paper and stamps on you. So thanks.

J

August 12, 1981
Dear Meg,

You're not being very nice. Maybe you are not getting these letters because of the coma. Ha Ha. I am kidding and I hope you are not in a coma or dead either. It is late here and I am tired. Tonight my father went ballistic on Gabe for drawing a giant cow on our driveway with sidewalk chalk. I don't know why he got so upset but maybe because the cow had droopy utters that squirted milk. When he came inside he was trying to calm down. He told me to follow him into the den and to read to him from the Tanakh, the Jewish Bible. He likes to listen to it these days when he goes ape shit. I get very nervous and make more mistakes than normal. I read the English and the Hebrew and he sometimes cries right there. He likes the Song of Songs part of the Bible the most because he says it sounds like love poems. I think he is right.

> Upon my couch at night
> I sought the one I love
> I sought but found her not.
> I must rise and roam the town,
> Through the streets and through the squares;
> I must seek the one I love.

I don't think of you when I read this so don't think I do. You won't be reading this anyway. Are you in New Jersey? Do you hate me for doing you know what? I think I am lonely tonight.

J

September 18, 1981
Dear Megan,
This is my last letter. Maybe you are married or maybe you are a nun now and can't write to boys. Maybe you are just a jerk. I don't like you right now and I won't waste my time and ink. You owe me stamps.
From,
Done writing to you

November 2, 1981
Dear Megan,
I think I should get paid money for leading the Tot Shabbat. I've done it six times now and I fucking hate it because the room reeks like baby diarrhea and it's all just bullshit so my father can get on the *beema*. He says it's a mitzvah and I should see it as an offering to God. I want to say, To whom? The burn-

ing bush guy? He says if I keep up the good work I'll be able to read from the Torah at the adult service and that this will make him the most proud man alive. *Who goddamn cares?* is what I say to that. Not me is who. I don't even believe in God! Do you? Ms. coma, married, nun, who can't even write me or call me or stop by to say hello. I don't believe in you either! I'm moving away from here and you'll be the one who never hears from me. And it doesn't matter that I haven't seen Asher in a while because I opened my father's atlas and found out how to get there on my own. It says it takes three hours and fifteen minutes by Amtrak train and that it's 195 miles from here. I could take a bus too. A Greyhound. It goes 280 east to the turnpike and then north toward 80. The turnpike then becomes 95 N and then I just wait for a long time and exit at number 21. I'll need to ask where the school is from there. It would be stupid to get there and learn he's at Brigitte's house or something. I'd have to stay in a hotel. Maybe one with a pool. But I'll find it on my own. Got it? Oh, the plant that looks like an old man's elbow with leaves is very dead. The leaves fell off the elbow—and I don't care.

From,

See ya never

November 31, 1981

Dear Jerk-off,

It is eleven o'clock at night and I am in my room in bed. I am supposed to be at my mom's this week but she went to Indiana for an adoption conference. I think Asher lives at Brigitte's house now because he once said her mother's a "wino" who doesn't know what the hell is going on. I really wish he would come here once in a while. Last night I dreamed Asher jabbed my dad in the toe with an orange Popsicle and he roared like a lion and fell down a manhole. It was very real. Tonight at dinner my father said he wants me to read from the Torah in a few months. At the adult service. I really don't want to. The president now is Mickey Bloomfield's dad, Ira Bloomfield, and Mickey did the Tot Shabbat services for two whole years before anyone asked him to do the adult service. My dad says I should be honored that they want me so fast. When I told him I don't care he slammed the table with all his strength. Everything tipped and spilled and he told me to clean it up. I was surprised that I said that. I may not send this letter. I'm saving every penny. I may need to catch a train.

December 26, 1981
Dear coma bitch nun,

Asher came to my dad's house yesterday. When I asked him about Rhode Island he said something I couldn't hear and ran up the stairs to look for a painting he did of a fat lady riding a seesaw. It made me so fucking mad. A few minutes later his door was closed and locked. I knocked on it but he didn't come out so I knocked again and again until he got all pissed and flung the door open. He said, "What's your problem?" right into my face and I said, "Tetzaveh, you asshole," and walked off to my room. That's the Torah portion my father's making me read and it's a nightmare how long the thing is, much longer than the one for my Bar Mitzvah. It's about this guy Aaron and his sons and this ram they need to bludgeon for no good reason. When Asher came in my room he apologized and couldn't believe I had to read from Tetzaveh this long after my Bar Mitzvah. I was so glad that he was so mad for me and wished my dad could hear all the words he used. I wanted to hug him and talk about Rhode Island and tell him what I'd learned about living there from a travel book I found at Jonny's. Did you know that the capitol building in Rhode Island has the third largest unsupported marble dome in the universe? Also, Providence, the place where we'll be living, is known as America's Renaissance City. But we didn't get to any of that because he had to go find the seesaw painting and get out of here before my dad got home. This is my last letter. The next time you hear from me I'll be writing from America's Renaissance City. So don't try to find me or write me. It's too late.

Sincerely,
None of your fucking business

February 16, 1982
Dear Megan,

At Dad's right now. It's really late. Mom and Nate went to Lincoln, Nebraska, for a conference yesterday. I guess it's a hotbed for the adoption industry. Tomorrow morning is my Torah reading. I've practiced and practiced for so many hours with my father that I practically know the fucking thing by heart. I'm still very nervous. All my dad's friends and colleagues are coming. He's even more nervous than me and this makes him very unpleasant to be around. I sometimes wonder how much God would like him if he knew him. I think about leaving here almost every day now. I think about walking off the *beema* in the middle of Tetzaveh and running out the back of the temple onto Glendale Avenue. I keep going to Piedmont Avenue and to the bank and take out all my Bar Mitzvah dough. I then get a cab to Newark, Penn Station, and then a train that goes to New Rochelle to Stamford to Bridgeport to New Haven to Old Saybrook to New London to Mystic to Westerly to Kingston and on into Providence. I then just wait for my brother in a hotel with a pool. I haven't seen him for almost two and a half weeks now. Tomorrow when the Torah is open I'm going to ask God to please let him get a scholarship to RISD so we can live together in an apartment somewhere between the historic College Hill neighborhood and the edge of the Providence River. I bet you don't know anything about Rhode Island. I bet you don't even know how to get there by train or how many firsts Rhode Island has. The first golf tournament, the first circus, the first polo match, the first discount department store ever in America. Did you know this, Megan? No, you didn't. And that's what I thought. Don't try to reach me there. Think of me as dead.

Hate,
You

# III

# 1983

## Fifteen Years Old

*May 22, 1983*

*Dearest Friends,*

*P*lease join me on June 12 of this year to again hear my fifteen-year-old
son Jacob read from the Torah at temple Beth Tikvah at 9 A.M. sharp.

*I feel that this reading is quite a significant one.
It marks yet another pinnacle in Moses and Aaron's plight
to bring the slaves of Egypt to a better understanding of God's intentions for
them in the wilderness of Zin. What makes this day even more special is that
I have just been reinstated as president of the shul and will again be on the
beema with my "blond boy" for his fifth reading this year.*

*Rabbi Shapiro has said that "Jacob's Torah readings have a very natural
cadence and that you [I] should be very proud of him." So with that said,
I look forward to seeing you. Please also join us for brunch
afterward at our home.*

*Bring nothing but your beautiful selves.*

*Love,
Abram*

## The Deep End

"I'm gonna *shoooooot!*" Asher screams from my mom's tiny front lawn. Brigitte sits up on the hood of Nicky's Camaro in her bra and cut-offs while Beth stays vertical, rewinding a cassette with her pinkie. It's graduation time at Piedmont High and never have I seen my brother's smile this deep. I watch from the upstairs bathroom of my mom and Nate's rental on Bickley Street. Asher's got a bottle of Korbel between his knees and feigns a mounting orgasm with fluttering eyes. His best friend Nicky loves it and laughs with his head back, awaiting this bullet-to-be. "She's gonna blooooow," my brother says next, and pumps the bottle a few more times. I lean my chin against the window. I find a smirk of my own.

"Three . . . two . . . *one!*"

RISD said yes on the first of this month. A "full ride" as he puts it, a scholarship to paint. I stood behind him when he opened the letter in my mother's front hall. I watched him, the back of his head, and waited quietly to hear the news. "We're gone!" I thought I might hear. Get packed, it's time, let's roll— any of those would have worked just fine. But it was his time, which he earned, and he chose to say all of nothing. Since then he's been booked solid with drinking and giggling and performing wobbly cartwheels in the halls of this house. The specifics of leaving have yet to cross his mind.

The cork rockets into the air with a *fump*, landing seconds later on Dr. Nate's Buick in the driveway. Asher laps at the foam that covers his hands and wrists. He takes a long sip and hands it to Nicky who swigs it and gives it to Beth. I watch her tip the bottle high with both hands and place it carefully between her lips.

"Jaaacob?" my mother calls from the stairs.

I leap to my feet and collect the tatters of my report card off the tiled floor. I cram them in my suitcase but some drop and float like ash around the room.

"You up there, Jacob?"

I flushed history and science but then cut my palm on the dull knife I was using, which was awkward on the tile, but I couldn't find a scissor. I had to tear the rest into confetti shreds and some of them stuck to the side of the bowl. "I'm in the bathroom," I yell softly. Now I'm collecting bits of paper and trying to clean the dots of blood off the floor and toilet seat— fucking ridiculous.

Beth screams something after she drinks and I look up from my knees. She's easily the sexiest metal-chick in my high school. An "aluminum-siding diva" from the north side of Roswell Avenue.

"Answer me if you're up there, please?"

"In the bathroom!"

Nicky's been dating her for two weeks now, says he found her in the deep end at the Piedmont pool. Her long peroxide hair hangs to her navel and today she wears a vinyl miniskirt with fish nets and a "Blizzard of Oz" T-shirt. She also has these airbrushed breasts that move when she walks, a Barbie-sized tush and a very approachable, just-took-a-bong-hit smile that tilts her head just so. Whenever I see her in the halls at school she's surrounded by a gaggle of Lita Ford look-alikes with tasseled white-leather jackets and big Aqua Net hair. But when masturbating I give her silky red panties, a see-through bra, and always have her arrive unexpectedly. Occasionally she wears a wig or some type of sharp and curvy shoe but I always smell Marlboros and record vinyl on her skin, and a splash of something boozy on her lips. We laugh when her *Houses of the Holy* necklace bonks me in the chin and I run my fingertips down the smooth of her silky long back. And after an hour or two of intercourse, she begins her ladder climb down, down, down my chest and soon with eyes closed I feel this tickle of warm breath against my wang.

"Jacob?" she says through the door.

I check the floor and toilet for more blood and confetti. There's a piece of Spanish pinned to the shower curtain. "Be right out." She knocks. I open the door just a slit, and hide my hand.

"I've been calling your name for five minutes. Why don't you answer me?"

"I'm in here."

"I see that," she says, trying to look behind me. "Ya got Hebrew school, babe. Chop, chop, Dad's on his way to take you."

Blow jobs have been on my mind a lot these days. I think

about how glorious the concept really is and how fortunate we are that someone's willing to do it. Jonny wins the race to fellatio. I'd been ahead on hand jobs 1 to 0, but who cares about that now. He gets one from this thirty-year-old lady in Mendocino, some wacky, hippy, California friend of his dad's. He says they were drinking margaritas straight from the blender and before he knew it she was shimmying toward him and picking at the knot in his sweatpants. I asked him if he came too quick, but not because I always do or worry that I forever will or struggle with that helpless, can't-stop-it-now rising that occurs when female fingers get so close to my pubic hair, but more just to know the details. He says he was doing fine until she put her pinkie on his butthole and "shoved a little."

"Are you even packed?" my mother says.

I keep the door nearly closed and point at my suitcase on the toilet. "You mean *that?*"

"Don't be flip, Jacob. You know I don't like that. If you're angry with me just say it."

"Flip?"

"Flippant. Don't be flippant."

"Flippant?"

She looks at her watch and sighs. "Will you wait outside for him today, please? I really just . . . don't have the energy."

I nod and gently shut the door. I check the toilet and glance out the window once again. Asher's holding his plastic-wrapped cap and gown. He takes two quick steps and punts it into the hedges.

"Come on, babe," my mother says from the hall. "He should be here already."

I splash water on my face and widen my eyes in the mirror. "What about Gabe and Dara?"

"What?"

"Where are Gabe and Dara?"

"They're at your father's already . . . with Janice." The new boarder. A Haitian nurse from Irvington who can already bless bread and wine in Hebrew and make grenade-sized matzo balls. My father's in heaven.

I grab my suitcase, open the door, and head for the stairs. My mother follows me down.

"We'll be in Atlanta until Sunday," she says, "and then Boca for the night."

"Boca?"

"Just a little R&R. You're back with me as soon as we land. All three of you. I'll come to Dad's from the airport. Now, Asher's gonna stay here and I want you to call him if there are any problems, all right?"

"What's in Atlanta?"

"Same. An adoption consortium. Nathaniel's the keynote."

After serving as a professional witness for a nationally publicized egg-donor case, Dr. Nate is in very high demand. It leaves them traveling a few times a month now. Asher gets to live here with his girlfriend when they're gone, while the three of us get my father, a very recent graduate of some group called est. Last month he allowed a new woman friend, Rona, to shave his beard off while he wept in the woods during an Outward Boundish self-help retreat. "At least he's trying" is the way my mother puts it.

"I'll call you when we get settled," she says. "All right? And here, put this twenty-dollar bill in your room for emergencies."

I open the front door and toss my suitcase on the porch. It rolls a few times and settles upside down.

"All right, Jacob?"

"All right." I take the money from her hand and squeeze it in my palm.

"Can I have a kiss?"

Beth sees me before the others do. She smiles and exhales a stream of smoke through her nose. We've hung out twice before and she's been sort of flirty both times. I've come to think she knows she's the queen of my skanky dreams. My mother kisses the back of my head. "Good luck in temple on Saturday. I know you'll do wonderfully."

I ignore this and await what comes next.

"When I get back I'll . . . talk to your father again. No more of these after this one, okay? Last Torah reading. Promise."

I want to laugh but I don't. Asher sees me and starts to walk over.

"Okay?"

"Right."

"I love you."

"Okay."

"'Okay'? Just 'okay'? You're not gonna say it back?"

"Fine. I . . . do, all right?"

"Then say it."

"I do."

"So say it."

"I *said* it!"

She walks in front of me and lifts my chin with her finger. "Why are you yelling at me?" she whispers.

I turn away and can feel her staring at the back of my head.

"Jacob, please look at me."

"Throw that thing in the air," Asher says to Nicky, and lifts a stone from the driveway. "Try underhand."

Nicky lifts his cap and gown off the front lawn and begins to windmill it around and around.

I hear my mother sigh.

"Out over the street," says Asher. "I don't want to hit the house."

"I'll try."

"What's he doing?" my mother says.

"*Pull!*"

Nicky hurls the bag into the air and Asher fires the stone at it. It misses by a mile and bounces off the Kissler's garage. They both laugh their asses off.

"Jesus," she says. "Asher! No more of that."

"Oh. Hi, Ma."

"No more. You'll break a window."

"That's it, Nick."

"I'm going inside, Jacob. Take care of your brother and sister over there, okay? I'll call you when I can." She kisses the back of my head again.

Pause.

I hear the door shut behind me.

My brother retrieves the robe from where it lands in the street and walks toward me on the porch. "Looky here," he says waving it. "Freedom in a bag."

I nod and sit on the front stoop.

"It's fuckin' over," he says, cradling the plastic bag in his arms.

I lay my open hand on my knee so he'll see the blood on my palm. He doesn't look down.

"Hey, I got somethin' to tell you," he says.

He found an apartment in Providence. That's what it is. There's a bedroom for each of us and the bigger one has a view of the river. He gets it of course. Mine has a tapestry for a door and no closets but the toilet's closer to me and his room can get noisy on weekends. Pack your shit and load it in Nicky's trunk, he says. Write a note to Mom if you want but do it soon. I want to hit the highway by dusk. No, be ready to bolt by dawn. Be ready by noon tomorrow. Say your good-byes and be ready to fire up the engine by . . .

"Little Greeny!" yells Nicky, and I face his way. He looks like a cross between Sid Vicious and Dennis the Menace these days: short, blond, boy-next-door meets aggressive, whiskey-loving nutcase with immeasurable issues and a passion for arena metal. He lives in an old, ignored Victorian with his extremely elderly grandmother and a piranha named Swallow. "New speakers, ya ready?"

Brigitte and Beth put their fingers in their ears. Nick flashes devil-horn fingers with his pointer and pinkie and starts his ignition through the window. The engine roars and the bassy thump of Iron Maiden makes his windshield wipers hop. Asher takes a smiling swig from the bottle of champagne and his eyes meet mine. "Pretty fuckin rockin'," he says, with a squinty, buzzed grin. "A Blaupunkt. Graduation gift from his dad."

I nod and look down at Asher's cap and gown. He sees me admiring it and sends it spinning into the air. "*Fuck yeaaaaaaah!*"

I watch it climb into the sky and dream that when it lands it'll be mine. Like a lonely bridesmaid I scurry underneath but it hooks right and drops like a brick into the rhody bushes.

"You didn't wait for me to get a rock," Nicky says, and pulls one from his pocket.

Asher holds the Korbel out for me. "You want a swig of this shit? Still cold."

"What'd you want to tell me?" I ask.

He takes a long sip and offers me the bottle again. "Have some."

"I can't. I got—" Beth is staring right at me—"Hebrew school," I whisper.

"Oooooh, you poor fuck."

"Why don't ya come along?"

"Um . . . can I have my testicles hacked off instead?"

Asher got officially expelled from Beth Tikvah the day after he heard from RISD. Est training and all, my father still went berserk and flung a full coffee mug at his bedroom door. Luckily, Asher wasn't home for all the fun. They've "talked" once since it happened.

"Here I am wavin' around this thing and you're headed to that shit hole. How ya getting there?"

"Ride."

"Mom?"

"No. Dad's on his way."

"*Here?*" he says, pointing at his bare chest. "*Now?*"

"I thought you knew."

He runs his hand through his long hair and peers down the street for my father's car. "I better get outta here. We gotta go!"

"What's up?" says Brigitte.

"My fuckin' dad's on his way."

Brigitte hops off the car and walks toward me. I look at the hooks on the front of her bra and the baby oil she put on her cleavage. "Your brother's getting cuter than you, Ash. Look at this pretty blond hair," she says, and I feel her fingernails against my scalp.

Nicky lets out an extended belch and says, "Real purty. And he got a *reeeeal* nice mouth too. Squeeeeel, *squeeel* like a hog, Jacob."

Beth and Brigitte both laugh.

Brigitte circles me while fanning herself with her hand. "Ooh-wee. I don't even care that you're leavin' anymore, Asher.

You can just take off and do all that disappearing you've been dreamin' about. Give your little brother and me some breathin' room."

Quintessential Gitte. Obligated to the Nancy Spungen persona she's honed for years, rumors often fly about the pills she's popped and the dicks she's sucked. The current gossip is that she blew her own brother, a coke fiend named Nigel who wears eyeliner and hiked-up kilts to school. Asher says he'd be amazed because Nigel's a flat-out homo who can make himself gag just thinking about pussy. Now Brigitte cups my chin in her hand and gives me a lengthy Eskimo kiss and a peck on the lips. Her hair is Big Bird yellow at the moment and shaved nearly to the skin on one side. And there's a cross pierced high in the cartilage of her ear that's made the skin puffed and shiny with infection.

"Lady killer," she says, with a tiny slap to my butt.

"Here, Nicky," Beth says, and hands him the cassette she fixed. She tugs her miniskirt down on her hips with a snap and stretches her arms high above her head. Belly button, ribs, the body on this girl! When she walks past me she winks and I look away.

"Um . . . hello?" she says.

"Oh . . . hi."

"Stop flirtin' with my girlfriend," says Nicky. I push out a laugh and watch her open his car door.

"He can if he wants."

"Get in the car, Beth. And you, little Greeny. Hose those lonely blue balls down," he says, and pretends to punch me in the stomach.

A car turns onto our street and Asher pulls his shirt on and squints at it. "That him? Let's go Brigitte," he says, clapping. "Right now. Fast."

The car gets closer to the house. It's not my dad but it stops right in front.

"Just clients," I say. Dr. Nate sees patients in the basement of this house. This means I can sit on the staircase and listen to people air out their miseries past ten each night. The couple walk quickly across the lawn, she in front of him. It's the Newmans—money's tight, she's the breadwinner, caught him napping in the afternoon with cereal milk in his navel, and she punched him in the chest. They walk along the side of the house and will enter from the rear.

Asher blinks a lot as he approaches me and wraps his arm around my neck. "We have to talk and it's gotta be quick."

I'm already packed. Just say when. Dusk? Noonish?

"It's not something I was planning on and—"

"Just tell me."

He pulls away from the embrace and glances over his shoulder at the street. "I gotta leave," he says, with his head lowered. "Tomorrow. In the morning. I was keeping it a secret because I wasn't sure if—"

"What did you say?"

"I know. I should have told you. There's this professor named Bovitz who said he'd rent me his attic if I showed up by Monday. There are so few places for the money I have, you wouldn't believe it. I had to talk to the high school and all this crap . . . Anyway, they don't give a shit if I'm at graduation or not. They said they'd mail me the fuckin' diploma." He chuckles and looks back at his friends. "Isn't that . . . cool?"

As I stand there in the driveway looking in his wide eyes, I tell myself it's a gag. It's got to be a joke. I start to smile and turn to face Nicky. "Are you fuckin' kidding me?"

Asher looks stunned but more offended. "Kidding?" he says. "Why would I be kidding?"

As my smile fades Brigitte comes into view behind him.

"But I'm going with you," I say.

He glances over his shoulder at her and faces me again. "No," he says. "No, I'm going alone."

In the blur of that second I turn and step toward the house. The words stick to me and expand as I try to outrun them, to be where I was.

"Jacob," he says, and jogs up behind me. "Talk to me."

I shake my head, not wanting to speak, and pinch back tears that fight to rise.

"Please."

I feel his hand on my shoulder and I yank away. When I get to the porch he snags the back of my shirt and stops me.

"Just relax . . . and listen to me!"

I see Beth on the lawn over his shoulder. She moves carefully as she stares at the wreck we are, and I turn from her view.

"Hear me," he says.

"No."

"I said—"

"You said you'd bring me," I say as soft as I can.

"I . . . don't . . . have . . . a . . . *dime*. Mom gave me a thousand bucks and that's it, that's all I have."

"*I* have cash."

"No."

"Bar mitzvah."

"*My* cash, the *only* cash in question went into supplies and getting my ass to Rhode Island. I *have* to get there like . . . yesterday and get a fuckin' job and a cheap as shit place to sleep. This is what I'm up against."

"You're not listening," I announce, walking closer. "It's in the bank. It's a lot."

"That's yours."

"That's ours."

"No," he says, and glances at the street for my dad. "The man, the . . . fella on his way here? The guy who raised you? Remember him? He'll *ne*-ver stop."

"Yes he will."

"You're lying to yourself."

"He'll give up."

"He'll find you."

"No."

"With *me*. He'll find you with me."

"No."

"And I've earned this."

"Listen."

"*No, J!*"

I flinch from the bark and look up at him. He lowers his eyes to his shoes.

"I *have* to go now," he says. "I really have to go. He starts to walk away and I follow him and reach for his arm.

"Wait . . . Wait."

He glances down at my hand on his wrist. "You've got to let go."

"I'll get a job too."

"You live here."

"You said if you got into school."

"I can't just . . . lift you outta here."

"Why?"

"It's a crime."

"A crime? You're my brother."

"It's kidnapping."

"Let me to talk to Mom," I plead. "Wait two days."

"I told you. I got to get there and be settled and find a place to live. Start painting. I can't bring you. I *can't*. Not now." He leans closer to me and takes my cheeks in his hands. "Root for me," he whispers. "Be happy for me. Ya know?"

He takes a step backward and I'm surprised to see tears in his eyes. "It's only Rhode Island," he says with a shrug.

"Let's go, Ash," Nicky says, and revs his engine. Brigitte pulls a bent mascara brush out of her purse and starts applying it on the move. "*I'll* see you soon, J," she says with weighty sad eyes. "I promise."

"Let's go, Beth!"

Asher holds my shoulders in his hands. "You're my family," he says softly, and leans close to my ear. "My brother."

I turn to see his face.

"I'll call you," he says.

I watch him run to the car and dive through the open passenger window. The thing screeches out of the driveway and I see sparks where it scrapes the curb. When Asher pulls his feet in, he climbs out the passenger window and rests his ass on the sill. He blows me a dramatic kiss that flings his arm above his head and I walk into the street so he can see me. And I can see him. Disappear.

## Erhard's Prayer

Out the back window of my father's long car, I count the suburban sick-amores that line the north side of Stanyon Road. Like on Saber Street, some of them rise through the seam of sidewalk and grass and have all but crumbled the cement meant to keep them aligned. Rona Milkin sits in the passenger seat in front of me and speaks quickly about something—a luncheon gone awry, greens steeped in oil. My father nods with moderate interest and searches for discourse on his digital radio. From the speaker behind my head I listen to the smear of what he cannot find and vow to leave for Providence before it gets too dark.

"Drenched," Rona says. "A pool of it at the bottom of the bowl. So, I'm livid. The thing's soaked. Okay? Soaked. Long story short, I tell him I'm not interested in who handles decision making in the kitchen. I'm *interest*ed in eating my lunch the way I ordered it."

"Good for you," my father mumbles.

"I knew the guy was trouble from the get-go. He was chewing something when he brought our waters."

The Hebrew word for recess is *hafsaka*. It begins about an hour into my first class and will allow me a chance to leave the building unseen. Bagels are left for us during this time and the halls are quiet and unpoliced for the entire fifteen minutes. Twice before I've walked to Jon's house three blocks away and put cream cheese on my bagel. A woman named Ida calls your house if you're late. She's got my father's home and office numbers but he may not be at either. I'm probably going to need to run.

"What are you looking for, Abe? Let me do it. You drive."

"I got it, Rone. I can do both."

The basement door beneath the sanctuary plops you out on Lemur Avenue. In theory I could be in Jon's driveway about five minutes from the time the bell rings. Whether he's there or not I'll take his bike from his garage, ride to Carteret Savings, withdraw as much bar mitzvah cash as they'll let me, and take a taxi to Newark's Penn Station.

"Abe, you're swerving."

"I'm not swerving."

"What are you looking for?"

"NPR."

"You're on AM."

The six fifty Amtrak for Providence leaves from track 6 unless it's raining or snowing—I'm not sure why. Get on the train. Ride for three hours and fifteen minutes and have a room at the Narragansett Inn around elevenish. I block my face with my suitcase and stare at the back of my father's head. He switches the radio off and yawns so wide his eyes squeeze closed.

"How 'bout a little preview for Rona?" he says through it.

"What?"

"The Torah reading. Let's hear it. A little preview for Rona."

He turns onto Glendale Avenue toward the temple and searches for me in the rearview. Rona starts to twist her rings when the silence gets long. "Piedmont in June," she finally says. "Look at all this green."

"Jacob?"

When I look up at the mirror his eyes are there. "Did you hear me?" he says.

"Yes . . ."

"Then let's hear it. 'Vaydabaaaaaaaare Adonai.'"

Rona glances back at me and smiles with warmth. "Don't feel like you have to do it for me," she says.

"*Yes*," my father says. "Feel like you have to. I'm asking you to do it. We have two days to make this thing perfect."

"It's okay, Abram."

"It's not okay. He knows the beginning by heart, we've been doin' it for weeks. Are you sick?" He cranes his neck to see me and reaches for my knee. "Anybody home? *Knock, knock.*"

"Who's there?" says Rona, trying to keep things light.

My father faces her.

"Let's talk about something else," she says.

"You'd think I'd asked him to cut his chest open."

"It's okay, Abe. Don't get upset."

"I'm not upset!"

"I didn't say you were."

"All I want is a little of it," he says.

No. All he wants is his crank monkey to sing his girlfriend a little Torah ditty before he drops it off at Jew school for three hours. All he wants is what he wants and this time it's inside my head. Naso, from Numbers 4:21–7:89: "Va'yidaber Adonai el Moshe lemor naso et rosh b'nei gershon gom hem laveit avotom l'michpachtom . . ."

My father thumps the steering wheel with the heel of his palm. "Do you know it or not? We've got two days."

I know it like I know my own name. "I know it," I say softly. "I'll do it later."

"Great," says Rona. "Later's great."

My father slouches in his seat. "Great. It's all fine with me," he says. "*I'm* not the one who has to get up there and do it."

"I hear you sing beautifully," Rona says. "I was telling your dad I know two other Libras who also read Hebrew very well. Does Jamie Berkowitz still go to your temple?"

Rona's got her back to the passenger door so she can talk and see me at the same time. She's an attractive, middle-aged Jewish lady from Landview who once played Dolly to my father's Horace Vandergelder. She has merlotish brown hair, overly attentive eyes, and enough memorized self-help clichés to sink a battleship. Married three times to "moronic male assholes" she's now painfully open about the "festering matters of her psyche," which were "virtually erased" after a series of epiphanies during her first "est-capade." These matters included her father's rampant adultery and her mother's neglect and addiction and her sister's chronic bulimia and her only son's amphetamine issues and all of this I learn in the first six minutes of knowing her in a booth at Friendly's. At the time she was in full tennis-club regalia—the visor, the head and wrist bands, the pleated pink skirt, and had a rock on her pointer finger the size of a plum. Today she's in a gray suit, having come from yet another in a series of training sessions. By August she says she'll be a certified "body catcher" and "confronter," roles that assist the leader in these Werner Erhard Self-Training Seminars. Rona's Lord God is a man named Randal, who leads the gatherings from a lawn chair on a portable stage. And ever since my father bumped into her at a Purim carnival this spring, he's been quite smitten by Randal's vision and the outcome of his drive-through redemption.

"I'm embarrassed," my father says to her. "He's never done this before."

"It's fine, Abram."

"You can't sing two lines, Jacob?"

"I have a sore throat," I say.

My father's neck pivots toward me as if I shot a gun. "You've *got* to be kidding me."

"Abe. It's okay."

"Rona. Please."

"He said his throat hurts."

"I heard him."

"Hold on," she says. "I think I have a sucker." She reaches into her Louis Vuitton and heads for the bottom.

I see the back of my father's head shiver with frustration but he is somehow able to speak with calm. "How 'bout if I start it and—?"

"My throat hurts," I whisper.

Our eyes meet again in the rearview. I look away from him, out the window, and begin my escape from the top: (1) *hafsaka*, (2) sanctuary door, (3) Jonny's bike, (4) bar mitzvah cash, (5) Penn Station, (6) New Rochelle to Stamford. Stamford to Bridgeport . . .

"Found it," says Rona, lifting a mashed butterscotch above her head. "Here, J, this'll soothe your throat."

I slowly reach for it. "Thank you."

My father faces me as I plop the thing in my mouth. Like a furious two-year-old, he cannot have what he wants. He'd do the stupid Torah portion himself but his Hebrew ranks in the third grade. Of all the academic balls I've fumbled at his feet I'm somehow cursed with the gift he most admires. To stand amid the stained glass of this holy house of God and combine the texture of the Judaic language with a musical performance is his wettest dream. The best he could pull off was president, the only secular role on the *beema* but one that still allows him a pulpit to address the audience. Someone has to announce upcoming calendar events and gift-shop hours and whether anyone left her umbrella under her seat. I used to get a certain pleasure from being able to do what he could not. Read and sing from these ancient scrolls. Even the most hunched and hairy-eared *shoolies* were impressed with my ability to lead them in prayer. But as I became the little blond sidekick to the *nasi*-at-large, I soon saw my kudos rerouted to their source. My manager, my trainer, my liaison to God. After all, it is he who gave me life. He who gave me Judaism. And he who gave me the gig. So it only makes sense, dear congregants, that the achievement would be his.

"Let's start over," he says. "Okay? Hi, Jacob, how are you? You've met Rona. Great. Would it be *possible* for us to hear a little of Saturday's Torah portion? Ya see, it's been three days since I've seen you and I'd like to tell you how it sounds with a day and a half to go. I'd like to know how much more rehearsing you're going to require. These are *not* ridiculous requests. There are over a hundred people coming to this thing."

There *might* be six if he didn't send out invitations. Reading from the Torah or wearing tzitzit or keeping kosher or wrapping tefillin are all known as mitzvahs, or acts of obligation, in Judaism. Refusal to perform what is obligated by God would turn my father inside out. He knows the congregants all heard about Asher. Expelled from the Jew school for what they called *kcheebul amanoot;* or, in English, some pretty wacky vandalism. My father's horrified by this, can hear the gasps of the temple board members in his sleep. But this *nasi,* this temple president, has a second son who can chant from the Torah. A fair and blond-haired son who can sing the language more beautifully than most. So he needs me. He needs his trained yeshiva boy to blast that room and let all those people know how devoted we are to performing mitzvahs. I *am* my father's salvation for Asher's crime; I *am* his very hope to stay on this stage. And as I sit here with this sucker in my mouth, flying toward more Hebrew school, the only thing I can think to do is get my ass on that train. I click the butterscotch against my two front teeth, and then bite it with a crunch.

"Would you *please,*" he says, " just . . . finish that candy."

We ride in silence and it's making Rona tense. She can't seem to get comfortable. She faces me once again and asks how I'm feeling. I tell her the candy is helping and try to think of something else to fill the quiet. "So," I whisper, holding my throat, "you were in training today?" She takes a long and smiley deep breath, and prepares to talk.

"I was. Has your father told you about it?"

I nod. "A little."

"I really don't want to come off preachy . . ." she says.

Jesus Christ. An est pitch. I asked the woman about her day.

". . . but if you ever decided to do this for yourself and the lives of those you love, your days on this earth will be altered forever."

My father broadens his shoulders and consciously breathes out his nose. The topic excites him and it may just cool him off. "Can you hear her?" he says, facing me, a finger on the wheel. "Is it too windy back there?"

I shake my head.

"Go ahead, Rone. You've got all of him. He's listening. Listen *well*, Jacob. With your ears."

Listen with my ears. (1) *Hafsaka*, (2) New Haven to Old Saybrook, (3) Old Saybrook to New London, (4) New London to Mystic.

"Firstly, J, a huge and confusing misconception in our society is the notion of victimhood." Rona's got this memorized. She speaks in the robotic rhythm of an untrained actor. "But I'm here to tell ya that there just ain't no victims out there. Weird, huh? Maybe. But that's what you're gonna learn first. And 'compassion,' that ever-popular word of ours? You can get rid of that too," she says, balling up nothing like a mime and tossing it over her shoulder. "Now, I see the way you're reacting to the things I'm saying. 'No compassion? No victims? You've gotta be missing a few cards from your deck, Rona.' Am I right?"

I slowly nod.

"But compassion, Jacob, is reserved for victims. And there are no *what?*"

My father looks back at me. He looks at the road. He looks back at me.

"Victims?" I say.

"Right," she says and claps. "Because if you take responsibility for your own life than *aaaaaaaall* the horrible things that have happened to you become your *own* responsibility and the reason for this is that . . . you . . . alone . . . *what?*"

My father looks back. He looks at the road. He looks back at me.

"Um . . ."

"Caused them to occuu-*uuur*," she sings with hands high.

"You see?" my father says, shifting in his seat with excitement. "Only when we accept this, only when we realize that *every* being creates their own lives—"

"Their own *realities*, Abram."

"Lives, realities—either one, no?"

"Randal says 'realities.'"

"Okay . . . only when we realize that we create our own *realities* are we in a position to resolve the issues that plague us."

"Right, Abe." Rona hops up on her knees to face me. "Before I found est and the wisdom of Randal, I was in a bad, bad marriage, Jacob. I used to look out at the world and just feel helpless every single day I woke up. And along with my own horrible sense of self, I'd acquired the taste of all the many miseries of our society that we see on the news and read in the paper and I could taste it, taste it right on the end of my tongue. Right here," she says, pointing at it. "And I was vulnerable, partly because I'm a Gemini—sure, goes without saying—but more because I'd been *stripped* of what Randal calls my 'birth-skin.'"

Before Rona came aboard in the spring, my father was dating all the time. He overbooked Saturday nights almost every week and told the three of us to help him manage the overflow. There were dozens of conversations like: "If L calls don't tell her I'm with D. But if H calls tell her I'm with P or R but only if she asks. If P calls, tell her I'll call her tonight but never mention D." I panic on the phone once and tell a woman named Viv that he's in the bathroom when he's really out with Nancy or Bettrice or Donna Bickinstein. She calls back four times. "Just put him on, Jacob." "He's pretty sick, Viv," I say, knocking on his closet door.

". . . and Randal has to laugh at this because what he says

is, 'What is . . . is, and what ain't . . . ain't. And there just ain't
no in between.'"

The first year out he only seems to date stewardesses. My
theory is that he had all these pent up years traveling with a
fantasy, and suddenly it was legal to mount these women with
their coffee-stained smocks pushed up to their necks. I think
there were about five from various airlines and each of them
fell in love in minutes. To them he's like this fleeting assem-
blage of everything they've ever wanted in a man but couldn't
find: affectionate and present and glowingly receptive to whatever came out of their mouths. They saw a cuddly and attractive accountant with the listening skills of Gandhi. He saw a
lunch cart with its hair in a bun and two nights to burn in
Newark. They all get gooey with how they're treated, how
they're touched, and how it all might very well blossom into re-
tirement. Just before Rona there was a People Express em-
ployee named Valerie. I saw her hamburger-brown uniform
thrown over the shower rod one morning. She's in her thirties,
from Tuscon, wears tons of glittery blue makeup on her eyes
and knows every single Abba lyric. She brings her six-year-old
son, Dakota, to our house during a three-day layover, and he,
like all the stewardess offspring, hits it off great with Gabe and
Dara. And not long after, like most of them, Valerie's enamored
and slowly moving all her crap into the house. But just when
her presence starts to seem less weird, she informs my dad that
she's a born-again Christian. He hangs in there for a few more
weeks (he did convince my mother to convert to Judaism) but
then asks her point-blank, during "gratefuls" at Shabbat dinner: "If Hitler were to confess his sins, would he be forgiven
for the atrocities he inflicted on the Jews?" Valerie thinks about
it. She gives an answer. My father listens. After he zips her suitcase, he calls her a taxi and waits with her in the front hall. I

watch him pace a bit in the driveway that night after the cab pulls away. He loosens his neck with a few head rotations and soon comes inside. Within the hour he and Adina Meyer are on their way to Sardi's and balcony seats for Jackie Mason. He never goes goyim again.

". . . a learning curve in which all this useless pain can be lifted in two glorious weekends of self-reflection and 'mind maintenance.' And after I wept in front of Randal and thrashed about on the carpet of the Oak Room at the Parsippany Hilton, I felt this huge burden of guilt lift from my 'I-cage' being, *me,* wrapped in my birth-skin, and my "You-cage" being, all the desperate and seemingly hopeless people who *su-ffer* because I now understood that *they* . . . were responsible . . . in a way . . . for all their own derailments. *They,* Jacob, had created their own realities. Just as I had created mine."

This is a much more elaborate pitch than my father's ever done. He just says he'll give me the money for admission and I'll come out with a whole new respect for our relationship.

"So, to get back to your question, I'm training to be a 'confronter,' which means I'd stand nose to nose with you and say absolutely nothing as Randal paces back and forth, playing the roll of the 'bull-baiter.' This is when he shouts in your face and breaks us down into the children we all are inside."

"At the time I hated it," my father says, craning his neck to face me.

"Your father cried like a baby," she says, stroking his earlobe. "We're all so afraid of the school-yard bully. But he too is inside us, all of us, scratching away at our birth-skins."

"He was stripping me of my dignity," my father says.

"Yes. Or your locked-up I-cage. Your father *became,* in essence, a piece of garbage in Randal's hands. But in a good way."

I see the temple.

"Ya see, Jacob . . ."

(1) Mystic to Westerly, (2) Westerly to Kingston.

". . . Randal feels that the brain is a self-perpetuating machine, programmed to repeat the same mechanistic responses to similar situations facing people in their daily lives. And so, what he's ultimately saying is that true enlightenment is knowing you are a machine. Whether you accept this or not, it is so." Rona reaches out for my hand and I slowly give it to her. "He then tells you to accept the true nature of your own mind. Assume responsibility for creating everything that occurs in your life, and in doing so . . . you will become whatever it is you want to be. In a word, Jacob, you will be perfect. Just the way you are."

My father wipes his eyes on his sleeve as he pulls into the Beth Tikvah parking lot. Rona smiles and drops her head on his shoulder.

"All you have to do is show up," he says. "I'll pay every dime of it."

"I'd love to see you try it, Jacob. I'd love to see you give this to your father and to yourself."

"Oh, he'll be there," says my dad. "I can tell he's interested. He'll be there."

I slide on the interior toward the door and reach for the handle. Before I open it my father says, "Hey," and I stop.

"Practice in there, all right?" he says. "Tell me you will."

I look closely at the skin where his beard once was. I look into his eyes.

"Thank you for the butterscotch," I say to Rona, and step out of the car.

"You're very welcome," she says. "I hope it helped."

When I get out in the parking lot I see my father is also standing. He starts to walk toward me.

"What are you doing?" I ask him.

"I thought I'd walk you to the door," he says, and I flinch as he puts his arm around me. He leads me quickly down the back steps and inside the temple lobby through two sets of glass doors. And the second we get inside, he stops and swivels me to face him.

"What the hell's goin' on?" he says calmly. "Huh?"

"Nothing."

"Do you even know how many people are unable to do what you do? This is your gift, Jacob. Hank Greenberg hit baseballs. Chaim Potok—"

"I'm gonna be late," I say, lifting my watch.

"Don't interrupt me."

"If I'm late they—"

"Do you have any idea—*any*—how proud it makes me to see you up on that *beema*? Do you?"

I keep my eyes from him.

"Ask me how proud it makes me. Ask me how it feels to see all those people reacting to you, reacting to my son's voice."

I say nothing.

"Ask me, Jacob. Ask me how much I *love* you when you're up there."

A woman walks out of the ladies' room and my father steps back from me and smiles. She grins back and heads down the hall. One Mississippi, two Mississippi, three . . .

"Now. For a person who's . . . struggled so much in school, it's key that you realize where you shine and where you don't. *I* know my own limitations. None of us has *all* cylinders humming. None of us can be *all* things great. I learned this truth from Randal."

I look at my watch and then down the hall.

"There are so many, many things to absorb during these hours with this man, but . . . the thing that stayed with me most—the one phrase that kept popping up for me—was something that reminded me of you. Of you. Can I share it with you? Is your *throat* okay?"

A classmate named Jonah walks through the glass doors with a cherry Fruit Roll-Up hanging over his lip. He waves at me with his head and my father waits for him to pass by.

"Randal says, 'Wher*ever* you are today, you're there because you put yourself there.'"

My father looks up and down the hall, and takes a step closer to me. "Again. Wherever you are today—meaning, wherever you find yourself at this moment in your life—*you're* the one that put yourself there."

"Dad."

"Crap grades? Learning disabled? Rebellious? Angry at God? Angry at me? *Sore* throat? I don't care. You can try and rattle me in front of anyone ya want with your ailments and your subtle, cutesy games. But you can*not* blame me for your own life. Understand? So let's try one more time. I want you to *know* and *hear* . . . that wherever you are today . . . you're there because—"

"Dad?"

"What?"

"I'm in *Hebrew* school!"

He blinks a lot and steps back to fold his arms.

"I'm in Hebrew school today."

"So what?" he says. "What's your point?"

I glance out at the parking lot and see Rona looking back at me through the window. "I've never . . . in my whole life . . . *put* myself in this building. You put me here. *You* did."

The head shaking begins slowly and soon becomes a zoney stare. "You can't even grasp this fundamental idea," he says.

"Abram?" says a voice from down the hall. It's my teacher, Rabbi Seth.

"Oh. Hello, Rabbi," my father says. "Shalom."

The bell rings just above my head and my father is startled. He looks up at the gray device and would dent it if he could.

"Two days till Naso," the rabbi says. "We ready?"

"More than ready," my dad says, with a bounce on his toes. "And if he's not, he will be."

"We'll work on it today with the others," he says. "Let's get to class, Jacob. Ya need a yarmulke in here, buddy."

I check my pockets for one and look up at my father. In the game of the Unthinkable, I tell him I won't be on the *beema* on Saturday. I tell him about recess and Penn Station and my hope to meet up with Asher by noon tomorrow. I tell him in all the years that I've been praying to God, I've never truly believed I was heard. And I tell him in the all the years I've been letting him down, I've never truly believed I was dumb.

My father pulls a yarmulke from his coat pocket and spreads it flat on my head. "We'll talk later," he says softly. "Understood?"

I slowly lift my hand into a wave and nod at him. "Good-bye, Dad," I say.

He blinks at me skeptically but I don't look away.

Rabbi Seth walks a few steps down the hall but stops to wait for me. My father leans forward and gives my forehead a gentle kiss. "Every word a jewel," he says. "Go make it shine." He then turns and walks up the stairs toward the parking lot. The rabbi calls my name but I ignore him, to watch my father leave. And in the seconds that his car is gone and I no longer see him, I search my mind and heart, for what I'll now be without.

## Holy High

"All night, seas of flame raged and tongues of fire darted above the Temple Mount. Stars splintered from the baked skies and melted into the earth, spark after spark. Has God kicked his throne aside, and smashed his crown to smithereens?"

"Thank you, Rifkah," says Rabbi Seth. "Translation, please."

"Call halila ratchu yame lehavot vaheshtarbvu l-shonote . . ."

Rifkah Feldman holds a powdered mini doughnut between her thumb and pinkie and taps her foot to the rhythm of her words. Behind her head the Israeli flag hangs in permanent half-mast from a wooden pole in the corner. And all along the walls are dated travel posters for Netanya, Haifa, and Elat; a grainy Wailing Wall. Room *gimel,* or number three, is what they call this tiny basement classroom. It's down here, twelve feet beneath the *beema,* amid the stacks of musty prayer books and chalk-dusted yarmulkes, that I sit for nine hours a week and stew under an endless drip of superbly useless metaphor.

I rip a piece of paper from my notebook and write "Dear" in pencil at the top. Rifkah stops midsentence to glare at me. I broke her concentration.

"Sorry," I offer, and she eventually resumes. As long as I've know her, she's been a big-boned, curly-haired princess with a raisin-colored mole beneath her second lump of chin. She touches it as she speaks in her nasally buzz and reads quickly to impress and remind us of her fluency. Like the droves of lazily entitled Jewesses that go to my high school, Rifkah will make an ideal and horrific first wife for some dentist looking to marry his mom. Within days of the wedding, her lifelong obsession with food will surface and she'll be forced to rationalize it as her "traditional" role in her loveless marriage. When the dentist finally leaves her and her two yeshiva boys, Ethan and Shelly, he'll soon start humping a hygienist with an ass that could crack a walnut.

I look down at the letter on my desk and check my watch. Sixteen minutes until *hafsaka.* Dear Dad. Dearest Dad. My Dear Dad. DEAR DAD.

There are only three of us today and twelve in the entire school when it's full. No one attends Hebrew school after their bar mitzvah but the impenetrably forced and the squarely devout. Rifkah, for example, chooses to be here, like an outpatient in a mental ward who can leave at any time but won't. Jonah Bernbaum, on the other hand, would rather be bleeding. He, like me, attends only because his father pumps him full of a clear and odorless poison called "Jew guilt," which gnaws at and festers in our Eastern European bone marrow.

I've known Jonah since the fourth grade and have always admired his hatred of our circumstance. He's an actual boy genius with translucent skin, a smudgy-sad mustache, and enough visible ear wax to induce nausea. Forever frail and bookish, he now says "fuckin'" a lot around me and speaks in a forced and jive-ish slang that makes him walk with a little hop. I think he likes me because I let him be this nerdy, streetwise Heeb without laughing or reminding him that he's four foot ten and wearing sandals with tan socks. After earning a ridiculously high IQ score in the middle of the fifth grade, he achieved some celebrity when the *Newark Star* put him on the Sunday cover. But when you've seen him devour his own sneeze to avoid the ridicule of his classmates, you know he's about as lonely as a tube sock full of semen.

Rifkah takes a sip of Diet Pepsi and swipes her mouth on her shoulder. She then flips the page she's reading and begins from the top. "The fear of God was upon the distant mountains and terror seized the sullen rocks of the desert."

"Okay, thank you, Rifkah," says Rabbi Seth. "Who's next?"

I look down at my letter again. When I'm done, it will explain everything. That I'm safe. That I'm fine. That there's no need to worry about me. I lean forward in my desk chair and press my pencil to my note.

Dear Father, . . .

"Jonah," says the rabbi. "Please read. "

I look over at Jonah and then up at the clock. Fourteen more minutes until *hafsaka*.

Jonah yawns and glances over at the time. "Um . . . pass," he says.

Rabbi Seth rolls his eyes. "You can't pass. It's not a game show."

Jonah rummages through his backpack and looks for something to read. "What do you want to hear?"

"I don't care. Honestly. The Tanakh, the Scroll of Fire. Ya'akov's reading his Torah portion. Pick anything and read it."

"Fine. How 'bout this?" he moans, lifting a prayer book.

Rabbi Seth points at him. "Dynamite choice. From anywhere."

"Anywhere?"

"Anywhere, Jonah."

A rabbinical student in his twenties, Rabbi Seth Lerner wears Mets hats and faded jeans and calls the Torah his "drug of choice." As long as we show up he lets us snack during class, put our feet up, and even curse if you can justify the context. Before Asher got expelled he'd say Seth was the "hippest Jew-schoolteacher alive," and liked to envision a menorah-shaped bong somewhere hidden in his house. But the rabbi finally stopped ignoring Asher's attendance, or lack thereof. I was in the kitchen of my father's house when my father answered the phone. *"Twice?"* he kept saying. "What do you mean twice? He's been *twice* in seven months?" My brother was at my mother's at the time, still floating from the acceptance letter he'd received the day before. In the morning I see the lock has been broken off Asher's door. There are pencil drawings and paintings all over his carpet, crumpled but not torn. I lift them and spread them flat on his desk, trying not to fumble the chips of dried paint. I leave them all in a pile on his bed. When he arrives at my dad's that day I don't hear him until he's in his room. When I get there he doesn't see me at first. He's just standing by his desk with a portrait in his hand.

"I need to talk to you," I tell him.

He flinches and faces me. "Did he do this?"

"Rabbi Seth called last night."

Asher slowly nods and looks down at the painting.

"He told Dad you . . . haven't been in a while."

Asher stares at it for a few more seconds.

"None of them are ruined," I say, taking a step toward him.

He stops me with his hand and I see the muscle in his jaw move. "Don't."

"Some aren't bad," I say softer.

He then lifts the painting over his head with both hands and tears the thing in two.

I lie when my dad asks if I've seen him. And I lie when he asks where he is. In the morning Asher heads over to the temple, hours before Hebrew school, and decides to end his relationship with Judaism. The second I arrive that afternoon, Jonah is cackling and pointing at the top of the rabbi's desk. "What's so funny?" I ask from the doorway.

"It's a giant dick!" he squeals. "A fuckin' giant black dick."

When I walk in and look down at it, I know exactly who's been by.

"Look at the *balls*," Jonah roars.

An erect and velvety drawn horse cock in pencil with veins the size of thumbs and a mushroom-shaped head. I spit on the drawing and smear it with my sleeve. There are four minutes until the bell rings and I just know there are more. Jonah says he'll help me and we run from room to room. The human penises are done in chalk in rooms *yod* and *dalet* and are a little more cartoony. A flaccid one wearing tefillin has a bubble over it that says, "Please pass the white fish." I grab an eraser and start wiping it off the board while Jonah just stands there, his mouth pinned wide with laughter. The chalkboards in rooms *alef* and *bet* are covered in tits. There's no way I can get them all without a sponge and a bucket, but I try. As I work Jonah steps up to the board and pretends to lick each nipple. I'd never seen the boy genius so untamed.

"Jonah?" says the rabbi.

"I'm looking?" he says, still flipping through his prayer book.

"Forget it. We'll come back to you. Jacob."

I look up.

"From the top, all right? Ya singin' it?"

I shake my head.

"Fine."

I glance up at the clock and then down at my book. The last time. The very last time. "Va'yidaber Adonai, el Moshe lemor naso et rosh . . ."

Asher hid out at my mother's house for a week after the expulsion was announced. It seemed he knew better than to come near my father and was counting on time to lessen the calamity. Stay away, I told him, you might as well wait a year. But he strolled on in one night, as if nothing had gone wrong, using an air of nonchalance I would not have recommended. We were all eating dinner when I heard the front door open.

"Asher?" Dara called, and I prayed it wasn't him. My father glanced at me and tossed his napkin on the table.

". . . b'nei gershon gom hem laveit avotom l'michpachtom."

"Translation, please."

Another look at the clock. "The Lord spoke to Moses. Take a census of the Gershonites also, by their ancestral house and by their clans. Record them and—"

"Ida," Rifkah announces, pointing at the door with a doughnut. The temple secretary, Ida Gabirol, knocks and pokes her face in. As long as I've know her she's worn a flesh-colored Band-Aid on her nose but today it's gone.

"Come in," says Rabbi Seth and hops off his desk.

"Sawry to interrupt Rabboy. Jacob's father cawlled. He needs to go home right away."

I stare at Ida's face and slowly stand. "What happened?" I ask.

"He didn't say. You live nearboy, correct?"

I nod while gathering my things.

"He said ya should wawk home and he'll explain it awl when you get there. I hope everything's okay, Jacob."

"Yes," says Rabbi Seth. He walks over to me and rests his hand on my shoulder. "I'll call the house later, to check on you."

I throw my book bag over my shoulder and walk toward Ida in the hall.

"Ya'akov?" says the rabbi, and I turn to face him. He lifts the letter I'd begun off my desk and holds it out for me. I walk back in the room and he meets me halfway.

"Good luck," he says.

I slowly nod and take the letter from his hand.

THROUGH THE SANCTUARY and out the doors to the parking lot, I move as fast as I can down the driveway to Glendale Avenue. I picture my father on his knees with the phone at his ear and there's fire and smoke and I don't know if he can breathe. I listen for sirens but the drone of lawn mowers is all I hear, the sun still so bright. At the corner I turn on Saber and start running uphill past the climbing rows of mailboxes and square-shaped lawns. My mind says the worst, like someone's dead, someone I love. I could see it in Ida's face, a fire or a crash, some vicious news she knew. "Yaw muthu is dead, Ya'akov. Huh plane went down." She must have pointed at the smoke—she saw it first—white but barely visible. She turned to Nate as the plane's floor began to buckle and saw floating sparks like fireflies, but thousands, raining from the vents. They gripped each other's hands and nuzzled their heads before an explosion rocked the fuselage and the windows blew out. The fiery wreckage is on some farm in Upstate New York. I keep running up this hill past the Daffners and the Goulds and see Westlock up ahead. "It's your brutha who's dead, Ya'akov. His car flipped ova." It happened on the S curves of Piedmont Avenue. He's at the morgue right now under a sheet in a long silver drawer and they need me to identify him and say it's him, it's him, while covering my mouth and bending over his corpse. I lift his head with my hands and pull his cold cheeks up to mine—*no, no, no, no, no, no, no,* you promised, you promised we'd *go,* we'd *leave* here! A car drives by me and honks for some reason and I'm sure it's my dad until I look and it's not. There's a cramp in my side, deep beneath my rib and I pinch it.

"*Wrong!*" I can hear my father scream. "It can*not* be erased! It's a crime! A crime against *God.* You vandalized a synagogue, you *pig! Why?*" He shoves him backward into the kitchen table and Asher's hip smacks the edge. Every glass tips and spills, and Dara and Gabe both dart from the room. Asher says, "Calm the fuck down," and keeps his hands high and in front of him as my father comes again.

"Get the hell out," he says, into Asher's face. "I want you out of my house."

"Some chalk on a chalkboard, Dad. Chalk!"

"Ask me!"

Asher's shoulders rise and drop. "Ask you what?"

My father leans his face into Asher's. "Ask me if I love you right now," he says with great calm. "Try it. Do . . . you . . . love . . . me?"

I can see my house. It's lit in a summery, late-day orange and it's not on fire. When I get to the corner at Westlock I slow to a walk and hear another car racing up behind me on Saber Street. I turn and see it fishtailing and for a second I think it's Nicky and then it is, it *is* his car. He drives the right side of the

Camaro up on the curb behind me and I jump to get out of the way. Asher is alive. I see him in the passenger seat and it's not a dream. "Need a lift?"

I run to the window and lower my forehead on his arm. "Oh my God," I say, out of breath. "Listen. Dad called. Told me to come home. Something's happened."

"Get in," he says, and opens the door.

Beth and Brigitte are in the back so I climb on Asher's lap. My knees are mashed up against the glove box and my chin and cheek touch the fuzzy gray ceiling. Asher says, "Cozy," and slams the long door. Nicky floors the thing and my head jolts backward.

"What's your guess?" Asher says over the blaring music.

"What?"

"The reason he called."

"I don't know," I say, and rest my head against his. I close my eyes. "Asher."

No flames, no smoke, no charred sibling limbs. I'm surprised to see my father's car is gone. Nick slows down and even signals but then slams on the accelerator and the car takes off in a shot. I turn to see the house go past us through the back windshield. "Nicky!"

Asher grabs the yarmulke off my head and crams it in my lap. "Surprise fucker! "It was us."

I stare down at him. "What?"

"Let me get one of those brews for the boy, Bridg."

Brigitte and Beth start laughing in the back and Nicky goes into a fishtail once again. I spread my arms to the dash as the rear of the thing kicks back and forth with smoking tires. "Stop!"

The car rattles sideways to a frightening halt and stalls. "Relax, you puss," Nick says. He starts it up again, pumps his foot, and again we're flying toward nowhere on screaming tires. Brigitte reaches into a Styrofoam cooler behind the driver's seat and hands Asher a can of Stroh's. He cracks it open and holds it up to my lips. "*Exooooodddussssss!*" he screams, and tips it in my mouth.

"Wait!" I try to swallow it but it pours down my chin. "Asher—"

"And the Hebrew slave boy slurped beer from Pharoah's urn, which symbolizes—"

"Just wait."

". . . the tears and mortar and locusts and—"

"Drink up now," says Nicky. "You's *way* behind, little man."

I take the can from Asher's hand before he tips it again. "Does this mean I'm coming?" I yell. "Does this mean . . . ?" Asher catapults me into the backseat and I land shoulder first between Beth's knees.

"We got porno!" yells Brigitte, and gives my ass a smack.

"And it was *God*," Asher screams laughing, "who *freed* baby Moses with his mighty hand. Drink the precious hops of my fields he commanded and they did, yes they did. And it was *goooooooood!*"

When I finally get upright between the girls I have beer on my hair and jeans. The car is just soaring down these thin suburban streets and I cringe on every screeching turn.

"So I'm going?" I yell, but no one seems to hear.

"*Let my people goooooo*," Asher sings over the music. "*Gooo doooown Moseeees, waaaaaay down to Egypt laaaaand, tell old Pharaoh, let my Jacob gooooo.*"

When I turn to Beth she's wearing my yarmulke and admiring herself in the rearview. "'Barook . . . tata, do-anye.' Good, right?"

"Is he bringing me?" I ask her.

"'Elohaino melik kolom.' And I'm Catholic," she says, pointing at a purple cross on her ankle.

Asher swivels around to face me and lowers the radio. "Exiled into a land of debauchery and lust"—he's so hammered— "the Hebrew slave boy had only God to defeat now."

"Asher?"

"The Hebrew slave boy speaks."

I push off the girls and slide forward on my seat. My face is nearly touching his. "So . . . yes? I can go?"

He looks me in the eyes for a second and lets his head flop forward.

"I told ya he'd think that," Brigitte says.

"It's a party, J. You're coming to my farewell party."

I stare at the top of his head until he looks up. "*What?*"

"It's my last fuckin' night! I *had* to get you."

"You *had* to call that office and . . . pretend to be *him?*"

"Relax."

"So I could come to a fuckin' party?"

"It's . . . funny."

"For *you*," I say, and punch the seat in front of me.

"Hey," says Nicky. "Easy."

"Just relax," Asher says.

"Relax? Rabbi Seth's calling him right now, you dick."

"Good! Dad's not home."

"But he will be."

He takes a swig off his beer and swallows quickly. "I'll tell him it was me."

"No you won't."

"I will."

"You're a liar!"

"I'll get you back to the house by seven," Asher screams over the music. "He'll never know. Now shut the fuck up and drink."

He turns the radio up even higher and we all sit in the thump of Judas Priest. Nicky drives about ninety down Irving and squeals right onto East Robson. I press up against Brigitte, pinned to her shoulder, and she laughs and nibbles on my earlobe.

"Look at you!" Asher screams with a smile. "A second ago you were sittin' in that shit hole and now you're pimpin' between two hot chicks. What's not to love?"

I lean forward so he can hear me over the music and engine. "Can we talk?"

"Definitely! We'll party at Mom's, all right?"

"Is she still there?"

"No, long gone. Jew school lets out at seven o'clock, right?" I nod. "But what if Rabbi—?"

"What if he *what?*"

"Calls Dad!"

Asher takes a sip of his beer and seemingly turns around to think. My ribs are throbbing to the bass of the music. It's a crunching amplified beam of rock like a *jugjugjugjugjugjugjugjug* that swallows all other sound. The singer screams and Nicky starts to bang the steering wheel to the beat. "Livin' after midnight, rockin' till the dawn, lovin' till the mornin' and I'm gone—I'm gone."

"Asher!?" I yell, not sure if he hears me.

"Rollin'!" *Jugjugjugjugjug.* "Rollin'!" *Jugjugjugjujug.*

"Your brother won't let anything happen to you," Brigitte says. She then reaches into her purse for a pot pipe and matches. "He got all bummed when we left you today."

I look at her as she puts the thing between her lips.

"He loves you a lot, J." She winks and tries to ignite a soggy match. "Says he thinks your dad's gonna fuck you up." Beth pulls a lighter out of her purse and lays over me to light the pipe. I feel her breasts on my knees.

"Ont some?" says Brigitte with her lungs filled.

"I better not."

"It'll really help loosen ya up," she says, exhaling, and starts to cough in these tiny nostril spurts of smoke.

I take it from her and hand it to Beth. "I love your blond hair," she tells me, and puts the pipe to her lips.

Asher lowers the music, spins around, and has this to tell me: "If he calls him we're screwed."

I nod with wide eyes. "*That's . . . that's* the plan?"

"But he won't." Beth hands him the pipe and he takes it from her. "Try to have some fun, man. I'll get you back in time and you'll wish you smoked some pot and drank some booze and—anybody here want to suck J off?"

Beth raises her hand so only I can see. My penis starts to fill.

"I will," says Brigitte. She climbs on top of me and thrusts her pelvis. Everyone laughs.

Asher lights the pipe still laughing. "You are one wacky fuckin' chick," he says with lungs filled. He exhales. "I'm really gonna—"

"Miss me?" she says, climbing off me.

Asher looks all sheepish and wasted.

"Is that what you were gonna say?"

He sits back in his seat and taps the ash out the window.

"Asher!" she screams.

"What?" he says, annoyed.

"Is that what you were gonna say? I'm gonna miss you, Brigitte. I'm an asshole because I'm leaving you behind and I'm gonna miss sticking my *cock* inside you!"

Nicky's laugh sounds like a car engine trying to turn over in the dead of winter.

Brigitte throws her shoulders back into the seat and mumbles "asshole" a few more times.

"We've been drinking since noon," says Beth, still eyeing my hair. "Ya didn't dye this, did you?"

"Little Greeny ain't smokin' da ganj?" says Nicky.

I sit forward, away from Beth, as Nicky watches her touch my head.

"Can I talk to you, Asher?" I say.

Beth holds the pipe to my lips.

"Stuff's like lawn grass," she says. "Real harmless."

"Lawn grass?"

"Just a little," Beth says like a nurse. She lights it.

I take a small toke and hold my shoulders back like the burn-outs do. Brigitte starts to applaud and Asher smiles proudly and nods.

"We need more beer," Asher says. "Anything else?"

Nicky's currently steering the car with his knees. "Where's *your* girlfriend, little Greeny?" he says.

Beth puts an open palm on the center of my back and starts rubbing in circles.

"I don't have one."

"'Cause you're a homo, right?"

"No."

"You sure?"

"Yeah."

"Should we get him a whore, A. G.? How 'bout a transvestite off Broad Street?"

"How about Jonny?" says Asher.

"Oh, that's cold," says Nick.

"*No*," he says chuckling. "I mean where the hell is he? How often ya get kidnapped from Jew school? He should be here, join the liberation."

"He's probably home," I say.

"Does he like beer?"

I nod.

"Back toward Glendale," Asher says to Nick.

I lean forward and sort of smile. "You're gonna go get him?"

Nicky yanks the car into a massively hard U-turn that makes us all pile on each other once again. With my face against the window I suddenly think of crashing in this heap of bodies and weed and envision sirens and some red-haired cop lifting my yarmulke with a long pair of tongs. The car pulls out of the U and straightens out and we all fall back into place. "He's a terrible driver," I say, but only Beth hears. She looks at me with her smiley stoned eyes and quickly slips her tongue between my lips. As she pulls away I stare at her in disbelief. "*Please,*" I whisper, mostly with my eyes. "Nicky."

"Please what?" she says into my ear. "Please do it again?"

"O-*kay,*" I say, leaning forward, nearly hopping into the front seat. "What's this baby got, Nick, a six cylinder?"

"Try eight."

Beth touches my butt and I turn to scold her.

"Barook, tatta . . . aboniiiiie," she sings, and the Camaro soars toward Glendale Avenue.

## Rabbi Nudity

There aren't any telephone outlets in the bathrooms of my father's house. There aren't any in the living room or the basement or what he calls the "library" either. So if he's sitting or standing in one of these places he would hear it ring probably or definitely but he may just very well ignore it. I've seen him do this, not often, but I've seen it—times when he's groggy or reading or the Mets have runners in scoring position. Besides, it's a weekday, a Thursday, late afternoon, so he's either at his office or with Rona or somewhere in his car—a car that wasn't in the driveway when we were there, so there currently seems a greater chance of *not* reaching him than reaching him when one figures the time of day and the various rooms he may or may not be in when the phone finally rings. At home.

But the rabbi does it. He reaches my father at 5:06 P.M. and proceeds to ask if "Everything's kosher?" At the time Jon had just answered his front door with Elios pizza sauce on his lips and I'd told him I was stoned and kidnapped and that Brigitte didn't seem to be wearing a bra. And I don't think it's a matter of mistrust that leads the rabbi to call, but more respect for the president, the *nasi*, and what might have gone wrong in the *nasi*'s home. I can see my father's face, the phone at his ear, slow, paced-out blinks of astonishment that soon quicken as suspicion triggers in his mind. "Yes, yes, I'm here," he says into the phone. "What time did he leave?"

The first call to my mother's house comes at five thirty-three. We've all just arrived and made our way through Asher's unpacked clothes and toiletry crap, which is strewn all over the front hall carpet. As it rings, Asher whistles with his fingers and lifts his hands in the air like a bank teller in a western. "*Nobody* answers the fuckin' phone. Please repeat."

"Nobody answers the fuckin' phone," says the crew in broken unison. None of us moves until all nine rings are done. The silence brings an air of excitement, as if we've all just survived a shelling. Jon, Beth, Nick, and Brigitte move on into the kitchen with the beers. Asher says, "Soon be back," and runs up the staircase. I follow him.

When I reach the top he's staring at the ceiling in the hallway with his hands on his hips.

"What are you doing?" I ask him.

"You been in this attic yet?"

I look up at it and shake my head. "No. Can I talk to you?"

"Go ahead," he says, looking for something to stand on. "I'm listening." It's then he jumps and swipes at the ceiling with his hand.

I lean on the banister and watch him leap twice more. "Before you called the temple tonight . . . I was writing this letter."

"Can you boost me up there, ya think?"

I weave my fingers together and walk toward him. He braces himself on my shoulder and steps into my hands.

"The letter was to Dad," I say.

"Lift."

"You're too heavy."

"Forget it," he says, leaping down. "I need a chair or something." He walks into Gabe's room and looks around.

"The letter said I was going to catch a train."

He walks back in the hall with his arms folded. "Grab me that chair in Mom's room, will ya?"

He faces me when he doesn't hear me move.

"Please?" he says.

I drag the chair from her vanity table into the hall. He steps up and pulls open a hatch that leads to a ladder. In seconds his head and torso are rummaging through my mother's tiny storage space in the ceiling. I stand underneath him at the base of the ladder and talk straight to his ass.

"It leaves from Newark at six fourteen. And during *hafsaka* I was gonna leave. Just walk out of there. I was gonna be on it."

"Holy shit, it's a fuckin' mess up here."

"Asher?"

"I can't see crap."

"Asher?"

"Can you get me a flashlight or, oooh, never mind, there's a chain." He pulls it and the room lights up around his head.

"Much better. I'm looking for a box with my name on it. It had all these bones and shit like that in it. Ya seen it?"

"Bones?"

"Not human bones."

"I haven't seen it."

"I'm making a mobile for my first project and—oh yuck. Stretch Armstrong leaked all over the place."

"J?" Jonny says from the stairs.

I look over the banister. "Yeah?"

"Bottle opener?"

"I'll be down in a second."

The phone starts to ring.

"No one answers the fuckin' phone," says Asher from his hole. "Tell them."

"Don't answer the phone!" I yell.

"I hope to Christ that's not him," Asher says, tearing open a box.

I look into my mother's bedroom. I can see the phone on her bedside table. "It's him," I say.

"Shhhhh. It's still ringing." Asher freezes and I hear him sigh. "Could be anyone," he says.

Nine rings again, and it finally stops. "No, it can't."

Another rip into a taped box. "Remember that ram's femur I had?"

I look at my watch.

"Or that hoof I used to prop my door open with?"

"A what?"

"I have to find that fuckin' box. And where's all my Mongoloid drawings and my pump rifle and—? Oh nice."

"What?"

"Good box."

It's then he starts throwing things down. A male mannequin

wig with dried glue on the sideburns comes first. It bounces once and lands like roadkill against the carpet. A Barbie with painted nipples comes next, followed by a pair of flip-flops, a small animal's femur, and a tefillin I got for my bar mitzvah. This is going to be quite a mobile. "Gold mine" he says, and down comes his pump rifle and a small box of ammo. When he finds a loaded Polaroid and two clips of film, he jumps down off the ladder with a thump that rattles the walls. He swipes the cobwebs off his hair and points the thing right at me.

*Clickadee-vvvvv.* "Fuckin' works," he says. "Give me the finger or somethin'."

I choose not to.

*Clickadee-vvvvv.* I squeeze the flash from my eyes. "Did you hear anything I said?"

"Yeah, yeah, just come down to the kitchen for a minute." And he's off and running. "How drunk are you girls!?" he yells from the stairs. "I need nudie shots for the road!"

When we get there he aims the Polaroid at the open fridge. *Clickadee-vvvvv.* Pyramid of Milwaukee's Best. *Clickadee-vvvvv.* Nicky poking carrot into Jon's ass while Jon reaches for beer. *Clickadee-vvvvv.* Beth spanking Brigitte while Brigitte sticks tongue out at camera. *Clickadee-vvvvv.* Nicky and Jon "shotgunning" beers. *Clickadee-vvvvv.* Beth with hands on knees looking over shoulder with pursed lips. *Clickadee-vvvvv.* Brigitte winking with carrot deep in mouth. *Clickadee-vvvvv.* More of the carrot, flickering tongue at tip. *Clickadee-vvvvv.* Nicky pretending to urinate in sink. *Clickadee-vvvvv.* Beth smiling with middle finger raised as she heads down the hall to the bathroom. *Clickadee-vvvvv.* Brigitte mooning camera with cutoffs and panties at knees.

"Yow," says Asher. "Now *that's* ma-girl."

I can see the black patch of her pubic hair between her legs and a tiny blue bruise high on her thigh. Bottomless female in kitchen. *Clickadee-vvvvv.* I look away when my eyes meet hers but I'll need to look again. She wiggles her hips with her arms over her head and says something like, "Wahooooo!" Jonny stares at her vagina while raising his beer for a toast. "Nine minutes ago I was watching cartoons," he says, and sips. Brigitte slowly lifts her pants as Asher circles her and clicks off four more shots. "Oh, you're a *goddess,*" he says. *Clickadee-vvvvv.* "What a naughty little girlie . . . my girlie." *Clickadee-vvvvv.*

Beth walks back from the bathroom and sees Brigitte getting dressed. "You did it already?"

"Flashed her kitty," says Nicky.

"You did?"

Asher blows on the pictures. "They're developing."

"You were 'sposed to wait for *meee,*" she whines.

Brigitte zips her fly. "Asher dared me."

"I'm drunk *too-oo,*" she says in a baby voice, and starts to lift her T-shirt. I hear Jonny mumble, "Sweet," as Asher's camera cranes smoothly toward her chest. With a boozy smile and her eyes squeezed closed she unhooks her bra and out they come—four feet from my mother's Holly Hobby cookie jar. *Clickadee-vvvvv.* She shimmies briefly—*clickadee-vvvvv*— and reclasps her bra in the front. Jon and I share an "isn't life great" glance as Nicky bumps my shoulder and moves right in.

"Show's over," he says. "Get dressed. Now."

"Don't tell me what to do," she slurs.

"I tell ya whatever I want to tell ya." He attempts to pull her shirt over her head, and she ducks him and scoots away.

Nicky comes at her again. He flicks her earlobe and presses his index finger against her forehead.

"Ow, you *fucker!*" she says, and runs out of the room without her shirt. He goes after her.

Jon's got his beer in the air again. "To unexpected titties," he whispers, and shrugs his shoulders.

"Amen," says Asher, and points the camera at us both.

"Asher?" I say.

"Say snatch," he says.

"Snaaatch," says Jon with his arm around me. *Clickadee-vvvvvv.*

"Asher?"

"Where's Brigitte?" he says and runs out of the room. "Bridg!"

"Up here," she says, and I watch him dart up the stairs.

Drinking games begin in what we call the den—a small room with corduroy couches just off the front hall. "Shoot to Thrill" just cranks from Dr. Nate's Kenwood and I pray his dusty speakers won't explode. I have no idea where Asher and Brigitte are but Nicky flutters his tongue when I ask. I take this to mean they're fucking or sucking or tonguing each other behind Gabe's cardboard puppet theater. I walk to the front hall and look up the staircase. I can see nothing but a framed picture of Dr. Nate's mother on the wall. She wears cat glasses and a beehive hairdo and holds a gardening hoe in one hand. Beth walks up behind me and bumps her hip into mine.

"Could be a while, ya know. Those two go for hours."

I glance up the stairs at the dark hallway. "Hours?"

She nibbles on her thumbnail. "Maybe longer."

I picture Brigitte tied up in electric tape with a racquet ball in her mouth. A quarter clinks off the table in the den and Jon says, "Yes! Drink . . . please . . . Nick."

When I turn to Beth she's looking at my butt. "You have *really* broad shoulders. I like that," she whispers, and points with her thumb toward Nicky. "Built like a little girl."

I shake my head. "No, he's, he's . . ."

She takes a step closer to me and I can feel her breath on my chin.

". . . he's your boyfriend."

"Have you seen me in school?" she says, and my eyes go straight to her mouth.

"Yes."

The front on her miniskirt is touching my belt. The quarter clinks again.

"Drink!" says Nick. "Drink it all."

Beth leans forward and kisses my bottom lip only. It sticks a little as she pulls away and my penis turns to stone. I see an eyelash on her cheek before she presses her open mouth against mine. I taste girl and beer off the slick of her tongue. I close my eyes.

*Thump* is the sound from upstairs, as if two bodies fell off the bed. Beth starts to laugh and bend at the knees.

"What the fuck was that?" says Nicky.

Beth's mouth is wide with giddy disbelief. She shuffles back into the den, clapping her hands. "Some kinky-ass sex is what that is."

I sit on the bottom step with my erection and glance up at Dr. Nate's mom. I think I hear Brigitte giggling.

"Jacob?" says Jon. "You playing?"

The phone rings and I quickly look down at my watch. When I run in the den Beth is reaching to pick it up and I have to yelp to stop her. "No, *don't!* Please."

Her hand yanks away as if she touched a stove.

"Just . . . let it ring."

"I almost forgot," she says.

"No one answers the fuckin' phone!" Asher yells from the second floor. We all sit there in silence as it rings six times. When it ends Jon clinks the quarter in the glass and picks Nick to drink. I walk to the window and look out at the street. A neighbor, Mr. Vargus, stands on his front lawn with a garden hose and waters the stones that surround his driveway.

"You in or out, Jacob?" says Nick.

I walk over to the couch. "I have to leave now. Right now. Someone get Asher for me."

"No way," says Nicky. "Who *knows* what's goin' on up there."

"*Asher!*" I yell, moving toward the stairs. "Asher?"

"Laaaaaaadies and gentlemen!" says an unseen Brigitte from atop the stairs. "Put your hands together for the one, the only . . . Rabbi *Nudity!*"

Thundering down the stairs comes my brother. And he's got nothing on. I mean naked, nude, stripped, wearing zero on his body but the tefillin he found in the ceiling, strapped to his forehead and arm. Lunatic. His girlfriend is cackling bent-kneed behind him as she tosses Asher's *talit* on his shoulders like a prize fighter. Asher plus alcohol often equals nudity plus religious contempt, which equals uninhibited displays of sexual repression which often equals a funny dance of some kind. Somehow I'm never prepared. Brigitte's wearing his underwear and one of Dr. Nate's velour bathrobes. She points the Polaroid at Asher as he hops up on the coffee table with his fists on his hips. Everyone's laughing, including him. His penis looks wet. Lunatic.

"Shalom!" he slurs. "I am Rabbi Nudity." He whirls the *talit* around like a matador and Brigitte whistles from her teeth. "The *only* naked rabbi in all of Bethlehem."

*Clickadee-vvvvvv.*

Jonny rolls off the couch onto the carpet, laughing and pointing.

"Able to leap small Jews in a single bound." He jumps off the table and bends over a cowering Jon. "Faster than a hasty circumcision."

"Hail, Rabbi Nudity!" says Brigitte from her knees.

Asher folds his arms and kicks a few times like a Rockette. He then runs out of the room and in seconds returns with his jeans on.

Everyone claps but me.

"It's almost seven, Asher," I say.

He reaches for my wrist and looks at my watch. "If we leave in ten you'll be fine. Doesn't he have rehearsal or something?"

"I don't know."

"He's probably not even home yet," he says.

"But he might be."

"But he *might* not."

"But you're not . . . you're not even listening to me," I say, trying to speak only to him. "Can I talk to you? Can I talk to you alone, Asher?"

"Fine, let's talk."

"Now. It has to be now."

"Go ahead."

"*Alone!*" I yell, and everyone looks at me. "Alone."

"What's your problem?" he says with a crinkled brow.

I walk over to the stereo and turn the music down. "I told you all this before and I know you heard me. I . . . wrote dad a letter. Okay? I wrote him a letter."

Asher looks at the others and starts shaking his head.

"It says I'm leaving."

"Leaving for where?" Jon says.

"He's not leaving, Jon."

"*Yes*, I am. I am, Asher. I am."

I stare at him for a second and then look down at my watch. "That's why I need to leave. My train leaves in twenty minutes."

"Are you fuckin' kidding me?"

"No."

"What train?" says Jon, and I face him.

Asher plucks at the teffilin on his arm. "Yeah. Good question, Jon. What fuckin' train?"

I slowly walk toward him and look him straight in the eyes. "I need a ride to Penn Station. Take me there now, please."

"You have lost your mind, friend. I mean, really, what the hell are you talking about?"

"You know exactly what I'm talking about. I know you heard me. You're just afraid. Say it. You're afraid."

Nicky makes a siren noise and faces Asher with a tilted head. "I think little Greeny just called you a puss, Ash."

Brigitte lifts the Polaroid and decides now's a good time for posterity. *Clickadee-vvvvvv.*

Asher swigs one of the beers on the table and asks Beth for a cigarette. He lights it and walks over to the fireplace, squinting as he goes. "Afraid? Afraid of what?"

When I look at the others they're all staring back at me.

"Of what he'll do to you. If you keep your promise."

He turns and walks quickly toward me, clenching the jaw my father gave him. I try not to flinch. "I never promised you *shit!*"

"Boys, boys," says Nicky standing. "This is a party."

"No it's not," I say to Nick. "It's a shtick. A gag. To make you all see how *insaaaaaane* Asher is."

Asher shakes his rage off and tries to smile through his flushed cheeks. "Listen to this guy."

"You just used me to fuck with Dad."

"*What?*"

"You did."

"You're wrong."

"You did."

"You're high!"

"Only one of us is gonna pay for this."

"I don't need *you* to fuck with Dad."

"Then why am I here?"

"I told ya six fuckin' times I'd get you back in time."

"You called the front office! You said there was a problem at home. He's the president, they look out for him over there. You *know* this."

He looks at the others with a shrug of his shoulders. "I thought you'd want to be here."

"Because you're *selfish*, like *him!*" The tears rise so I turn and begin to walk out.

"Is that right?" Asher says, following me. "I'm selfish. Is that what you said? I don't fuckin' need this."

"I don't fuckin' need you!" I say, spinning to face him. "Surprise! Before you leave me. I'm leaving *you*." I walk out of the room and straight for the front door.

"J," says Jonny. "Where you . . . uh . . . ?"

Asher comes running after me and grabs my elbow. "He's not goin' anywhere, Jon."

"Get the fuck off me."

"Just relax."

*Clickadee-vvvvvv.*

"Wouldja fuckin' *stop!*" Asher barks at Brigitte. ". . . with the goddamn camera." She looks as if he punched her. "It just went off," she says.

"I don't give a rat's ass, just stop!"

"Prick," she says, and throws the camera on the couch. Asher moves toward me and pulls me by the arm through the front hall.

"Ow."

"You wanna talk? *Talk*."

"You're pinching my—" I yank my arm away from him and walk on my own.

He follows me into the kitchen and pulls a chair out from the table. "Sit. Talk. Go."

I stand by the chair and say nothing.

"I'm listening," he says, and opens the fridge. He grabs a beer and cracks it open. He takes a sip. "Go. Say what you want to say."

I glance over at the clock on the stove. Asher starts to uncoil the tefillin from his arm. "That's it?" he says. "We done?" He sits heavily and his chair squeaks on the floor. "Talk to me."

For the moment the house is so quiet, just the hum of the fridge in my left ear. Asher drinks again and places the teffilin on the table. The seven twenty-five leaves in ten minutes. I lean my chest over the place mat beneath me and talk as quietly as I can. "Asher?"

He looks up at me for a second before lowering his eyes to his hands.

"You need me," I say, "so much less than I need you."

"That's not true."

"Yes it is."

"Maybe to you."

"You don't want to need me."

He sniffs and picks at the flap on his can. "What the hell does that mean?"

"It doesn't matter. I have money and you need money and all I want is to live—"

"Wait, wait, wait. I don't want your money."

"You do so."

"I *don't* want your money!" he screams. "I want to be gone. I *get* to be gone. I've waited my whole life to be outta here."

I shove my chair back from the table. "Why'd you pull me out of temple tonight?"

"Because I'm *leaving,* Jacob. Because it's a party and I wanted you here so you could drink with me and leave all that . . . bullshit behind for one goddamn second."

"You came and got me to fuck with him."

"No!"

"Say it."

"I wouldn't do that."

"It's payback, Asher. Admit it. For every word he's ever screamed in your fuckin' face."

"You're wrong!"

"Then why? Why am I in this house right now?"

"Because."

"Because *why?*"

He stands and slams his hand on the kitchen table. "Because I *love* you! All right! Ya happy now?" He flops back into his chair and dips his face into his hands.

I stay still, holding my breath, as these tears I've never seen begin to run down his cheeks. And it's a gift. It is. So precious and unwrapped. These words he gives me. I listen to them again in the echo of my mind as he swipes at his face with his bare shoulder. Like jewels. That's what my father would say. Words can be like jewels. A quarter clinks in the den and I slowly walk behind my brother in his chair. Me too, I say to myself. "I love you too."

He reaches his hands up and grips each of my wrists. "I can't bring you with me," he says.

I shut my eyes in the wake of these words, and feel the light squeeze of his fingers near my palms. "I get to go alone."

I look down at the floor, trying not to cry, trying to see who I am without this parachute I've stitched. And it's vicious I'm afraid, this lonesome I taste. I think to beg, I do, and step closer to air my plea. A risk-free plan in three easy steps, a feasible escape to this campus in my mind. But I stop myself and watch instead my brother's face, his eyes, the slow shaking of his head. "Stop," he says softly. "No more." I stare at him as he swipes again at his eyes. "I get to go alone."

*Alone.* "Va'yidaber Adonai el Moshe lemor." It's how the Torah portion begins on Saturday morning. And I already know there's no part of me that will sing these words for me, or any God above. And when the Torah is closed that day, and the final prayer is said, my father will approach me with reward in his eyes and tell me he's never heard it done better. But what I will have done is nothing more than feed some emptiness in his pride. For I am an appendage. One paid in hollow bursts of love.

Asher sighs and runs his hand through his hair. "You all right?" he asks me.

I begin to nod but the tone of his kindness trips me up. I turn from him, and let myself cry as quietly as I can. When I hear him approach I move away, avoiding his touch. He follows me and I soon feel his hand on my arm.

"Don't," I say, and step further from him. "Just don't." I walk to the door.

"Jacob?" he says.

I ignore him.

"You need to fight," he says, and I stop to face him. "Find a way." A sermon, ladies and gentlemen, from the honorable Rabbi Nudity.

"Is that what you did?" I ask. "When you drew testicles and tits all over the Hebrew school? Huh, Rabbi? Was that you *finding* a way?"

It takes him about four seconds to arrive at "yes," but he says it with apology. "I think it was."

I force out a laugh. "Terrific. I guess I'll need some chalk."

"You'll find it."

I shrug my shoulders. "I'll find what?"

"Your own way."

"What does that mean?"

"It'll be *your* way. It has to be your way."

"What *way*? Asher. Tell me. What's my way?"

"Just tell him!" he yells, his eyes enraged. "It's *over*, Dad! Tell him tonight! You want to impress a room full of Jews, *you* do it, *you* sing about the . . . goddamn wilderness of Zin! *You* study it for months and *you* get up there and *you*—"

"Listen to you! The all-knowing. The runaway. He doesn't even know you're leaving."

"It doesn't matter."

"Oh, it *doesn't*?"

"I'm already *gone*," he says. "Okay? I've set my boundaries and I'm long gone. Long fuckin' gone."

The footsteps behind us grow louder quickly. When I turn I see Brigitte skipping toward Asher with a flathead screwdriver in her hand. She lifts the tip of it to his neck, and presses it just below his ear.

"Time out," he says, his hands carefully rising. "Crazy girl alert."

"Apologize for being an asshole!" she says.

"Okay, okay. Sorry, girl. Sorry."

"Say it again."

"I'm sorry."

She lifts it off his neck, and finds a drunken smile. "So, what are you guys doin'?"

The phone rings the loudest in the kitchen. Asher cringes

and sits, lowering his forehead to the table. "No one pick that up," he mumbles. As a quarter clinks in the den and Beth screams, "Drink!" in a wobbly screech, I turn to Holly Hobby and the clock above the stove, and watch the seven twenty-five head to New Rochelle. Rhode Island is not to be, for me. In fact it's no island at all. Three rings.

When I move toward it, Brigitte asks me where I'm going. Four rings. "What the hell's he doing?" Asher doesn't answer her. "Hey. Jacob? Jacob?" Five rings. "Don't you pick that up," she says. "Jacob!"

Six rings.

Standing before the kitchen phone I feel a great and sudden urge to laugh. Seven rings. I look over my shoulder at my brother. He nods with a subtle smirk and asks me, "What's so funny?" Eight rings.

"You," I say, with a descending smile. "Me. The wilderness of Zin."

Asher's eyes seem to unplug as he drapes his arms over Brigitte's shoulders. I wait a beat with my hand on the receiver. Nine rings.

And then lift the phone to my ear.

## Saturday

I can see it now. Now that it's morning. A tan body bag from Saks with a tiny oval window over the right lapel. Another beginning is what it means. A pardon for what's been done. It's been two days since my father picked me up at my mother's house. The tantrum was mild and quick and ended in the car. The silence that followed has lasted much longer.

I'd guessed "temple clothes" when he entered my room in the middle of the night. Could smell the beach-ball plastic of the bag from my bed. I sit up now and stare at it, hanging from my doorknob. A suit, no doubt made special for the day, tailored off some dummy my size. I walk to it and slowly unzip the bag. A charcoal three-piece. A black belt, new shirt, and maroon loafers with tissue paper crammed into the toes. A new yarmulke rests next to the shoes. It's large and boxy with earth-tone rams and menorahs on the sides.

I pull out the suit, toss it on my bed. It's time to get dressed.

**Rule Number 10 of the Green House Rules**

*When dressing for synagogue:*

    *a. Slacks go on last and must hang or lay paper flat with hard crease intact until other garments are donned.*

    *b. After the briefs start with the feet. Socks must always match and should never reveal shin skin when seated. Only black or brown socks are allowed, and be sure the elastic is intact and snug around shin.*

I see myself in the long mirror on my door. The suit pants are roomy in the crotch, but the jacket seems fine. My tie has a very large head and a short body: "hobo clown," as my dad would call it. I try again, but it comes out worse. The third time I get it right. Sort of. I step closer to the mirror and tighten it. I gaze hard at my own reflection. My eyes are green. Maybe hazel. The right one has a smeared trace of brown in it. That's weird. I never saw that before.

"Jacob?" My father calls from downstairs. "You dressed, J? It's time."

    *c. Shirttails should never be noticeably bunched around waist and rear of slacks. Lay them flat against under-pants and skin of upper legs. Fasten slacks only when tails are flat so that shirt is taut against stomach at entry to belt.*

    *d. Cuffs and collars need to be stiff with starch. Collar*

> *must fully blanket all appearances of tie around neck,
> and tie must never gather or twist against fabric in
> question.*

I walk out of my room and to the stairs. My new shoes are slippery on the carpet. For a second I'm on ice and lose my footing. I recover, walk halfway down the staircase, and see my father looking up. He grins when he sees me, his head high. "There he is," he says, and I slip again, grabbing the banister for support.

"You need to scuff up the bottoms. Go out to the driveway and scratch 'em up a little. But be quick, okay?" He looks at his watch and then back to me. "Look at you," he says, folding his arms. "You look like a million bucks. They're gonna weep today, Jacob. Just look at you."

I walk past my father, and open the front door. In the driveway I remove my right shoe first and begin to rub the bottom against the pavement in circles. Two giggling girls ride by on bikes, and a third soon follows. I watch them pedal down the street until they turn onto Saber and disappear. With my shoe back on I walk out to the sidewalk. When I hear my father open the screen door, I turn to see him. He taps his watch and waves me toward him. "You ready?"

"I think I'm gonna walk."

"What?"

"It's a nice day."

"You're going to walk to temple?" he says, another glance at the watch.

I nod and step further into the street. "Scuff the shoes."

"Jacob?"

I stop and face him.

"I'll meet you there," he says.

I wave and cross the street. And then I don't see him. I begin to walk slowly, but in seconds my steps get longer and faster until my shoes are so scuffed that I begin to run. And I mean run. But it's funny because you don't see people racing on foot down the road with their ties flapping over their shoulders very much. And if you did, you'd wonder, wouldn't you? You'd wonder—where the hell is that kid going so fast? Where the hell is that kid going?